"Will you help me

Carlo looked away from Samantha's hopeful face and tried to regain control of his emotions. Would it really be so hard?

Returning his attention to Samantha, he said, "Yes, I'll help you."

The smile she aimed at him as she surged to her feet transformed what had been a lovely face into one that was heart-stoppingly beautiful. Endless seconds passed as he stared at her, unable to summon the power to do anything else.

Lord, he had to be the biggest fool in town. If ever there was a woman who was off-limits, it was Samantha Underwood. Because if he ever told her the truth, she would never smile at him again.

Dear Reader,

Have you noticed our new look? Starting this month, Intimate Moments has a bigger, more mainstream design—hope you like it! And I hope you like this month's books, too, starting with Maggie Shayne's *The Brands Who Came for Christmas*. This emotional powerhouse of a tale launches Maggie's new miniseries about the Brand sisters, THE OKLAHOMA ALL-GIRL BRANDS. I hope you love it as much as I do.

A YEAR OF LOVING DANGEROUSLY continues with *Hero at Large,* a suspenseful—and passionate—tale set on the mean streets of L.A. Robyn Amos brings a master's touch to the romance of Keshon Gray and Rennie Williams. Doreen Owens Malek returns with a tale of suspense and secrets, *Made for Each Other,* and believe me…these two are! RITA Award winner Marie Ferrarella continues her popular CHILDFINDERS, INC. miniseries with *Hero for Hire,* and in January look for her CHILDFINDERS, INC. single title, *An Uncommon Hero.*

Complete the month with Maggie Price's *Dangerous Liaisons,* told with her signature grittiness and sensuality, and *Dad in Blue* by Shelley Cooper, another of the newer authors we're so proud to publish.

Then rejoin us next month as the excitement continues—right here in Intimate Moments.

Enjoy!

Leslie J. Wainger
Executive Senior Editor

Please address questions and book requests to:
Silhouette Reader Service
U.S.: 3010 Walden Ave., P.O. Box 1325, Buffalo, NY 14269
Canadian: P.O. Box 609, Fort Erie, Ont. L2A 5X3

Dad in Blue

SHELLEY COOPER

Silhouette

INTIMATE MOMENTS™

Published by Silhouette Books

America's Publisher of Contemporary Romance

To Kari and Mitchell, for making motherhood an
incredible challenge, a thrilling adventure and my
greatest joy. I never fully understood the meaning of
total, unconditional love until those two miraculous
February days when I first held each of you in my arms.

 SILHOUETTE BOOKS

ISBN 0-373-27114-X

DAD IN BLUE

Copyright © 2000 by Shelley Cooper

Visit Silhouette at www.eHarlequin.com

Printed in U.S.A.

Books by Shelley Cooper

Silhouette Intimate Moments

Major Dad #876
Guardian Groom #942
Dad in Blue #1044

SHELLEY COOPER

first experienced the power of words when she was in the
eighth grade and wrote a paragraph about the circus for
a class assignment. Her teacher returned it with an A and
seven pluses scrawled across the top of the paper, along
with a note thanking her for rekindling so vividly some
cherished childhood memories. Since Shelley had never
been to the circus and had relied solely on her imagination to compose the paragraph, the teacher's remarks
were a revelation. Since then, Shelley has relied on her
imagination to help her sell dozens of short stories and to
write her first novel, *Major Dad*, a 1997 Romance
Writers of America Golden Heart finalist in Best Long
Contemporary. She hopes her books will be as moving to
her readers as her circus paragraph was to that long-ago
English teacher.

IT'S OUR 20th ANNIVERSARY!
We'll be celebrating all year,
Continuing with these fabulous titles,
On sale in November 2000.

Desire

#1327 Marriage Prey
Annette Broadrick

#1328 Her Perfect Man
Mary Lynn Baxter

#1329 A Cowboy's Gift
Anne McAllister

#1330 Husband—or Enemy?
Caroline Cross

#1331 The Virgin and the Vengeful Groom
Dixie Browning

#1332 Night Wind's Woman
Sheri WhiteFeather

Special Edition

#1357 A Man Alone
Lindsay McKenna

#1358 The Rancher Next Door
Susan Mallery

#1359 Sophie's Scandal
Penny Richards

#1360 The Bridal Quest
Jennifer Mikels

#1361 Baby of Convenience
Diana Whitney

#1362 Just Eight Months Old...
Tori Carrington

Romance

#1480 Her Honor-Bound Lawman
Karen Rose Smith

#1481 Raffling Ryan
Kasey Michaels

#1482 The Millionaire's Waitress Wife
Carolyn Zane

#1483 The Doctor's Medicine Woman
Donna Clayton

#1484 The Third Kiss
Leanna Wilson

#1485 The Wedding Lullaby
Melissa McClone

Intimate Moments

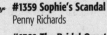
#1039 The Brands Who Came for Christmas
Maggie Shayne

#1040 Hero at Large
Robyn Amos

#1041 Made for Each Other
Doreen Owens Malek

#1042 Hero for Hire
Marie Ferrarella

#1043 Dangerous Liaisons
Maggie Price

#1044 Dad in Blue
Shelley Cooper

Prologue

Carlo Garibaldi stood at the foot of the twelve cement steps leading up to the police station's main entrance, and willed himself not to run in the opposite direction.

The impulse was one he had been fighting daily for longer than he cared to admit. This morning, as he examined the three-story, red brick building, whose cracks and crevices he knew more intimately than a lover knew the lines and curves of his beloved, the dread that filled him at the prospect of the climb was even more paralyzing than normal.

It didn't take a genius to figure out why. Today was the anniversary of his cowardice and his shame. It was not an event he planned on celebrating.

After drawing a steadying breath of the crisp, November air, Carlo placed his shaking left hand on the cold iron railing that bisected the stairs. It took him another twenty seconds to summon the energy to raise his right foot and place it on the bottom step.

The climb seemed to take an eternity. Despite the chill

air, when he reached the top, he could feel a thin layer of perspiration coating his forehead. Beneath the lapels of his leather jacket, his heart thundered.

He pulled open the heavy, white-painted oak door, and the familiar aromas of coffee, stale cigarette smoke and ancient linoleum greeted him. But when he stepped inside, the place was deserted. Like Virginia's lost colony, everyone, from the dispatcher to the janitor, seemed to have disappeared.

Chairs stood askew from their desks, as if they'd been hurriedly pushed aside. Here and there, a cigarette sat in an ashtray, burning unattended.

"Lon? Dennis? Mary?" he called. "Anyone here?"

The gurgling of the coffeepot was the only answer he received.

Sudden fear had adrenaline pumping through his veins. Where was everyone? What had happened? Had what he'd been dreading finally come to pass? What further sins would he have to atone for?

Shouldering past the empty desks, Carlo stumbled to his office and threw open the door. He came to an abrupt halt when he saw the sea of smiling people who had gathered there. The mayor. His five brothers and his sister. His missing staff.

"Mr. Mayor," he said, blinking against the sudden glare of flashbulbs that told him the press was also in attendance. From behind him, someone relieved him of his jacket.

"Chief Garibaldi," Douglas Boyer cried jovially. A wide grin split the mayor's round face as he pumped Carlo's arm. "I trust you're feeling well."

Slowly, Carlo's heartbeat returned to normal. He'd dodged another bullet. This time.

"I'm fine, sir."

"Good, good. I suppose you're wondering what we're all doing here."

"The thought crossed my mind."

Douglas Boyer broke into a hearty laugh. "Hear that, everyone? The thought crossed his mind. Not only is he the best police chief this community has ever had, but he's also got a first-rate sense of humor."

The mayor's expression grew solemn. "We know this past year has been difficult for you, Chief. In one random act of violence, our town, and your force, lost a good man. For that we all still mourn. Because your injuries kept you away from the job for so long, we've been remiss in thanking you for your actions that day. But today, on the anniversary of that terrible event, I'm here to rectify the oversight. Without your quick thinking and selfless act of bravery, the loss of life could have been so much worse. On behalf of the good citizens of Bridgeton, Pennsylvania, I would like to express my gratitude by presenting you with this plaque."

A familiar knot tightened Carlo's stomach as he stared at the words that had been engraved on a brass plate. He was being honored for bravery above and beyond the call of duty.

You've got it all wrong, he wanted to shout as applause filled the room and more camera flashes blinded his eyes. *I'm not who you think I am. I'm certainly no hero.* Because of him, one of his men was dead. Because of him, a woman and her young son would forever grieve.

Incredible as it seemed, he was the only one who knew the real truth of what had happened that day. In the three hundred and sixty-five days that had passed since then, no one had publicly, or even privately, denounced him. No one had righteously stepped forward to set the record straight.

Coward that he was, he hadn't been able to do it, either. He hadn't even been able to tell his family the truth.

And now he was being hailed as a hero. Talk about a perversion of justice.

Forcing a polite smile, Carlo nodded at all the well-wishers and tried not to flinch at the words of encouragement and the handshakes and pats on the back his staff gave him as they filed out of the room. After everyone left, and before anyone else could interrupt, he fled to the washroom and locked the door. He needed time alone to compose himself before facing what was left of the morning.

Leaning forward, he peered into the mirror. The face that stared back at him was drawn and pale, his eyes red-rimmed and haunted, his mouth a tightly sketched line. He looked worse than a cruiser that had been battered unmercifully in a high-speed chase, then run through a mile of mud puddles for good measure. The only things fresh about him were his crisply pressed blue uniform and the shiny badge that, until a year ago, he'd worn with pride. He wondered what his men would think if they knew how badly his hands shook every morning when he strapped on his gun belt.

Carlo sighed, and the sound echoed heavily in the small room. He was thirty-six years old, and all he'd ever wanted out of life was to be a cop, like his father and his grandfather before him. He'd joined this midsize, suburban Pittsburgh force straight out of college. Over the years, he'd risen steadily through the ranks, until he'd been named chief of police at the astonishingly young age of thirty. And he'd thrived on it all.

Until that awful day a year ago, he'd walked the streets of Bridgeton, confident he'd be able to face any challenge that crossed his path. His brother, Antonio, who worked undercover for the city of Pittsburgh, liked to needle him that he had the cushiest job in the world. According to Antonio, while drive-by shootings were commonplace on his beat, the worst crime Carlo could expect to encounter in Bridgeton was a drive-by shouting.

Joking aside, Antonio's words hadn't been far from the mark. On a typical day in this bedroom community of twenty thousand people, arrests were made for theft, vandalism, disorderly conduct and the occasional domestic disturbance. Murder, rape and aggravated assault were almost unheard of.

Carlo had been so proud of his force's safety record and the fact that there were few unsolved cases on the books. Truth to tell, he'd been overly proud. And cocky as hell.

Then the unthinkable had happened. There was an old saying about pride going before a fall. Carlo's certainly had. Along with it, so had his confidence. Where once he had reveled in the responsibilities of his office, now he didn't trust himself to tie his shoes properly, let alone coordinate the efforts of the people in his charge.

He'd thought hard work was the solution to the feeling of helplessness that consumed him. He'd thought it would take away the nightmares that bedeviled him whenever he tried to sleep.

He'd thought wrong.

He second-guessed himself on every decision. Each time a call came in, each time one of his men climbed into a squad car, he tensed. For months now, he'd been living on automatic pilot, just going through the motions, and he'd been lucky. Nothing terrible had happened. But if the events of this morning proved anything, it was that his time was running out.

Squaring his shoulders, Carlo faced what he'd been denying for so long. Automatic pilot wasn't good enough where his people, and where the citizens of this town, were concerned. The way he was feeling, he had no business being anywhere near here. Until he came to terms with the demons driving him, he wasn't going to be any good to anyone.

Back at his desk, he jotted a quick note to the mayor, asking for an unpaid leave of absence. Then he called Lon Sumner, his deputy chief, into his office and informed the man that he was now in charge. When Lon asked when Carlo would be returning, he didn't answer. Truth was, he didn't know if he would be returning at all.

What would he do if he wasn't a cop? The question that would have been unimaginable a year ago echoed over and over in his brain. As he climbed the stairs to the second floor, and the mayor's office, Carlo was certain of only one thing: He never wanted to be responsible for anyone, or anything, again.

Chapter 1

Dozens of wooden animals littered the kitchen table. Deer. Horses. Dogs. Cats. Sheep. Goats. An elephant. Even a skunk. Picking up a square of wood, Carlo used a carving knife to make several rough cuts across the grain. An owl, he decided, was what he would carve next, and after that, perhaps a camel.

The unexpected peal of the doorbell made him jump. His knife slipped, nearly taking a chunk out of his thumb.

Muttering a curse beneath his breath, Carlo carefully placed the knife on the table. He knew exactly who he'd find when he opened the door: his brothers. All five of them. For the past six days, since he'd gone on his leave of absence, they had taken turns checking in on him. Hourly.

For sheer convenience, the telephone was their preferred method of reaching out and touching him. They'd instituted their phone check-in system years ago, when his baby sister, Kate, had left home to strike out on her own. A year and a half ago they'd relied on it heavily when a stalker had threatened her. Kate had always hated their constant surveillance, even when she'd been in danger, and Carlo finally understood why. His brothers were driving him crazy.

They were worried about him, and for that he felt a twinge of conscience. Just as he hadn't told them what had actually happened on that day a year ago, neither had he told them the reason for his leave. In his opinion, his justification for not doing so was sound. If he told them the truth, one of two things would happen. They would either turn away from him in disgust, thus giving him the blessed peace he craved. Or their concern for him, and for his state of mind, would deepen, in which case they'd insist on setting up camp in his living room so they could monitor his every move. The way his luck was running, he'd give odds on the latter.

Which was why, two hours ago, after countless how-are-you-doing calls, he had taken the phone off the hook. He should have expected that, when his brothers couldn't get through to him via Ma Bell, they'd show up at his front door instead. It just went to show how muddled his thinking had grown lately that he hadn't anticipated an unannounced visit.

The doorbell echoed again.

Carlo had half a mind to pretend he wasn't home and to let them stand there, out in the freezing cold. He would have, too, if he hadn't been certain they'd do something drastic in response. Like bashing the door down. Or dragging out the police force and the fire department to bash it down for them.

With a resigned sigh, he placed the square of wood beside the carving knife and stomped into the living room.

"Don't worry," he growled, throwing the door wide. "I haven't died...yet...."

Instead of his brothers, a woman stood there. She was lovely. Clad entirely in black, from the turtleneck encircling her long neck to the slacks and leather boots peeping from beneath her thigh-length wool coat, she was the picture of elegance. Even her purse and gloves were black.

A short silence greeted his announcement before she softly replied, "I'm happy to hear it." Her voice was low and husky, as if she were fighting a cold, or on the verge of hoarseness.

Hair the color of corn silk fell to her shoulders and glinted in the sunlight. Her features were delicate, well defined, her cheeks rouged by the cold air. Her mouth was full and parted in an *oh* of surprise. And her eyes... Death by chocolate was the only term Carlo could think of to describe them.

He suddenly grew conscious of how he must appear to her in his rumpled jeans and flannel shirt. He searched his memory, but couldn't remember if he'd even bothered to comb his hair that morning.

"I'm sorry," he said, smiling and running a hand over his hair, hoping to flatten down any stray strands. "I thought you were someone else."

"Obviously." She sounded amused.

He hadn't looked at a woman in over a year. Initially his injuries, and the months spent in recovery and rehabilitation, had been the cause for his lack of interest. Later, when he'd gone back to work, he'd immersed himself so thoroughly in his job that he'd lacked both the desire and the energy called for when embarking on even the shortest-term relationship.

Today, however, he was definitely looking. Oh, yes, he was. And that took him by surprise. For six days he hadn't been able to work up an interest for much of anything, except whittling.

Maybe this was what he needed. A temporary diversion to take his mind off his troubles. Why, he wondered, hadn't he thought of it earlier? The good news was, she was staring at him with an equal measure of startled surprise and unexpected awareness. That was promising. Very promising indeed.

She was probably some do-gooder, out collecting for charity. Or an Avon lady going door to door. Whatever it was she was selling, Carlo was definitely buying. In bulk.

"Can I help you?" he asked.

"I suppose I should introduce myself."

She offered her hand, and he took it, marveling at the perfect fit when his fingers wrapped around hers.

"My name is Samantha Underwood."

Carlo felt his fingers go rigid with shock. It couldn't be.

"James Underwood's wife...er, widow," she amended, confirming his worst fears.

He dropped her hand like a hot potato and took a step back. His chest felt suddenly thick, as if it were congested with flu. Only it wasn't the flu he was suffering from. It was something worse. Far worse. Guilt. And shame.

First he'd been honored for bravery he didn't possess. Now the wife of the man whose death weighed on his conscience was standing before him.

What could possibly happen next? he wondered in near desperation. Would James Underwood pay a personal visit, the way Marley's ghost did Ebenezer Scrooge, and demand retribution for Carlo's misdeeds?

This couldn't be happening, he told himself as his heart thudded madly and a wave of anguish surged through him. Fate was simply having a huge practical joke at his expense.

Yet it was happening. For there Samantha Underwood stood, plain as day and twice as beautiful. And he'd been leering at her as if he was the Big Bad Wolf and she was Little Red Riding Hood.

What could she want from him? To denounce him? But if that were the case, why had she offered him her hand?

"You weren't expecting me, were you?" she said at his continued silence.

Not even in his worst nightmares.

Given that the Bridgeton police force was not the largest

one around—then again, it wasn't the smallest, either—some people might think it odd that he and Samantha Underwood had never met. But James Underwood had only served under Carlo's command for a little over a year when he died. And Carlo made it a practice not to socialize with his men, or to form close friendships with them. Things got too messy when personal feelings intruded on professional relationships.

He drew a ragged breath and struggled for composure. "Should I have been?"

Consternation crossed the fine features of her face. "Didn't the mayor call you?"

Douglas Boyer? Why would he be calling Carlo about Samantha Underwood?

"No."

"I'm sorry. When I spoke to him earlier today, he told me he'd clear the way for this meeting."

Knowing the mayor the way Carlo did, the man had, in all probability, tried. Unlike most politicians, Douglas Boyer made a point of following through on his promises, campaign or otherwise. He would have fulfilled this one, too, if Carlo hadn't taken his phone off the hook.

"It's obvious my being here is inconvenient," she said, sounding embarrassed. "I'll come back another time. Have the mayor contact me with whatever is good for you."

A rush of cold air alerted Carlo to the fact that she was still standing on his doorstep. It also alerted him to the fact that his manners were woefully lacking.

He couldn't let her go like this, not without first discovering the reason for her visit. It would drive him crazy if he didn't.

"There's no need to come back later. Please, Mrs. Underwood, come in."

He led her into a living room that literally sparkled with cleanliness—not because he was a normally fastidious housekeeper, but because, whenever his hands tired from whittling, cleaning provided a welcome distraction to the thoughts that crowded his mind whenever he had an idle moment.

When he relieved her of her coat, he saw that she was model slender. That slenderness, however, didn't stop her from having curves in all the right places.

"You have a lovely home," she said, looking around her as she took off her gloves.

"Thank you."

"Is that an antique?"

She inclined her head toward a mahogany writing desk. It was one of several heirlooms that had belonged to his mother, and that his father had distributed among his children when he'd sold the family home three years ago in preparation for his move to a Florida condo.

"Yes."

"It's beautiful."

"Thank you."

She was stalling for time, Carlo realized. Whatever the reason for her presence in his home, it made her as nervous as it did him.

"Can I get you something to drink?" he offered. "Some coffee or tea, perhaps?"

"No, thank you." Squaring her shoulders, she turned to face him. "The reason I'm here is that I have a favor to ask of you."

That took him aback. "You do?"

"It's about my son."

Both hands clasped firmly around her purse, she sank gracefully onto the sofa and lapsed into silence. So he wouldn't tower over her and make her even more nervous, Carlo took a seat across from her in an overstuffed armchair.

"How old is your son?" he prompted, when she didn't say anything more.

His words seemed to jolt her out of some inner reverie. "Eight." She paused. "I suppose I should start at the beginning."

"That always works for me," he replied in what he hoped was an encouraging tone.

She nodded her agreement. "Mayor Boyer has been wonderful to my family since James's...death. He calls every other week or so to check in on us and to see how we're doing."

Her words picked up speed. "I haven't wanted to burden him with our troubles, but when he called me this morning..." Her slender shoulders rose and fell in a helpless shrug. "I guess you could say he caught me at a low point. To make a long story short, I unloaded on him."

Because he was trained to notice details, Carlo glimpsed the dark circles beneath her skillfully applied makeup. Apparently Samantha Underwood wasn't sleeping any better at night than he was. His throat tightened. Whose fault was that?

Her fingers whitened around the purse she clutched in her lap. "I told him about Jeffrey and how withdrawn he's become. He doesn't speak much to anyone but me or my mother. He refuses to participate in group activities at school. At lunch and recess he sits by himself and rebuffs all attempts to include him in play. His classmates no longer invite him to come over to their homes. He won't even ride his bike anymore, and he rarely plays outside. Basically, he either plays by himself, reads a book or watches TV."

She broke off, her eyes wearing a look of torture that Carlo longed to erase. Though he dreaded the answer, he knew the question was one he had to ask.

"How long has he been like this?"

"Since his father's death. He's seeing a grief counselor, but so far she hasn't made much progress. Ditto a whole host of specialists I've taken him to. He…he has nightmares.''

She couldn't know the impact her words were having on him. Each was like a single bullet, and they were fired with the deadly accuracy of the bullets that had filled the air on the awful day that James Underwood died.

''What is the favor you have to ask of me?'' he said.

''After I confided in him, Mayor Boyer told me about the program you and he were involved in. He suggested I call you.''

''The Buddy System,'' Carlo muttered dully.

''Yes.''

Patterned after Big Brothers and Big Sisters of America, the goal of The Buddy System was to match local children from single-parent homes with an older buddy of the appropriate sex. The program was the mayor's baby, part of a community-oriented project he was heavily promoting in the year before his reelection. Carlo had agreed to oversee the project's operations under duress, Douglas Boyer having twisted his arm a time or ten.

''So you want me to match Jeffrey with a buddy when the program is formally introduced a few months from now.''

''Not exactly.'' Her big brown eyes bored into him, making him wonder if she could see into the darkest recesses of his soul, to the guilt that ate away at him like a cancer. ''I want *you* to be Jeffrey's buddy.''

Shock momentarily robbed him of the ability to speak. ''Me?'' he finally asked, blinking at her.

''Yes. Mayor Boyer seemed to think you would be the perfect buddy for my son. Especially now, since you've taken a leave of absence and have some time on your hands.''

Carlo had had to give the mayor some kind of excuse for his sudden request. He couldn't recall exactly what he'd said, although he thought he'd muttered something about coming back to work too soon and needing more time to regroup.

Had the mayor seen through Carlo's excuses to the underlying truth? The man was quite perceptive. Carlo couldn't stem the thought that, by sending Samantha Underwood to him, Douglas Boyer was playing amateur psychologist.

If so, it was a dangerous game.

Carlo couldn't help Jeffrey. He could barely take care of himself. How could he possibly be expected to act as a buddy to an eight-year-old boy? Besides, he couldn't give the child the one thing he needed and wanted most: his father. If Jeffrey's grief counselor hadn't been able to help, surely Carlo wouldn't be able to do any better.

"I'm sorry, Mrs. Underwood," he said as gently as he could. "I'm afraid I can't be Jeffrey's buddy. But I will promise to match Jeffrey with the most suitable buddy once the program is in place."

Her face fell, and her voice was a whisper of pain. "I don't think Jeffrey can wait that long."

Her disappointment, and her obvious anguish, were almost too much for Carlo to bear. Harder yet to bear was that she had come to *him*, hat in hand, asking for his help. And he was letting her down. The way he'd let James Underwood down a year earlier.

"Why does it have to be me?" he asked, hearing the note of desperation in his voice. "Why not someone else on the force? I could give you the names of several men, all of whom would be more than qualified to do the job."

"James respected you more than any other man he knew," she told him. "He often spoke to Jeffrey about you. Although he hasn't met you, Jeffrey knows who you are. You wouldn't be a total stranger to him. Besides, I need someone who can help now. With Thanksgiving coming in a couple of weeks, and Christmas so soon after, I don't think too many people will have the time to devote to Jeffrey that he needs. Especially if they have families of their own."

"And I have the time," Carlo murmured.

"Yes," she agreed. "You do."

It felt as if the walls of the room were closing in on him. "What about an uncle or a grandfather? Wouldn't a relative be a better choice to spend time with Jeffrey?"

She gave him a sad smile. "Ideally, yes. Unfortunately, there are no uncles. For the most part, we're a family of women. Jeffrey's only surviving grandfather lives in Des Moines, and he's not in good health. That leaves you, Chief Garibaldi."

The walls closed in on him tighter, making it hard for him to breathe.

Samantha Underwood's eyes pleaded with him. "I know I'm asking a lot. Too much, probably. But if you could see your way clear to helping Jeffrey, I'd be forever in your debt."

That was it, then, he realized dully. He had no choice. Because the question had changed from could he do this to did he have the right to refuse Samantha Underwood's request. And the answer was that he didn't. He had to at least give being Jeffrey's buddy his best shot. Because he wouldn't be able to live with himself if he didn't try.

Carlo couldn't help thinking—wishing?—that, if he was able to help the child, it would quiet some of his own demons. Leaving his job certainly hadn't accomplished that task. Cleaning his house hadn't. Neither had carving endless quantities of wooden figures. Maybe, if he could somehow reach Jeffrey Underwood, draw the boy out, he'd be able to come to terms with the past, which would in turn help him to come to some sort of decision about his future.

On the heels of that hopeful thought came doubt. What if he blew it? Because of him, Jeffrey Underwood didn't have a father. Because of him, Jeffrey's mother had been reduced to the point of begging so that the boy could have a male influence in his life. What if Carlo tried to help and only succeeded in making matters worse? Samantha Underwood had already lost her husband because of his incompetence. Could he bear it if she lost her son, too?

"Will you help me, Chief Garibaldi?" she asked again. "Will you help me help my son?"

Swallowing hard, he looked away from her hopeful face and tried to regain control of his emotions. Would it really be so hard? All he had to do was entertain the boy for a few hours each week. Having practically raised his four younger brothers, the youngest of whom had been more than a handful, Carlo felt fairly confident he could at least accomplish that task.

Returning his attention to the woman sitting across from him, he said, "Yes, Mrs. Underwood, I'll help you. Until the program is up and running, and I can find someone else, I'll be Jeffrey's buddy."

The smile she aimed at him as she surged to her feet transformed what had been a lovely face into one that was heart-stoppingly beautiful. Endless seconds passed as he stared at her, unable to summon the power to do anything else. For a moment he even thought she was going to reach out to him, to wrap her arms around him, and his heart thundered in anticipation.

When he came to his senses, self-reproach left a bitter taste in his mouth. What had he been thinking? That she was going to embrace him? And, if she had, would he have ruined what surely would have been a gesture of gratitude by covering her mouth with his own?

Lord, he had to be the biggest fool in town. If ever there was a woman who was off-limits, it was Samantha Underwood. Because if he ever told her the truth, she would never smile at him again.

"I can't thank you enough, Chief Garibaldi," she said. "You've taken such a weight off my mind."

Carlo didn't want her thanks. What he did want was for her to go, so he could think clearly again.

When he helped her into her coat, his hand accidentally grazed her cheek. He heard her indrawn breath of surprise in the second before he pulled away from the contact.

"Where do we go from here?" he asked, feeling decidedly shaky.

"You meet Jeffrey. Are you available Saturday morning?"

"Is ten o'clock okay?"

"Ten o'clock would be perfect." She handed him a piece of paper with her address and phone number.

At the front door, he forced himself to meet her gaze. "I'm sorry about James," he said. She'd never know how sorry. "He was a good man. It was a privilege to serve with him."

The sorrow that filled her beautiful brown eyes let him know that, despite the spark of interest he thought he glimpsed earlier, her heart still belonged firmly to her late husband.

"Thank you."

Carlo didn't know what was worse. Receiving Samantha Underwood's thanks, or realizing that, for the next several months, he would be spending a lot of time in her company.

"I really wanted to pay my respects, after James died," he felt compelled to say. Unfortunately, his injuries had made that impossible.

She nodded her understanding. "And I meant to visit you in the hospital. Thank you again, Chief Garibaldi."

He followed her out onto the front porch and watched while she climbed into her car and drove away. He was still standing there five minutes later, eyes shielded against the sun, when his brothers arrived.

* * *

"Did you speak to him?" her mother asked the minute Samantha walked through the front door.

Samantha shrugged out of her coat and hung it in the closet. "Yes."

"And?"

She turned to face the older woman. "He'll do it."

Maxine Miller's hands went to her heart. "Oh, thank goodness."

"Yes," Samantha echoed hollowly. "Thank goodness."

Her mother frowned. "You don't sound happy about it."

The euphoria she'd felt after Carlo Garibaldi had agreed to be Jeffrey's buddy had worn off during the drive home. While she was still thrilled that he'd agreed to help her, she was less than happy about the method she'd used to earn that agreement.

"That's because I guilted him into it."

"How did you do that?"

"By basically telling him that he was the only man who could do the job. He would have been heartless to refuse."

"A less than honorable man would have had no problem refusing," Maxine pointed out.

"Yes," Samantha agreed. "And, as we all know, Carlo Garibaldi is an honorable man. Which just proves my original argument."

A look of sympathy crossed her mother's face. "You did the right thing, honey. In this case, the ends definitely justify the means."

"Knowing that doesn't make me feel any better." Samantha sighed. "Where's Jeffrey?"

"Upstairs in his room."

Her already heavy heart grew heavier. "I suppose it was too much to hope he'd be outside, playing with one of his friends."

"Oh, Sam." Maxine's eyes filled with tears.

Samantha felt her throat thicken, and she quickly looked

away. Though she longed to, she couldn't allow herself the luxury of a good cry. She was afraid that, once she started, she would never stop.

"I hate to see you worry like this," her mother said. "You have to understand that what happened to Jeffrey is a tragedy few children his age experience. It's only natural he would withdraw the way he has."

"I didn't." Nineteen years earlier, under circumstances eerily similar to the ones that had cost James his life, Samantha's father had been killed in the line of duty.

"You were thirteen when your father died, not seven. And you had your two older sisters to help you through."

"Maybe. But it's been a year, Mom. What should have been the hardest part is already behind us. The first Thanksgiving without James. The first Christmas. The first birthday. Yet Jeffrey isn't getting any better. If anything, he's getting worse."

"Have patience, honey. And faith. He'll come back to us. I know he will."

Samantha wished she could be so certain. She drew a long, shuddering breath. It tore at her heart to think of her child being so alone. Before James's death, Jeffrey had been so outgoing, so alive. And now...

Swallowing, she said, "To tell you the truth, Mom, I don't know how much more of this I can take."

She was a nurse. She'd dedicated her life to helping others. It tortured her that she couldn't do anything to help her own son. She could bandage a cut, soothe a fevered brow, but she had no idea how to heal the bruising of Jeffrey's soul. With every day that passed, he slipped further and further away from her. No matter how hard she tried, Samantha couldn't reach him.

"Would you like me to come over for a couple of evenings this week, so you can get out on your own?" Maxine asked. "Maybe some time by yourself would help."

"It wouldn't do any good. I worry about Jeffrey whether I'm with him or not."

"I could just come and keep you company."

Once again, Samantha found herself blinking back tears. "I'd like that, Mom. Very much."

"I think going to Chief Garibaldi was a step in the right direction. Having Jeffrey spend time with someone who knew and worked with his father might just be able to bring about the breakthrough we've been praying for."

"I certainly hope so," Samantha said fervently. So much rode on this relationship working out. The stakes were incredibly high. Too high?

"What's he like?" Maxine asked.

"Who?"

"Chief Garibaldi."

Samantha's heart thudded as she recalled her first glimpse of him. "Oh."

"Well?" Maxine gazed at her pointedly.

"He's…just like James described him." And so much more.

"His picture was in the paper last week. He was honored for his actions that day."

"I know," Samantha said softly. "I saw it."

After speaking to Mayor Boyer that morning, Samantha had dug the newspaper in question out of the pile to be placed at the curb on recycling day. Though grainy, the photograph on the front page had arrested her attention. She'd seen his cap of unruly black hair, his broad forehead, his piercing brown eyes that gleamed with intelligence, his classic Roman nose and his determined chin, and had known exactly what to expect when she met him: a man who, like her husband, was filled with an unswerving dedication to right all wrongs.

What she hadn't expected was his smoldering sensuality, or the helpless way she had responded to it.

Guilt stabbed at her as she faced a truth she'd been trying to hide from since the moment she'd laid eyes on her son's buddy. Her husband, whom she'd loved more than life itself, had been gone just over a year, and she'd stood on Carlo Garibaldi's front doorstep, gaping at him like a hormone-struck teenager. Her son needed help desperately, and all she'd been able to think about was the breadth of his shoulders, the depth of his brown eyes, and the fullness of his lips. What had gotten into her?

She supposed it had something to do with the fact that he was nothing like she had anticipated. When he'd answered his door, her first reaction, before awareness set in, had been amazement that he wasn't taller. After the way James had sung Carlo's praises, Samantha had expected him to be almost Paul Bunyanesque in stature. To discover that he was a good two inches shy of the six-foot mark had been a surprise.

What he lacked in height, however, he more than made up for with his dark good looks, sheer force of personality and well-muscled physique. He'd looked so strong, so capable, that Samantha had found herself repressing a ridiculous desire to lean her head on his shoulder and tell him all her troubles.

When she'd realized how he affected her, she'd almost turned on her heel and walked away. Instead, for Jeffrey's sake, she'd forced herself to offer him her hand.

Since there was no way she could talk to her mother about this, Samantha decided that a change of subject was in order. "When do you leave on your cruise?" she asked.

"A week from tomorrow."

Because Lawrence Miller had been killed on Thanksgiving Day, Maxine always took a cruise over the holiday—the exception being the preceding year because it had been too soon after James's death. Getting away was her mother's way of dealing with her loss.

"You really don't mind me going?" Maxine asked.

"Why should I mind?"

Her mother shrugged. "I'm not sure I should be leaving you alone just now."

"I'm not alone, Mom," Samantha said gently. "I have Jeffrey. We'll be just fine."

She was stretching the truth somewhat. Things wouldn't be truly fine until Jeffrey was himself again. But the last thing Samantha wanted was for her mother to worry about the two of them while she was on her cruise.

"If you say so." The doubt in Maxine's voice made her ambivalence clear.

"I say so."

"If only your sisters didn't live so far away."

Bridget, Samantha's oldest sister, was a financial analyst on Wall Street. Colleen, the middle child, was an electrical engineer and lived in Los Angeles. Both were so wrapped up in their careers that they rarely made it back home.

"It's a sign of the times," Samantha said.

"A sad sign, if you ask me," her mother replied.

Silence reigned while Maxine followed Samantha out to the kitchen. Against her will, Samantha's thoughts returned to Carlo Garibaldi and her reaction to him. Her mother had grieved for nineteen years now for the man she had lost. To the best of Samantha's knowledge, in all that time Maxine had never looked at another man.

Samantha had looked long and hard at Carlo Garibaldi. What did that make her?

Her unwelcome awareness of him wasn't important, she told herself. She certainly wasn't going to act on it. All that mattered was that Jeffrey get well again.

Pairing Jeffrey with Carlo Garibaldi was a last-ditch effort to break down the walls he had erected between himself and the rest of the world. With all her heart and soul, Samantha prayed it would work. Because, while she herself didn't know how to reach her son, she was certain of one thing. If someone didn't get through to Jeffrey soon, she stood a good chance of losing him altogether.

Chapter 2

Hands in the pockets of his leather jacket, Carlo slowly walked the twelve blocks separating his home from the Underwood residence. Overhead, the sky was covered by a blanket of gray clouds that did or did not, depending upon which meteorologist one favored, hold the promise of the first snow of the season.

When he reached the foot of the cement path leading up to 221 Lincoln Drive, he came to a reluctant halt. At first glance, the house where Samantha Underwood lived with her son looked a lot like his own: older—probably built in the early twenties—constructed of brick, square in shape and two-and-a-half stories tall. It was only when Carlo peered closer that he glimpsed the subtle signs of neglect; signs all pointing to the absence of the man who had been in charge of its upkeep.

Leaves from an old oak tree carpeted the yard. The forest-green paint on the shutters flanking the front windows had begun to flake. A jagged crack marred one of the windows of the detached two-car garage.

Carlo shivered when an icy wind stung his cheeks and snuck its way into the folds of his jacket. Once again, he pondered the wisdom of the decision that had led him here. He'd half decided to walk back home when Samantha opened her front door and stared out at him.

She wore a pair of brown corduroy pants and a matching cotton sweater with a deep V neck that drew his gaze to the long, slender column of her throat. Her straight blond hair had been combed back off her forehead to fall freely to her shoulders.

At the sight of her lovely face, Carlo's breath clogged in his throat. She was like the sunlight to a man who had been trapped in a dark cave for far too long. Try as he might, he couldn't look away.

Damn. The awareness was still there. If anything, it had intensified. He'd hoped—prayed, actually—that it had just been a fluke, the result of a desperate man latching onto the sight of a beautiful woman standing on his doorstep. Especially now that he knew the impossibility of there ever being anything between them.

But it wasn't a fluke. The way she made him feel inside wasn't fading. Which meant he had to ignore it.

"Are you going to come in?" she called.

Since the choice of beating a hasty retreat had been taken away from him, Carlo moved up the walkway and climbed the steps of her front porch.

"Sorry I'm late."

That she looked happy to see him made his breathing grow even more erratic. Actually, maybe relieved was a better description, an impression she confirmed with her next words.

"For a minute, I thought you weren't coming."

"For a minute, I almost didn't," he answered honestly.

Hand still on the brass knob of her front door, she tilted her head back to meet his gaze. "Having second thoughts?"

"And third and fourth and fifth. Aren't you?"

"No," she replied, without a hint of hesitation.

The way she stood firm in her conviction that he was the one person who could help her son illustrated how deceptive appearances could be. To look at her, a man might mistakenly believe that Samantha Underwood was as delicate as blown glass. But, though she looked slight and insubstantial, the woman had an inner strength that transcended her seeming fragility. Something told Carlo she was as fiercely and stubbornly independent as his sister. But then, she would have had to be, to survive the past year.

Unfortunately, her strength made her all the more attractive to him. He never had been drawn to women who clung tighter than the rose vines that climbed the trellis in his front yard every summer.

"So you're having second thoughts," she commented.

About more than just his promise to help her son. "Yes."

"Why? Don't you like children?"

"I like them well enough. It's the responsibility that's getting to me."

She seemed to mull his words over. "From everything I've heard about you, you're a man who thrives on responsibility. You wouldn't be chief of police otherwise."

A year ago, that had been more than true. He'd once been a man who'd prided himself on his ability to look out for others. The operative word being once.

"That may be so," he said, "but while I'm responsible for directing the actions of the people under my charge, I always leave their mental welfare to others. I'm no mental health expert, Mrs. Underwood. I've never pretended to be."

She seemed to relax. "He's just a little boy, Chief Garibaldi. A lost little boy who needs a man's guidance. That's all. How about we leave his mental health to his grief counselor?"

Put that way, the task didn't seem so daunting. "Carlo," he said.

She blinked. "I beg your pardon?"

"The name's Carlo. Since we're going to be seeing each other rather frequently, it only makes sense to drop the formalities."

She stood aside. "Would you like to come in…Carlo? And please, call me Samantha."

He stepped into a small foyer, the walls of which were lined with framed photographs. While Samantha collected his coat and hung it in a closet, Carlo rubbed his hands together to restore their warmth and allowed his gaze to rove over the gallery. Some of the pictures were very old, a few appearing to have been taken more than a century earlier; others had been shot more recently.

One in particular caught his eye. In it, Samantha smiled her radiant smile at the camera. Her arms were wrapped around a small boy who wasn't more than three or four, and her chin rested lovingly atop his head. The openness of that smile, and the look of supreme contentment and quiet joy in her clear, brown eyes, held him riveted.

Suddenly, he wasn't in such a hurry to leave. Not only did he want to stick around, but he wanted to see her smile that way again. Worse, he wanted that smile to be for him only. He wanted to take away the cares and worries weighing so heavily upon the pair of shoulders that appeared too delicate to bear them.

And he really was losing it, if a mere picture could affect him so deeply.

The click of the latch on the closet door signaled that Samantha had finished hanging up his coat. Tearing his gaze away from the photograph, he turned to face her.

The picture's impact didn't even come close to how she affected him in the flesh.

"Why'd you grow a beard?" she surprised him by asking.

His hand automatically went to the growth covering his cheeks. Since the day he'd handed in his request for a leave of absence, he hadn't shaved or gone to the barber. In that short period of time, he'd managed to cultivate a fairly respectable beard, and for the first time in years his hair now brushed the collar of his shirt.

The question was, how had Samantha known that his beard was a recent addition?

"I saw your picture in the newspaper," she added, as if reading his mind.

"Oh."

What had she thought when she'd seen it? Had she wished it were her husband, alive and well, receiving the award instead of him? If he were in her shoes, he knew that was what he would have wished.

"I decided I needed a change of pace," he said.

"It suits you."

"Thank you." He felt oddly pleased.

"Jeffrey's in the den," she said. "I've prepared him for your visit. I want to warn you, though, that he probably won't respond very…well, positively to your presence. At least at first. Don't let it discourage you. Would you like to follow me?"

The house was neat and comfortably furnished. Samantha led him past a living room, through a brightly decorated kitchen and into a room that was obviously the den. A fire crackled in the brick fireplace, the sound and smell of burning wood both welcoming and comforting.

Deliberately forcing his awareness of his hostess to the back of his mind, Carlo turned his attention to the child sitting stiffly on the edge of the sofa. Jeffrey Underwood wore blue jeans and a Steel City Wrestling Alliance sweatshirt. His head was bent, his gaze focused on the coffee table. There was a stillness about him that Carlo had never seen before in an eight-year-old. He seemed small for his age, and like his mother, way too thin. He was also unnaturally quiet.

"Jeffrey," Samantha said gently. "Remember how we talked about finding you a buddy to do things with?"

The boy nodded without raising his head.

"Well, he's here. I think you're going to like him very much."

Samantha gestured to Carlo, and he crossed to the sofa, where he took a seat next to the child. Though the boy didn't move, Carlo could sense him mentally shrinking from the contact.

"Hi, Jeffrey," he said. "I'm Carlo."

The boy refused to look at him.

"Jeffrey," Samantha prompted.

"Hello," the child said in a flat voice.

"Carlo worked with your father," Samantha offered. "He's Bridgeton's police chief."

Jeffrey raised his head, and Carlo saw a flash of emotion in the child's eyes. That was a good sign, at least. It meant he wasn't totally withdrawn.

"My dad's dead," Jeffrey announced baldly. "He's never coming home. And I don't want a buddy."

"Jeffrey!" To Carlo, Samantha added, "I'm sorry. He's not usually so rude."

In Samantha Underwood's eyes, Carlo saw the pain she fought so hard to hide. And a worry that tugged at his heart.

"No need to apologize," he said lightly, although his conviction that he wasn't the person who could help this child had grown. Samantha might believe him capable of working miracles, but Carlo knew better. From the looks of him, Jeffrey was going to fight him all the way.

"Jeffrey's just being honest about his feelings," he continued. "I, for one, always appreciate honesty. I'm hoping, though, that once he gets to know me, he'll change his mind about wanting a buddy."

Jeffrey's response was to pick up a toy car from the top of the coffee table. Making revving noises, he began running it across the smooth wood surface. Though he didn't say the words, they vibrated on the air nevertheless. *Fat chance.*

Despite the fact that Carlo was fairly certain the battle had already been lost, he wasn't ready to raise the white flag just yet. He owed Samantha, and her son, that much. Hoping to capture the boy's attention, he reached into his jeans pocket and pulled out a pocketknife and a small piece of white pine.

"Do you know how to whittle? My grandfather taught me when I was about your age. It looks hard, but it's really very easy, once you get the hang of it."

Though Jeffrey seemed focused on the car that was now making circles on the floor, Carlo could swear the boy was watching him out of the corner of one eye. Encouraged, he glanced over at Samantha.

"Do you have something I could use to catch the wood chips?"

She handed him a magazine, which he opened on his lap. In a matter of minutes, the knife moving deftly in his hands, Carlo had fashioned a man's head. He offered it to Jeffrey, who held it for a few seconds before giving it back.

"Would you like to learn to whittle?" Carlo asked.

Jeffrey gave an indifferent shrug.

A sudden thought occurred to him. "If you'd like, I could buy you a pocketknife of your very own—that is, if it's okay with your mother."

The boy shrugged again. "Maybe."

Jeffrey uttered the word in the tone kids used to indulge their elders when they found the subject under discussion too boring for words, but didn't want to hurt any feelings. Carlo wasn't fooled; he'd seen the interest that had flashed in Jeffrey's eyes. It had been brief, lasting only the fraction of a second, but it had definitely been there. After all, what eight-year-old boy could resist the lure of a pocketknife?

When Carlo had been eight, weapons of any shape or size, even sticks and stones, had been endlessly fascinating.

Elated at his tiny victory, and thinking that maybe things weren't so hopeless after all, Carlo looked up at Samantha for permission. "Is it okay if I buy Jeffrey a pocketknife?"

The gratitude in her eyes took his breath away. That the emotion was for him was enough to render Carlo speechless. It also made the blood race through his veins and obliterated all rational thought as he stared at her and tried to remember what question he had asked.

She was the first to look away, her fingers plucking at a nonexistent piece of lint on her sweater. "I think Jeffrey's old enough to handle the responsibility. So yes, you can buy him a pocketknife."

A deep breath did little to restore Carlo's equilibrium, or lower his heart rate. "It's settled, then." He turned to Jeffrey. "I'll bring it with me on my next visit."

Jeffrey didn't say anything. Still, Carlo couldn't help feeling a faint glimmer of hope.

Samantha pulled a tray of chocolate chip cookies from the oven. Lowering her face, she basked in the warmth of their heat and breathed in their comforting aroma. Some people ate when they were nervous. Others wore out the carpet with their pacing. Samantha baked.

How was it going in there? she wondered as she closed the oven door. From her position at the kitchen's center cooking island, she could see into the den if she leaned forward far enough and craned her neck like a contortionist. She did so and saw Carlo reading a book to her son. Though Jeffrey seemed to be paying more attention to the car he continued to push around on the floor, every once in a while he grew still as he listened. She could swear that, when Carlo read the part about the evil witch getting turned into a toadstool, Jeffrey actually smiled.

Her heart ballooned with hope. This was the first time her son had responded to someone outside their immediate family. She *had* done the right thing by going to Carlo Garibaldi. She could feel it in her bones. If things continued to go well, she just might get her miracle. For the first time in what seemed like forever, she wasn't afraid to trust that everything would turn out okay.

Ignoring the growing crick in her neck, her gaze returned to the man who had occupied so much of her thoughts over the past couple of days. Everything about him was larger than life: his broad shoulders, his muscled arms, his stubborn chin. The faded jeans that fit his thighs like a second skin, and the white cotton shirt that he wore with the sleeves rolled back to his forearms only accentuated his maleness. He was definitely the most forceful man she had ever met.

He turned the page of the book, and she followed the movement with fascination. His fingers were long and capable looking. Without consciously summoning the memory, she vividly pictured the way they had moved so expertly over the piece of wood he'd held earlier. From there, it wasn't much of a stretch to imagine how they would skillfully caress a woman's body. Samantha's stomach fluttered at the unbidden thought.

It didn't mean anything, she told herself. She could easily think of two or three movie stars who made her feel the same way when she watched them on screen. She didn't lose any sleep over them, and she wasn't going to lose any over the new man in her son's life.

Carlo chose that moment to look up, caught her watching him and flashed her a grin. Samantha went all hot inside. Resisting the urge to fan herself like a menopausal woman in the middle of a hot flash, she pulled back out of view and busied herself removing the cookies from the tray.

She shouldn't be looking at him that way, she told herself.

She had no business looking at any man that way, had never been tempted to, until she'd met Carlo.

She'd never felt this way when James looked at her. She'd never burned inside like a forest fire raging out of control. She'd never yearned…for exactly what she couldn't say.

Her love for James had been gentle and sweet. It had been quiet and steady, a rock upon which to depend in this crazy, topsy-turvy world. It had been real and lasting. There had been nothing frivolous about it.

And every thought she had about Carlo Garibaldi that didn't relate to her son definitely fell into the frivolous category.

Even though the attraction was purely physical and meant nothing, it still felt like a betrayal. She loved her husband. She missed him with every fiber of her being. How, then, could she fantasize about the touch of another man?

The love she and James had shared was a love to last a lifetime. But it hadn't lasted a lifetime. Because of a cruel twist of fate, they'd had only ten short years together. She wasn't about to sully James's memory by giving in to a foolish infatuation.

It was time for more baking, she told herself, and began mixing up a batch of snickerdoodles. Wryly she acknowledged that if she didn't calm down soon, the welcoming committee at church was going to have more than its share of refreshments for their reception tomorrow.

She didn't hear Carlo enter the kitchen. When she turned and nearly collided with his warm, hard body, she let out a gasp and her hand went to her heart.

"I did call your name," he said with a smile.

"I'm sorry," she said breathlessly. "I didn't hear." Then, after a steadying breath, which helped slow her heartbeat appreciably, she asked, "Done already?"

"I think that'll do it for today," he confirmed. "I don't want to push my luck."

"What's Jeffrey doing?"

"Watching a Disney movie."

Because she didn't know how to act around him, and because he made her feel so unsettled, Samantha picked up a plate mounded high with cookies and clumsily thrust it at him. "Would you like one? They're fresh from the oven."

"Thanks. They smell delicious." He took a bite, chewed and his smile widened. "Incredible. Is that real butter I taste?"

"Yes. Thank you."

She watched in fascination while he quickly devoured three cookies, then demurred when she offered him a fourth, saying he didn't want to spoil his appetite for lunch. The appreciation in his eyes warmed her heart.

Then he spoiled it all by reaching out a hand and brushing it across her forehead. Samantha nearly dropped the plate of cookies in her haste to get away from the contact.

"Don't!" she cried.

"Sorry," he said stiffly, pulling his hand back, and she knew she had offended him. "You had some flour on your forehead. I was just brushing it off."

She forced an uneasy laugh. "I'm the one who should apologize. I don't know what made me overreact like that."

But she did know. It was Carlo and the way she had no control over her body's response to him. And the guilt that swamped her because she couldn't.

"Forget about it," he dismissed, adding what had to be the understatement of the year. "We're both a little on edge today."

"You did a good job in there," she told him, feeling more in control now that she wasn't standing so close to him. "I think you made some progress."

Carlo gave a short laugh. "That depends how you measure progress. To my way of thinking, I made a millimeter's worth of headway, and we still have miles to go."

"Baby steps," she said.

"Baby steps?"

"You take one step forward, teeter for a bit, fall down on your butt and climb back to your feet. Over and over again, until you get where you're going. Baby steps."

"Baby steps," he repeated with a nod. "I think I get it."

"And I think, based on what I saw this morning, given time Jeffrey will come to trust you. If we're lucky, he'll even open up to you." Samantha felt her throat close with emotion and drew a ragged breath. "And then I'll have my son back."

"You really think I can do all that?"

"Yes," she answered softly. "I really do."

His eyes darkened with emotion in the seconds before he tore his gaze from hers. "I hope your faith in me is justified," he said gruffly.

The oven timer went off. Thankful to have something to occupy her attention, Samantha bent to remove a tray of cookies.

"Who's the photographer?" she heard him ask as she scraped snickerdoodles onto the wax paper she'd spread across one counter.

"What photographer?"

"The one who took all the photos in the front hallway. I couldn't help noticing them earlier."

"The older ones are family hand-me-downs," she replied, her back still to him. "The more recent ones are mine, along with a few from a professional studio."

"The pictures of you and Jeffrey, you mean."

"Yes. Those were professionally taken."

"So, you're into photography?"

Dusting her hands, she turned to face him. "I dabble a bit. What I really like is covering the walls of my home with pictures of the people who mean the most to me. It gives me pleasure to look at them. Plus I find gazing through a lens relaxing.''

He eyed the cookies covering her counter. ''Does baking relax you, too?''

She had to smile. ''No. Baking helps me use up nervous energy.''

''Do I make you nervous?''

Her smile faltered at the unexpected question, and her heart started pounding. Thank goodness he didn't realize exactly how nervous he did make her. At least she thought he didn't.

''This whole thing with Jeffrey has my nerves frayed,'' she said quickly. ''I've been baking up a storm for months.''

He seemed to hesitate briefly before saying, ''About the photos in the front hallway. I couldn't help noticing there weren't any pictures of James.''

As little as a few months ago, the mention of her late husband would have filled her with a rush of pain. Now she felt only a dull ache. And an emptiness that seemed to go on forever.

''There used to be dozens. Everywhere I looked. I took them down after…you know.''

''After he died,'' Carlo supplied.

''Yes.'' Sometimes she still found it hard to say the ''d'' word. ''It hurt too much to look at them.''

And now, at night, when she closed her eyes, she had trouble picturing him. She was terrified that she was starting to forget James. The way she responded to Carlo Garibaldi wasn't helping matters.

''How are you coping?'' he asked.

She busied herself scrubbing down the counters. ''I have my good days and my bad days. For months there was only pain. And denial. I simply couldn't believe James was gone. I wondered if the day would ever come when thoughts of him wouldn't consume my every waking minute. Then I got angry and screamed at God for letting James die, and I screamed at James for dying. When the anger faded, I moped around for another couple of months. Finally I accepted that James was gone, and he wasn't coming back. Somehow, I had to make a life for Jeffrey and me without him. Now that you're here, I think more good days just might be in our future.''

She glanced at him over her shoulder and was surprised at the look of consternation on his face. Poor man. She'd made it sound like she was depending on him to solve her every problem. No wonder he looked terrified.

''I'm sorry, Carlo. I don't know why I told you all that. What I meant to say is that I've been one of the lucky ones. My mother lives close by, as does my best friend. They've both been a wonderful support to me. So has Douglas Boyer. And now you. Jeffrey and I are doing just fine.''

''Except for the fact that he won't talk to anyone,'' he muttered.

She looked down at her hands. ''Except for that.''

''I want you to know something.''

A quality in his voice she couldn't quite define made her look up. ''What?''

''If it were in my power, I'd wave a magic wand and make things the way they were before. I'd make it so that day never happened. I'd give you back your husband and your little boy.''

His sincerity was unmistakable. Why he should seem to care so much, she didn't know. But he obviously did. And she was grateful for the sentiment.

''James was right,'' she said.

He looked startled. ''About what?''

''You really do take your responsibilities to heart.''

''Doesn't everyone?''

''You're a cop, and you can ask me that with a straight face?''

His smile was wry. "You have a point."

"Actually, what I think James meant was that you take things too much to heart. When you agree to do something, you don't take any half measures. You give it everything you have, and then some."

"I believe in honoring my commitments." His voice sounded stiff.

"And I've made you defensive. That's not what I was trying to do."

"What were you trying to do?"

"To say thank you. Thank you for helping me with Jeffrey, Carlo."

He seemed to grow even more uncomfortable. "I don't want your thanks, Samantha."

What did he want? she wondered. Now wasn't the time to ask. What it was time for was the truth. She had to be honest with him, or she'd never get rid of the guilt.

"I have a confession to make."

"You do?"

She nodded. "I shamelessly manipulated you to get you to help me with Jeffrey."

"What do you mean?"

"I mean that I used what James had told me about you to get you to do what I wanted you to do."

Understanding dawned in his eyes. "You knew I wouldn't be able to turn you down when you came to me."

"I didn't know for sure. But I hoped. And I definitely prayed. Thank goodness my prayers were answered." She paused. "Are you angry?"

"I should be, I suppose," he said on a sigh. "But no, I'm not angry. I understand why you did what you did. If Jeffrey were my son, I probably would have done the same."

She was almost afraid to ask. "Does this mean you'll be back next Saturday?"

Long, agonizing seconds passed before he finally answered. "Yes, Samantha. I'll be back."

Chapter 3

The Samantha Underwood who answered her door the following Saturday bore little resemblance to the woman who had bowled Carlo over the week before. The thick, lustrous blond hair that had gleamed like a badge in the sunlight was uncombed and hung lankly to her shoulders. Her eyes were sunken and red-rimmed, her lips chapped. In contrast, her cheeks were flushed with color. Though it was after noon, she wore a pair of flannel pajamas beneath a loosely belted, red terry cloth robe. It was a good thing the day was uncharacteristically mild, because she looked as if even the hint of a breeze would knock her off her feet.

Any other woman would have made an excuse for the way she looked. Samantha simply stood there, waiting.

And any other man—if he had a shred of decency, anyway—wouldn't have found the sight alluring. But Carlo did. Heaven help him.

Guilt left a sour taste in his mouth. She was James Underwood's widow. He had no business lusting after her like an awkward youth fumbling through his first crush.

"Are you okay?" he asked.

She brought a tissue to her mouth and sneezed. "Just fine."

"You don't look fine."

She stood aside so he could enter. "I picked up a bug at work. The hazard of being a nurse, I suppose. It'll run its course in a day or so."

His gaze roved over her again. So she was a nurse. It seemed appropriate, given what he knew about her.

"Must be some bug, to make you look like that."

Her smile caught him off guard. "Do you have to work at it, or are you naturally this charming? Much more of this flattery, and my ego will be totally deflated."

Carlo amazed himself by doing something he hadn't done in years: he blushed. He wasn't normally so clumsy around women. But then, Samantha was unlike any woman he'd ever known.

Her words echoed in his ears. *Much more of this flattery, and my ego will be totally deflated.* Could she have wanted him to flatter her? His heart gave a wild leap in the seconds before reality jolted him roughly back to earth.

"Sorry," he said stiffly, "I didn't mean to be rude."

"I was just teasing," she chided. "Can't you take a joke?"

Apparently not. The old Carlo would have taken it in stride. Not only that, he would have given back as good as he got, and thoroughly enjoyed himself in the process. But the old Carlo had died, and a new Carlo had been born in his place. A Carlo who had made the decision to drift aimlessly for a while, to go with the flow and see what happened. The old Carlo would have been appalled at this lack of direction and purpose. But then, the old Carlo hadn't turned out to be such an admirable fellow, so who was he to complain?

And the new Carlo had had enough self-examination for

one day, he decided, when the unpleasant memories threatened to push past the barriers of his subconscious.

"Is Jeffrey ready?"

"I'll check." Samantha turned to call up the stairs. "Jeffrey, Carlo's here."

Considering that she could have been the poster girl for
Webster's definition of death warmed over, her voice was
surprisingly strong.

Carlo decided that he liked the way his name sounded on
her lips. He liked it a lot. As a matter of fact, he liked it so
much he wanted to hear her say it again. How would it feel,
he mused, to hear her cry his name during the throes of
passion, and then again, softly, once that passion had been
sated?

Two thumps echoed from the ceiling. When Samantha
turned back to him, he gave a guilty start at the realization
of the direction his thoughts had wandered. He felt his
cheeks grow even ruddier as he tried to school his expression
into neutrality, so that those very thoughts weren't visible
on his face. What on earth was wrong with him? Why
couldn't he control himself when he was around her?

"That's Jeffrey's signal that he'll be down in a minute,"
she said. "We were a little late getting started this morning,
and he just got out of the shower." She swayed and reached
out for the newel post at the foot of the stairs.

Mentally cursing his wayward libido, Carlo moved
quickly to her side and took her by the arm. The heat coming
off her skin seared him as he led her into the den. The pillow
and blanket already lying on the sofa bore witness to the
fact that his arrival had disturbed her rest.

Samantha's strength seemed to ebb out of her as he helped
her settle onto the sofa, and he wondered exactly how hard
she'd had to work not to let on how rotten she was feeling.
If her sudden weakness was any indication, she'd used up

valuable stores of energy; energy that should have gone to fighting her fever.

"You're burning up," he said, tucking the blanket securely around her.

"It's just a slight temperature."

"Right," he muttered. "And the Nile is just a stream. At a guess, I'd put that slight temperature of yours at 102.4 degrees."

Her eyebrows climbed. Despite her weakness, she managed to look amused.

"Do you always estimate to the tenth degree?"

"For temperatures, I do. And, I might add, I'm usually right."

He made sure the pillow was centered beneath her head before straightening and looking down at her. She seemed so small and defenseless that he was overcome by an urge to stay by her side until she was well again. For a man who didn't want any responsibilities, he seemed to be racking them up right and left: first Jeffrey, and now the boy's mother.

"Just how did you come by this talent of yours?" she asked, her voice a near whisper.

It took him a beat to realize what she was talking about. "Let's just say I've nursed a fever or two in my time. You've got a doozy. While it won't kill you, it will sap your strength. What you need is plenty of fluids and rest."

"Yes, doctor."

He had to smile. Samantha Underwood was a nurse. She didn't need him telling her how to treat her illness. Still…

"Is there anyone I can call to come in and stay with you? A friend? Neighbor?"

"I'm not an invalid," she protested. She tried to rise up on her elbows and fell back against the sofa. "I've been taking care of myself for quite some time now. I think I can manage for a while longer."

How did she expect to take care of herself, let alone an eight-year-old boy, when she could barely lift her head off the pillow? Carlo knew better, however, than to give voice to the question. Pointing out the obvious would only make her even more defensive.

"What about your mother? Maybe she could come over and keep Jeffrey occupied, so you can get the rest you need."

Samantha closed her eyes and turned her face toward the wall. "Mom's away on a cruise. Besides, you're taking Jeffrey out for the afternoon. That'll give me all the rest I need."

Considering the thinness of her body and the circles under her eyes, Carlo doubted it. Samantha was in need of a lot more than a few hours sleep.

If he couldn't talk her into getting help, at least he could do everything in his power to assure the outcome she seemed so certain of. For Jeffrey's sake, of course. Turning on his heel, he headed for the kitchen.

"Where are you going?"

"To get you some water," he called over his shoulder.

The countertop that had been covered with freshly baked cookies a week ago was a mess. An open loaf of bread teetered on the edge of the white Formica surface; two slices had already fallen to the floor. Beside the bread lay a knife that was smeared liberally with peanut butter and grape jelly. Equally smeared were the countertop itself and the two open containers from which both substances originated. An empty glass sat in a puddle of milk. Obviously, Jeffrey had fixed his own lunch.

Under normal circumstances, Carlo would never consider rummaging around in a stranger's cupboards. But these weren't normal circumstances, and he didn't have the heart to disturb Samantha to ask where she kept things. He'd just have to rely on his intuition to lead him to the items he needed. After all, he'd once been able to find a cache of stolen jewels in under one minute by letting his intuition lead him to the most likely hiding spot. How hard would it be to find things that were meant to be found?

After cleaning up the mess Jeffrey left, it took him less than thirty seconds to find a tall glass, a tray and a pitcher, which he filled with ice and water. When he spied the bottle of aspirin on the counter, he called, "Have you taken anything for the fever?"

"Not yet," came the weak reply.

He'd placed the aspirin bottle on the tray and was about to return to the den, when his glance landed on the telephone. His brother Marco was a doctor. While he had the opportunity, he might as well get the opinion of a professional.

Carlo felt a lot better after speaking to Marco. So long as Samantha got plenty of fluids and rest, so long as her fever didn't rise to a dangerous level, and so long as she didn't exhibit any worrisome signs like convulsions, she should be okay.

"Hold out your hand," he ordered after placing the tray on the coffee table. When she complied, he shook two aspirin into her palm, then helped her to a sitting position before pouring a glass of water and handing it to her. "Drink."

He waited until she drained the glass to say, "You should be all set here. There's plenty of water for you whenever you're thirsty. There are also some crackers, in case you feel like nibbling on anything. Can I find you something to watch on television? Bring you the remote control? A book?"

"No, thanks. I think I'll take a nap after you and Jeffrey leave."

"Sounds like a good idea to me. And don't worry about Jeffrey. He and I will be just fine. I thought, since it was such a nice day, we'd rake some leaves and jump in them."

"I love jumping in leaves," Samantha said wistfully.

"Unfortunately for you, the only jumping you'll be doing today will be in your dreams."

"In that case, will you take a flying leap for me?"

He laughed. It was a good sign that she was still able to joke with him. Yes, he decided, there was definitely a mischievous light gleaming in those big, brown eyes of hers. Maybe she was getting better.

"You're teasing me again, right?" he asked.

"You catch on fast."

"I try."

"You should do that more often," she said.

"Catch on to things?"

"Laugh. It makes you look more human."

It came to him then that he couldn't remember the last time he'd laughed out loud. It felt good.

"What did I look like before?" he asked, still smiling. "Godzilla?"

"You know what I mean."

He sobered, and the good feeling faded. "I guess I haven't had much to laugh about lately."

Her sigh was low and heartfelt. "Boy, can I relate."

"Yes," he said carefully, mindful that she'd had even less to laugh about in the past year than he had. "I suppose you can."

"Thanks, Carlo," she said.

He blinked. "For what?"

"For the aspirin and the water. For coming back today. It means more to me than you'll ever know."

Warmth filled him as his heart swelled with pleasure. Then he remembered exactly why Jeffrey needed him, and the warmth was replaced by a sudden chill.

Carlo glanced at his watch. Jeffrey was taking his grand old time getting ready.

"Let me guess. He's not any more anxious to see me today than he was last Saturday."

"No," she admitted. "But he'll be down."

"What did you bribe him with? A new toy?"

Her mouth curved. "I don't believe in bribery, no matter how tempted I am to resort to it. Jeffrey is aware that he has a commitment to spend time with you each week, and that I expect him to honor it."

The clump of feet slowly descending the staircase echoed into the room. A minute later, Jeffrey appeared in the doorway. His hair was still wet from his shower. When he glanced at Carlo, a wary light filled his eyes. It changed to worry when he caught sight of his mother on the sofa.

Somehow, Samantha managed to dredge up a brilliant smile. Carlo felt a spark of admiration for this spunky woman. Whatever her worries and fears were for her son, she wasn't about to let the child see them. Nor was she about to let worry for her ruin what would hopefully be, for Jeffrey, a good time.

"Come here," she beckoned to the boy. When he knelt by her side, she smoothed a hand back over his hair. "I want you to promise to be on your best behavior while you're out with Carlo. Okay?"

"Okay." Jeffrey nodded grudgingly.

"She'll be just fine, sport," Carlo reassured. "See? She's all set. Water. Glass. Blanket. Pillow. The best medicine for your mom right now is for us to get out of her hair. Once she takes a nice long nap, she'll be feeling much better."

As he followed Jeffrey out of the room, Carlo couldn't help tossing a worried glance over his shoulder. Samantha was already asleep.

It was the kind of Indian summer weather that, on a school day, inspired many a young boy to play hooky; the kind of weather Pittsburgh rarely saw in November. There wasn't a cloud in the sky, and the air was unseasonably warm. A light jacket or sweatshirt was all a person needed, and even that seemed too heavy when the sun blazed its brightest.

After closing the front door behind them, Carlo said, "Want to rake some leaves?"

Hands in his pants pockets, his gaze cast downward, Jeffrey toed the ground in front of him. "I guess so."

Okay, Carlo reasoned. Put that way it did sound pretty much like a chore. He couldn't blame Jeffrey for being less than enthusiastic.

"I was thinking of something along the lines of a race. I brought two rakes with me. What I thought we could do is see who has the biggest pile of leaves once the front yard is all raked up. Of course, after the winner is declared, we get to jump in those leaves before sweeping them into the street for the maintenance crew to pick up on Monday. You game?"

Carlo gazed at the child, expecting him to eagerly agree. After all, what red-blooded American boy could turn away from healthy competition?

Apparently Jeffrey could. His answer to Carlo's challenge was an indifferent shrug.

"If you want."

Strike one, Carlo thought wryly as he headed for the rakes he'd propped against the oak tree.

Twenty minutes later, he was lying face up in a pile of leaves. Ten feet away, Jeffrey stood playing with a yo-yo he'd pulled from his pants pocket.

To give the boy credit, he had tried. Well, he had pushed his rake around for ten minutes or so before abandoning both it and Carlo. Carlo had kept raking until he'd built a nice, high pile. He'd hoped to at least entice the boy into jumping into the leaves. So far, though, he'd had no luck.

Gazing up at the brilliance of the sun, Carlo felt its warmth caress his face. Despite his lack of success with

Jeffrey, it felt wonderful, and he wished for nothing more than to lie there for a while longer. Until that moment, he hadn't realized how much the guilt and regret he'd been carrying around had weighed him down; how it had dragged at his shoulders, his conscience and his heart as if an anvil had been hung around his neck. It felt good to let go of the load for a while.

He looked over to where Jeffrey was walking the dog with his yo-yo. "Neat trick. Could you show me how to do that?"

Jeffrey showed him his back.

Strike two. Carlo decided to try a different tack.

"When I was your age and my brothers and I raked leaves together, they would throw them at me. It always made me mad. There's nothing I hate worse than a bunch of leaves in my face."

Ignoring the blatant hint, Jeffrey sat down on the front steps and stared wistfully at the horizon.

Strike three. You're out. Carlo sighed. He might have been able to pique Jeffrey's interest a time or two last weekend, but so far today he was batting zero.

"Baby steps," he muttered, remembering what Samantha had said to him. He'd measure each success in terms of baby steps, ignore the failures and refuse to look beyond that.

"I have that pocketknife I promised you. Want to do some whittling?"

"Some other time," Jeffrey said.

Brushing the leaves from his clothing, Carlo sat up. "I'm pretty hot. I think I need an ice cream cone to cool me off. What about you?"

That, at least, got the boy's attention, Carlo thought with satisfaction. Samantha Underwood might be above bribery, but Carlo Garibaldi wasn't.

"Baby steps," he murmured to himself as they set off down the street. "Baby steps."

*   *   *

They were seated at the local Baskin-Robbins ice cream parlor, munching contentedly on a double scoop of Quarterback Crunch and Rocky Road, when Carlo felt Jeffrey's gaze on him. More specifically, on his upper arms. When he glanced at the boy, Jeffrey quickly—almost guiltily—looked away. A minute later, though, Carlo felt the child's gaze on him again.

He had a flash of understanding. "You want to know if I've always been this strong, don't you?"

Jeffrey nodded.

"The answer is no. When I was your age, I was built just like you. I've been lifting weights since I was eighteen. It took a lot of work to get to the point where I am now."

Carlo hadn't been to the gym for his daily workout since he'd taken his leave of absence. Though he'd wanted to, he simply hadn't been able to summon the energy to go. Surprisingly, given his idleness, he still had a good deal of muscle tone.

"Can I lift, too?" Jeffrey asked.

"Anyone can lift. You just have to make sure to use proper form so that you don't injure yourself. When you're old enough, you can join a gym."

Jeffrey frowned. "I don't want to wait till I'm older. I want to lift now."

Why not? Carlo thought. The day was still young, and he wanted to give Samantha as much rest as possible. Besides, this was the most he'd heard Jeffrey speak. If this was what it took to reach him, Carlo was all for it.

"Would you like to see the gym where I work out?" he asked.

The light in Jeffrey's eyes was all the answer he needed.

"Hey, Carlo," Pete Loring, the owner of Fit Bodies, greeted when they walked through the door. "Long time no see."

"I've been busy," Carlo replied guardedly.

Typical of Pete, he didn't pry any further. "Who's your young friend?"

"A prospective client."

Carlo watched Jeffrey's eyes go round at the sight of the giant man who wrestled professionally under the name of Killer. Never had a title been a greater misnomer. Though fierce-looking, when not beating his competition to a pulp in the ring, Pete Loring was one of the gentlest men Carlo had ever met.

Pete's smile broadened. "A prospective client, eh? Well, then, we'll have to see that he receives the star treatment, won't we?"

"I know you," Jeffrey said with the first real excitement Carlo had seen him exhibit. "You're Killer."

"You a SCWA fan?" Pete asked, obviously pleased.

Eyes shining, Jeffrey nodded. "You're my favorite wrestler."

"Ah," Pete said, settling a meaty hand around Jeffrey's shoulders. "A fan. For a fan, not only will I give you the star treatment, but I will also roll out the red carpet. Ready for a tour?"

Carlo stood off to one side while Pete showed a starstruck Jeffrey around the gym and patiently explained the purpose of each machine and exercise. The crowded room was filled with grunts of effort and the sound of weights clanking as men and women alike stared at the mirror-lined walls to ensure they were using proper form. Though they came in all shapes and sizes, they all had one thing in common: their bodies gleamed with the sheen of perspiration that could only be brought on by hard work.

There was a time when the sights, sounds and smells of this room had thrilled him, a time when he'd lived for that hour or two each day when he could lose himself in the sheer joy of pushing his body to its limits. A time when, the minute he walked into this room, his fingers would itch to lift a barbell or to do repetitions on one of the machines. Carlo looked down at the hands hanging limply at his sides. No itch.

He gazed around him with a curious detachment. He'd worked so hard to build and maintain his physique, especially after his injuries, and now he no longer cared if he ever lifted another weight. There were so many things he no longer cared about. And he didn't even care that he didn't care. Intellectually, he knew that should worry him, that he wouldn't be able to resume even the semblance of his former life until he could care.

At the moment, though, the only things he seemed able to work up any feeling for were an emotionally scarred little boy and his sick mother.

When his gaze found Jeffrey again, Carlo saw that Pete had finished the tour and had left the boy to complete a workout of his choosing. The grimness and determination on Jeffrey's face as he lifted weights with a purposefulness that was far older than his years startled Carlo out of his reverie.

"Whoa, slugger, slow down," he cautioned, moving to the boy's side. "You don't want to overdo it your first time out. What are you preparing for? Battle?"

Jeffrey kept pumping iron. "When I grow up," he said in a fierce voice, "I'm going to be big and strong like you and Killer. And then I'm going to find the man who killed my dad and kill him."

Dismayed, Carlo didn't know what to say. After all, Jeffrey wouldn't have to look far. The man who had killed his father was standing right beside him.

There was no answer when, darkness rapidly falling, Carlo pressed the doorbell of the Underwood home. At his side, Jeffrey held the autographed T-shirt Pete had given him and the set of weights Carlo had bought so that Jeffrey could continue his workouts at home.

Frowning, Carlo pressed the doorbell again. Still no answer. Inside, no lights shone in any of the windows.

She was probably still sleeping, he told himself, refusing to succumb to the feeling of dread that had his heart suddenly racing. Four hours was a long time for anyone, unless they were desperately ill, to sleep.

"Do you have a key?" he asked Jeffrey.

Jeffrey placed the weights and the T-shirt on the porch floor so that he could rummage through his pants pockets. He pulled out a crumpled pack of gum, a battered toy soldier, the yo-yo and three marbles before finally producing a key. When he slid it into the lock, the door swung silently inward.

"Why don't you run upstairs, put your things away and wash up, while I go check on your mom." Carlo needed to get the boy safely out of the way, just in case something really was wrong with Samantha. "It's important that you wash your hands and arms thoroughly, because you might have picked up some germs at the gym. Since your mom's sick, you want to be careful not to pass them on to her."

His reluctance obvious, Jeffrey slowly mounted the stairs. When he reached the top, Carlo headed for the den.

It was hard to see in the dimness, but he definitely glimpsed the outline of her body beneath the blanket. It looked as though she hadn't moved since he'd left with Jeffrey.

He hated to wake her. But he couldn't leave until he knew she was alert and able to care for her son.

"Samantha?" he said, switching on a light. She didn't answer, and he called louder. "Samantha?"

"What?" She sounded groggy as she opened her eyes and blinked against the brightness. "Oh, you're back. Did you have a nice time?"

"I think it went well." Except for Jeffrey's startling revelation about his plans for vengeance. "How are you feeling?"

"Thirsty."

He poured her a glass of water and helped her to a sitting position. "Better?" he asked, when she'd drained every drop.

"Much. What time is it?"

"Five o'clock."

Her eyes widened. For a woman who'd slept the afternoon away, she looked anything but rested.

"Already? It feels like I just closed my eyes."

"That's because you're sick." A lot sicker than she wanted to let on. Leaning down, he rested his hand against her forehead. While still not into dangerous territory, her temperature had definitely risen.

He knew then what he had to do. It was the last thing he wanted. But he would be less than heartless to leave an eight-year-old and a defenseless sick woman to their own devices.

"That settles it," he said. "I'm staying."

Chapter 4

Samantha was determined to stand, even if it took every ounce of her strength. Pushing the blankets aside, she swung her feet to the floor and placed her hands flat against the sofa cushions for support. If only her head wasn't so woozy and her limbs didn't feel like they each weighed a thousand pounds.

After drawing a deep, bracing breath, she leaned forward and centered her weight on her legs. For a second or two, she was certain she'd collapse. But finally, through sheer determination, and not a little perspiration, she gained her feet.

She didn't even want to think about how awful she must look.

"You don't have to stay," she said, locking her knees when they threatened to give way beneath her. After being huddled beneath a blanket all afternoon, the air in the room felt cool, and she shivered. "I'm feeling much better."

"Liar," he said mildly.

"No, really. I know you're used to taking charge, but it isn't necessary. I'll be just fine. You can go home now."

She heard a hint of panic creep into her voice and bit her lip. She couldn't concentrate enough to figure out why it was so vital that he leave. All she knew was that every instinct of self-preservation she possessed was screaming how it was imperative for him to go.

"Face it, Samantha, you need help."

Sick as she was, the sound of her name on his lips still managed to send shivers of awareness up her spine. Those six words, spoken softly and with concern, penetrated the haze clouding her mind. In a moment of clarity, she knew exactly why she was so desperate for him to leave. She didn't like the way he made her feel when he looked at her, all soft and feminine and trembly inside. Even less did she like the way her breathing went haywire when he smiled; how her heart raced when he spoke her name.

She'd had her chance at love, and it had been wonderful. No woman could have asked for more. Then James had died, and they'd buried her heart with him.

Apparently, however, her hormones had stayed behind.

When she was well again, none of this would matter, she told herself. When her weakness disappeared, so would her vulnerability.

"You need help," he repeated.

"I'll be just fine on my own," she maintained stubbornly.

"Who's going to cook dinner for Jeffrey?"

"Me."

"Uh-huh. And who will see to it that he's bathed and put to bed?"

"Me."

"Who will read him a story before he goes to sleep?"

"Again, me. I'm his mother. It's my job."

"You're weaker than a newborn colt," Carlo said. "You

don't have the strength to take two steps, let alone care for a small boy.''

She let out a shaky breath. "I'll manage.''

"How?'' he asked quietly.

The way all single mothers did. Because she had no choice.

"You can't stay,'' she insisted.

"Why not?''

"You just can't.''

A teasing light entered his eyes. "Worried what the neighbors will think?''

It was said in jest, but the remark had thoughts racing through her mind. Inappropriate thoughts that took all the stuffing out of her knees. Samantha sank back down onto the sofa.

"Of course not.''

The irony was, she was the one who had teased him about not being able to take a joke. This time, it seemed, the joke was on her.

"Then what's the problem?'' he asked.

He was. Not that she could tell him so.

It wasn't just that she was physically attracted to him. If that was all it was, it would be easy for her to ignore the way he made her feel. After James's death, she'd been amazed at the number of men, some of whom had called James a friend, who had gallantly—their opinion, not hers— offered to ease her sexual frustration. She hadn't even been tempted.

But Carlo Garibaldi wasn't trying to seduce her, the way those other men had. He wasn't even trying to flirt with her. In his strong, determined, macho way, what he was doing was trying to take over. The age-old tale of men thinking that women were weaker and needed their help. And still she went all soft and gooey inside when he smiled at her.

What none of those other men had understood was, as

pleasurable as lovemaking with James had been, it wasn't what she missed the most, now that he was gone. What she missed the most was holding, and being held by, a man. A man she could cuddle with on the sofa at the end of the day. A man to whom she could confide all her thoughts, hopes, anxieties and fears.

Carlo Garibaldi's shoulders were more than broad enough to cuddle her. If she asked, she knew he would willingly offer them to her. That was what made him so dangerous.

"Samantha?" he prompted, still waiting for her answer.

She sighed. "It's too much of an imposition. I can't ask it of you."

"You didn't ask," he pointed out. "I offered."

"I'm giving you an out," she sputtered in mounting frustration. "Why aren't you jumping at it? Surely, you can't *want* to stay."

The teasing light left his eyes. "What I want has nothing to do with it. The condition you're in, I can't leave you alone with Jeffrey. It wouldn't be safe, for either of you."

Jeffrey. The truth of what she was up against finally hit her. What if something happened? What if, God forbid, there was a fire? What if Jeffrey had an accident and needed immediate medical attention? How would she cope?

Carlo was right; she had no strength. Her mother wasn't around, and all of her friends had their own families to care for. Like it or not, he was offering to help.

"You could get sick," she warned.

A lethal smile curved his lips. "I'll risk it."

She was too tired to protest anymore. Matter of fact, she was too tired to do anything but lie down.

"Very well, stay." She waved a hand weakly at him as she placed her head on the pillow and turned on her side. "I don't have the strength to fight you anymore."

His hands were amazingly gentle as he tucked the blankets around her. "Don't worry. You can fight me when you're feeling better."

Was it her imagination, or was there a note of tenderness in his voice? She furrowed her brow and tried to focus on him, but all she saw was the wavy outline of his body. Why was the room suddenly so hot, and why was she so weak?

As if from far away, she heard Carlo telling her that she should get some rest, that he would fix dinner for Jeffrey. Unable to keep her eyes open a second more, and feeling unaccountably safe, Samantha allowed sleep to claim her.

Carlo looked up from Samantha's sleeping face and straight into Jeffrey's worried eyes. The boy stood just inside the doorway, his gaze riveted on his mother.

"Hey, sport."

Jeffrey seemed to become aware of Carlo's presence for the first time. "Is she…" He drew a shuddering breath and tried again. "Is she okay?"

Like it was only yesterday, Carlo recalled the way his younger siblings had feared for their father's health in the months succeeding their mother's death. A headache, a fever, even a sneeze, was cause for grave concern, so terrified were they that they would lose their father, too. The apprehension filling Jeffrey's eyes told Carlo the child was experiencing those same emotions.

"She's fine," he said in a reassuring tone. "Her body's fighting an infection, and to do that properly she needs to get lots of sleep. When you're sick, don't you sleep a lot?"

Gaze back on Samantha, Jeffrey nodded.

"Well, that's the way it is with your mom right now. A little help from us, and she'll be good as new. Okay?"

After a long hesitation, Jeffrey said doubtfully, "Okay."

"Jeffrey," Carlo said.

"What?"

"Look at me, please."

It took a minute, but Jeffrey finally tore his gaze from his mother.

"I know we don't know each other well," Carlo said. "I know also that you haven't made up your mind yet about whether you're going to like me or not. No matter what you decide, I want you to understand one thing. I will never, ever lie to you. If I tell you something, you can take it for the gospel truth. And I'm telling you right now, your mom's going to be okay. No ifs, ands or buts about it. She's just sick, that's all, and she'll be better soon. Understand?"

"Yes."

Carlo felt gratified by the relief that flashed in the boy's eyes. "Good. First thing we have to do is make her more comfortable, which means we should get her upstairs and into her own bed. Then we need to get some food in our stomachs. It wouldn't do for us to get sick, too, now would it?"

While Jeffrey ran up the stairs to turn down the covers on Samantha's bed, Carlo bent over her sleeping form. She cried out when he lifted her in his arms.

"Shh," he soothed. "Everything's okay."

Her eyelids fluttered open for a second before slowly drifting shut again. "Where are you taking me?" she asked drowsily.

"To your room. You'll be more comfortable there."

"Jeffrey?"

"He's fine. I won't let anything happen to him."

"My head hurts," she moaned.

"It's the fever. Go back to sleep. When you wake up, you'll feel better."

"Promise?"

"Promise."

His heart turned over when she wrapped her arms trustingly around his neck and laid her head against his chest. She felt incredibly light in his arms; too light. Although she definitely had curves in all the right places, she was practically skin and bones. Small wonder she had gotten sick. She was run-down, her system unprotected from any marauding germ that wanted to lay siege. Unfortunately, she worked in a place where the marauding germs far outnumbered the people doing battle with them.

As he climbed the stairs with her in his arms, a lock of her hair brushed his cheek. It was as soft as a whisper, and he found himself biting back an unbidden urge to wrap his fingers around it so he could press it to his mouth.

What kind of a man was he, to lust after a sick woman? Not only a sick woman, but the wife of the man whose death weigh so heavily on his conscience.

It hit him then. When it came to Samantha Underwood, more than his libido was involved. Somehow, she touched him on a level no other woman had. Yes, he wanted to make love to her. But, more importantly, he wanted to get to know her. He wanted her to know him.

Carlo felt his jaw clench. To nurture this unexpected yearning was a lost cause. She was the one woman in the world he couldn't have, and the sooner he got that through his thick skull, the better.

When he reached the top of the stairs, he saw Jeffrey standing in a doorway at the end of the hall. It was only after he'd settled Samantha onto the bed that he realized the child hadn't led him to the master bedroom. For one thing, the room was tiny, little bigger than a closet. For another, he'd tucked Samantha into a single bed.

Had Jeffrey led him into the guest bedroom by mistake? But why would he do that? What purpose would it serve?

Further inspection revealed evidence that Samantha had taken up residence in the tiny room. A pair of jeans and a sweater, obviously worn, lay draped across a wing chair. A stack of library books sat on the bedside table next to a clock radio whose alarm had been set. Arranged neatly on the dresser top were a brush, several hair combs and four bottles of perfume. Carlo knew that if he opened the dresser drawers and the door of the closet, he would find more of Samantha's belongings.

Why didn't she use the master bedroom? The answer was obvious. Ignoring the issue of the role he had played in James Underwood's death, and Samantha's undoubted reaction when she learned of it, if Carlo needed anything to illustrate the impossibility of her ever returning his budding feelings for her, this was proof beyond a reasonable doubt.

The reason Samantha slept in the guest bedroom was because it was too painful for her to sleep in the bed she had shared with her husband. And the reason it was too painful for her to sleep in that bed was because she was still deeply, irrevocably in love with him.

Jeffrey refused to leave his mother's side. Carlo prepared a tray of soup and grilled cheese sandwiches, and they ate in the guest bedroom while Samantha slept. Together, they pressed cold compresses against her forehead to soothe her fever, and ice chips to her mouth when she complained of thirst. Together, they pulled her covers back up over her when she kicked them off.

They worked in silence, Jeffrey having rebuffed all of Carlo's efforts to engage him in conversation. The boy refused to pass the time by playing a game, watching television or reading a book. After a while, Carlo gave up. It was obvious Jeffrey would allow nothing to distract his attention from his mother.

Samantha's fever broke at ten o'clock, and she fell into a deep, restful sleep. At eleven, Jeffrey lost the battle to keep his eyes open. An odd lump filled Carlo's throat when he placed Jeffrey in his own bed and pulled the covers over his sleeping form.

As a youth, whenever Carlo had dreamed of the future,

he'd always pictured himself as a father. Having grown up in a large family, he'd simply taken it for granted that he would have children of his own one day.

Now, here he was at the age of thirty-six, and he wasn't a father. Not only that, but he was no longer certain of what the future held for him. His life hadn't turned out at all the way he'd planned it would. But then, he supposed it was that way for most people.

"Sleep tight, sport," he murmured as he turned out the light and closed the door. "Pleasant dreams."

After checking to make sure the house was secure, he washed up in the powder room located in the downstairs hallway. Shrugging off his shirt, he settled onto the sofa in the den with a bone-weary sigh and pulled the blankets Samantha had used earlier up over his shoulders. Closing his eyes, he willed sleep to come.

The remnant of Samantha's scent, which clung to the folds of the blanket he'd tucked under his chin, was what finally broke him. For weeks, months, he'd battled to keep the memories at bay. Every conscious moment had been an exercise in calculated repression. But when Samantha's delicate scent tickled his nose and brought her lovely face so vividly to his mind that she could have been standing in front of him, the dam holding back his memories burst. They came roaring over him in a relentless flood that refused to be stopped, until he'd relived every damning, shameful moment....

It was the third of November. A beautiful, sunny day. The call came in at three minutes past noon, a time when Bridgeton's streets were at their most crowded, and the station house was all but deserted. Aside from the dispatcher and Carlo, everyone was either out to lunch or on patrol.

"Attention all units," he heard Mary Bell announce over the radio as he passed the communications room. "Officer

needs assistance on the twelve hundred block of Maple Avenue. I repeat, officer needs assistance. Proceed with extreme caution. Suspect is armed and considered dangerous.''

''What's going down?'' he demanded when she completed the transmission. His words were terse, clipped, his internal warning system on full alert.

Though her voice had been calm, the hand Mary pulled away from the microphone shook. When she turned to face him, her eyes were wide with alarm.

''It's Sergeant Underwood, Chief. He's being held at gunpoint. A Fred Bishop, who resides at number 1238, called it in.''

Carlo's heart tripped once, then steadied as his training kicked in and took over. ''Underwood's status?''

''Unknown. Bishop reported that he looked out his front window because a barking dog disturbed him. That's when he saw the suspect pull the gun. He ran to phone us immediately.''

Carlo's gut clenched. For now, he'd have to work under the assumption that, at a minimum, the suspect had succeeded in disarming his sergeant.

After checking to see that his gun was properly loaded, he said, ''Tell any unit who responds to cordon off both ends of the twelve hundred block of Maple. Call Lon at Rusty's Café and tell him he's in charge of crowd control. Have an ambulance ready to go in as soon as we clear the way. And tell everyone to proceed with the utmost caution. I don't want any heroics.''

Mary nodded. ''That goes for you, too, Chief.''

The way she said the words, her voice a near whisper, was enough to remind him that, in its two hundred plus years of history, Bridgeton had never faced a crisis of this magnitude. Though they'd all had training to prepare them for situations like this, it was one thing to face an emergency *in practice, and quite another to have to deal with the real thing.*

"Don't worry about me," he said. "I don't plan on being a hero."

With any luck, Sergeant Underwood was this very minute disarming the suspect and would report the arrest momentarily. With any luck, Carlo was raising the alarm for nothing. But in his gut, he knew that wasn't the case. The taste of dread was in his mouth, and it would take a lot more than a glass of water to wash it away.

The first of his ten units responded as Mary picked up the phone to carry out Carlo's orders. "This is unit three, dispatch. Our current location is the six hundred block of Oakwood. Proceeding immediately to Maple…"

Carlo ran. He didn't bother with a squad car, since Maple Street was just three blocks away. While he shouldered his way through a lunchtime crowd that parted in front of his barked commands like the Red Sea for Moses, he prayed that his sergeant was okay. James Underwood was a fine man and a damn fine cop. Carlo would hate for anything to happen to him.

The scene that greeted him when he rounded the corner onto Maple was out of his worst nightmare. A young woman, two crying children clutched to her breast, cowered in front of a house to his left. Directly across the street from her, an elderly man lay face down on a lawn, his hands held protectively over his head. The grocery bag the man had been carrying was tossed to one side, its contents spilling onto the street. Several people, a postal carrier among them, crouched behind parked cars. Their faces were white with fear. Barking fiercely, an agitated German shepherd strained against the chain that bound it.

An aging, rusted-out Chevrolet sedan, hood raised, blocked the middle of the street. Beside the car stood a man *wearing a camouflage jacket, jeans and army boots. In his hands was an assault rifle.*

Gasping for breath, Carlo took cover behind a tree and drew his gun. Where was Underwood? It took him a few seconds to realize that the assault rifle was trained on a body lying prone next to the disabled car. The familiar blue uniform had Carlo's heart surging into his throat.

He could shoot now, he realized. He had a clear target, and the suspect hadn't yet seen him. He could wound the man, disarm him, and it would all be over.

The use of force, deadly or not, was forbidden without at first issuing a warning. Carlo knew that as well as he did his own name. Still, in this case, with his officer's life in peril, not to mention the innocent civilians who had been drawn into the situation by virtue of their being in the wrong place at the wrong time, surely he would be forgiven for not following the rules just this once. His finger tightened around the trigger, and he took aim.

In the end, doubt prevented him from shooting. He'd never fired his weapon in the line of duty. What if he missed? What if wounding the man wasn't enough? What if the suspect started spraying the street with gunfire? Innocent people could be wounded, or worse, killed.

His first glance at the disabled car had told him the whole sorry story. The suspect had been driving through town when it had been his misfortune to break down in the middle of the street. Obviously there was something in the car—most likely drugs—that he didn't want the police to find. And it had been Sergeant Underwood's misfortune to approach the car to see what was wrong.

The scream of police sirens swelled on the air, and the suspect turned his head toward the sound. In a matter of minutes, the area would be secured.

It was time for Carlo to make his move. No SWAT team waited from above to swoop down and save the day. There was just himself. To delay any longer was to put lives at risk. Hoping the element of surprise was enough to catch the man off guard, he burst from his hiding place behind the tree and assumed a firing stance.

"Police!" he cried, gun raised high. "Drop your weapon and raise your hands over your head."

The man whirled. Instead of dropping his gun, though, he kept it pointed at the prone body of James Underwood.

"Back off, or he's a dead man," he warned.

"How do I know he's not already dead?" Carlo asked.

The suspect nudged Underwood with his foot. "Raise your right hand."

When Underwood complied, for the first time since Mary had informed Carlo of the situation, he felt in control. Underwood was still alive. The suspect hadn't shot his sergeant in cold blood, which meant that Carlo had a chance of reasoning with him.

While police cars barricaded both ends of the street, Carlo took a step forward. Selecting his words carefully, he spoke calmly, soothingly.

"You don't want to do that. If you fire that weapon, you're going to do some serious time behind bars."

Carlo could literally see the wheels turning in the man's head. He was trying to think of a way out.

"It's not that easy," the man said.

"Sure it is. All you have to do is put the gun down."

"You don't understand. It's not my first offense. Any way you look at it, if you take me in, I'm doing some serious time. I can't go back."

Carlo took another step forward. He could feel a sheen of perspiration coating his forehead. "You're already caught. Surely you can see that. Don't do anything to make matters worse. For your sake, please put your gun down."

A malevolent hatred filled the man's eyes. "You're not fooling me with that good cop routine of yours," he spat.

"You don't care about me. Now, I told you to back off, and I meant it. One more step, and I'll shoot."

All of Carlo's training told him to stay where he was, and not to lower his gun. *"At least let these good folks leave."* He nodded at the innocent bystanders. *"They're not part of this. Okay? Just let them walk away."*

"Why should I?"

"Because there are women and children here. They don't need to be seeing this."

Carlo could sense the man's hesitation, as what little was left of his conscience warred with the streetwise punk he'd become.

"Fine. They can go. But the cop stays."

"Okay." Carlo raised his voice. *"Would all of you please walk as quickly as you can to the end of the block? An officer will be waiting to assist you."*

The sound of running footsteps filled the air. Carlo's gun pointed at his adversary, and his adversary's gun pointed at Underwood. Neither of them moved. Neither of them flinched. Neither of them pulled his gaze from the other.

"What now?" the man challenged when the footsteps faded away.

Distract him, *Carlo thought.* Make an opportunity to take him down.

"What do you want?" Carlo asked.

"What do you think?" The man's lip curled. *"To get the hell out of here."*

"Look around you." Carlo nodded to the police cars at either end of the street, and to the cops crouched behind them, guns drawn and pointed. *"There's no escape."*

A deadly resolution filled the man's eyes. *"In that case, if I'm going down, I can at least take some of you with me. Starting with him."* His finger tightened against the trigger of the gun.

"No, don't," Carlo said quickly. Adrenaline surged

through him, and his heart thundered. "I have a better idea. Why don't I put my gun down, you let my sergeant go, and together you and I walk out of here. Okay?"

His men would never let the man go; they knew their job and would do as they'd been ordered. Carlo didn't know what would happen to him, but he hoped at least to assure James Underwood's safety.

"Yeah, right," the man sneered. "Like they're just going to let me walk on by."

"If I tell them to, they will."

"Why should they listen to you?"

"Because I'm their chief. They take their orders from me. Why do you think they haven't already started shooting? They're waiting for me to tell them what to do. You can walk out of here. But you have to let my sergeant go first."

"A minute ago, you were telling me there was no way I was getting out of here. Now you're telling me I can walk away. Why should I believe you?"

Carlo prayed he would say the right thing. "A minute ago, I thought I could talk you into surrendering. I know different now. If you let my sergeant go, I'll give the order for you to go free."

The man nodded at Carlo's gun. "Put that down first."

Slowly, Carlo laid the gun at his feet.

"Raise your hands above your head," the man ordered.

Carlo complied. "They won't let you go unless I tell them to. And I won't tell them to, until you let my sergeant go."

Once again, the man nudged the prone officer with the toe of his boot. "Get up. Keep your movements slow and careful."

"I don't want to leave you, Chief," Underwood said when he'd gained his footing.

"Go," Carlo said harshly. "That's an order."

With one last helpless look, Underwood turned away. He'd only taken a few steps, when Carlo saw a sudden *movement out of the corner of his eye. A middle-aged man burst from the shadows of number 1238. He was carrying a gun. Bishop, the man who'd called in the incident. The suspect's violent curse told Carlo he had seen, too.*

"No!" Carlo cried. "Get back!"

Bishop's shot was wide of the mark. The next thing Carlo knew, the air was filled with the sound of gunfire. He lunged for the pavement and his gun. Just as he grabbed it, he saw Underwood stumble and fall.

"No!" he cried again, pulling the trigger. He didn't even feel the bullets that ripped through his flesh. He just kept firing until the suspect's body hit the ground.

Ignoring the sound of pounding feet that told him of the approach of his men, Carlo crawled to James Underwood's side. One look in the lifeless eyes told him that he was too late.

Chapter 5

"Too late," Carlo moaned out loud. "Too late, too late, too late." Heart racing and drenched in sweat, he bolted upright on the sofa and buried his head in his hands.

Inevitably, as they always did after reliving the horror, recriminations echoed in his head. If only he hadn't put his gun down. If only he had squeezed off a shot when he'd had the chance. If only Fred Bishop hadn't come charging out of his house with that gun. If only Carlo's ineptitude hadn't cost James Underwood his life.

If only...

Don't worry about me, the fateful words he'd said to Mary Bell echoed in his ears. *I don't plan on being a hero.* At the time, he hadn't realized how prophetic they would turn out to be.

He could have lived with it if he had been the only one to be brought down. What he couldn't forgive himself for was that another man had fallen in his place.

"Face it, Garibaldi," he said bitterly to the darkness,

''you're a coward. You've got a yellow streak a mile long running down your back. The reason you didn't break the rules is because you were afraid. If you hadn't been so scared, James Underwood might still be alive today.'' And Carlo wouldn't be constantly tormented by images he couldn't forget.

Pushing the blanket aside, he climbed to his feet. Because he knew sleep would be a long time coming, he decided to check on Samantha.

She lay on her side, one hand outstretched above her head, the other clutched to her breast. To his relief, her forehead felt blessedly cool.

For untold minutes, he simply stood beside the single bed, staring down at its lovely occupant, while emotion tightened his throat. Heart thudding unevenly, he studied the play of shadows over her delicate features and watched with fascination the way she pursed her lips with each exhalation.

Obeying an impulse he was powerless to resist, he reached down trembling fingers to brush back a lock of hair from her cheek. For several seconds more, he allowed his fingers to linger against the warmth of her skin, to feel its softness. Though he knew it had to be his imagination playing tricks on him, he could almost swear she was leaning into his touch.

Had James Underwood watched her like this while she slept? Had he, like Carlo, been unable to deny the urge to reach out and touch her? Was she dreaming of her late husband right now, wishing it was his caress she felt against her skin?

Carlo snatched his hand away.

A soft cry from the room next door captured his attention, and he left Samantha's side. When he entered Jeffrey's bedroom, he found the boy tossing and turning in his bed. The sheets were twisted around the child's small body, and his blanket and comforter had been kicked to the floor. Carlo bent to pick them up.

"No, no, no," Jeffrey cried as Carlo smoothed the covers back over him.

He has nightmares, Samantha had told him on the afternoon she'd asked him to be her son's buddy. What could be plaguing the child so?

"Jeffrey," he called softly, bending over the boy. "Jeffrey, wake up."

"No. Oh, no, please." Jeffrey moaned again. "Don't leave me."

Wishing only to end the torment he heard in the child's voice, Carlo reached down and gently shook his shoulder. "Wake up, Jeffrey. You're having a nightmare."

Jeffrey's eyes flew open, and he shot to a sitting position. To avoid what seemed an inevitable collision of Jeffrey's head with his chin, Carlo dropped his hand from the boy's thin shoulder and took a step back. Jeffrey skittered away and huddled in a ball against the wall. Gulping in air like a fish out of water, the boy stared at him out of unseeing eyes.

"It's okay," Carlo reassured, not knowing how to give the child the comfort he so obviously needed. If it had been his nephew in distress, Carlo would have gathered him into his arms and held tight until the terror had passed. But this wasn't his nephew. This was Jeffrey, and Jeffrey would reject any such gesture from him. The only people Jeffrey let that close anymore were his mother and grandmother.

"Everything's okay," Carlo repeated, hoping his presence would somehow help. "You were having a nightmare. That's all. It's over now."

Several minutes passed before Jeffrey's breathing returned to normal and the terror left his face. Without looking at Carlo, he climbed back under his covers and closed his eyes.

Carlo took that as his signal to leave. "If you need anything, just call. I'll be in the den."

"Don't go."

The barely audible words stopped Carlo in his tracks. Had he imagined them? Slowly, he turned to face the slight figure in the bed. Jeffrey's eyes were open.

"You want me to stay?" Carlo asked carefully. He was treading on fragile ground, he knew. One misstep, and it would crumble beneath him.

The boy's nod was brief but emphatic.

Don't let it go to your head, Carlo told himself. *Jeffrey doesn't really want to be with you. He just doesn't want to be alone right now.* Still, it was a start.

"Cover your eyes," he said. "I'm going to turn on the light." They both blinked against the sudden brightness.

Pulling the chair from the desk located by the door, Carlo placed it beside Jeffrey's bed and sat down. "To tell you the truth, I'm glad you asked me to stay. You see, I was having trouble sleeping myself. I could use the company."

Jeffrey didn't say anything. Well, what had Carlo expected? That the child would hurdle all the barriers he'd erected between them and blurt out whatever it was that was bothering him?

"Want to tell me what your nightmare was about?"

No answer.

"Fair enough. How about school? Want to talk about that?"

Again, no answer.

"Okay. What about TV? Do you have a favorite show?"

The boy shrugged.

This game of twenty questions was getting them nowhere, Carlo thought in mounting frustration. If only they had something in common, something innocuous to talk about to pass the time until Jeffrey was ready to be left alone again.

A sudden thought brought him up short. They did have something in common. Unfortunately, the subject was hardly innocuous, and touched on areas Carlo wanted to avoid, but he didn't know what else to say to bridge the silence that echoed around them as loudly as a thunderclap. It was worth a shot, anyway.

"My mother died when I was seventeen," he said, and was encouraged by the spark of interest in Jeffrey's eyes. "Did you know that?"

"No." The boy shook his head. "How did she die?"

"Cancer."

"Did it hurt?"

Of course, Carlo realized. A child would think of the pain first. "A little. But she had medicine to make the hurt go away."

Silence reigned for a full thirty seconds, thirty seconds during which Carlo held his breath and hoped Jeffrey wouldn't let the subject go. He exhaled slowly when the boy offered, "My dad died because he was shot."

"I know."

Jeffrey raised himself up on his elbows. "You were there, weren't you? My mom said you were. She said you tried to help my dad."

It was all Carlo could do not to flinch. This was what he'd been afraid of. He'd wanted Jeffrey to talk to him, but he didn't want to talk about the way James Underwood had died.

"Yes, I was there." The words sounded strangled.

"Did it hurt him to get shot?"

Oh, lord, how was he supposed to deal with this? As a wave of fresh grief and guilt surged through him, Carlo looked down at his hands so Jeffrey wouldn't see the emotion on his face.

He didn't know if he could do this. The torture was almost unbearable. He would willingly endure hot pokers pressed against his flesh, slivers of wood shoved beneath his fingernails, crawling on his hands and knees across hot coals, anything but Jeffrey's questions about that awful day.

He had to do this. No matter the cost, he had to put his personal feelings aside. Because Jeffrey had been silent, and now he was finally talking. If this was to be Carlo's punishment, so be it. He'd endure it without complaint, so long as Jeffrey kept talking to him; so long as it enabled the child to have a good night's sleep.

Hardening his heart against his pain and his guilt, Carlo raised his head. "Remember how I told you I would never lie to you?"

"Uh-huh."

"Good. Then you'll know I'm telling you the truth now, that I'm not saying this just to make you feel better. No, Jeffrey. It didn't hurt. Your dad...died instantly. He didn't feel any pain."

Jeffrey seemed to relax. "That's good."

"You've worried about that a lot, haven't you?"

"Uh-huh."

"Have you ever talked to your mom about it?"

"I wanted to but..." Jeffrey bit his lip.

Carlo understood perfectly. He remembered all too well how paralyzed with grief his father had been after his mother's death.

"But you didn't want to burden her, did you? You didn't want to add to her pain."

Jeffrey's silence gave Carlo his answer.

"It's been more than a year now. I think your mom would want you to talk to her about this. Think about it, will you?"

"How did you feel after your mom died?" Jeffrey surprised him by asking.

"I missed her. So much that it hurt."

"I feel that way, too. All the time."

The admission was more than Carlo had dared hope for. It was probably because the boy was too tired to put up barriers. Whatever the reason, he decided to take advantage of the moment. He didn't know when, or if, he'd be presented with another opportunity.

"For a while, after my mom died, I felt guilty when I laughed or had a good time with my friends. Have you ever felt that way?"

"Uh-huh."

Recalling how the boy had reacted to his mother's illness, Carlo added, "I was also really afraid my dad would die, too. Do you ever feel that way—worried your mom might die, and you'll be all alone?"

Jeffrey turned his head away, but not before Carlo saw the tears brimming in the corners of his eyes.

"You do feel that way, don't you?" he pressed.

"Sometimes," Jeffrey admitted.

"Did you feel that way today? Because your mom was sick?"

"Uh-huh."

"Is that why you won't play with your friends? Because it hurt so much when your dad died, and you don't want to hurt like that ever again?"

Tears spilled onto Jeffrey's cheeks, and he drew a shuddering breath. Carlo's heart went out to the child. Jeffrey had endured so much for one so young.

"I want you to know I'm not saying all this to upset you and to bring back bad memories. I'm saying this because I understand how you're feeling. There's something else I think you should know. It's been almost twenty years since my mother died. In all that time, no one else in my family has died. No one. My father is still alive. So are all of my brothers and my sister. My friends, too."

He paused to make sure he had Jeffrey's undivided attention. "Know what? If I had pulled away from everyone I care about out of fear of losing them, I would have missed so much these last twenty years. Do you think your father would want you to live the way you are? Not participating in school? Turning your back on your friends? Not doing the things you always loved to do?"

"No." The word was a whisper.

Carlo swallowed the lump that had formed in his throat and said a silent prayer that he wouldn't botch everything right here.

"Death touches us all at one time or another. And it causes a lot of pain for those who are left behind. It's only natural to want to escape that pain. But when we shut out the people who love us, when we shut out our friends, we really don't escape. In the end, all we do is cause ourselves even more pain.

"Please don't hurt yourself anymore, Jeffrey. For your mom's sake. For your sake."

A sob escaped Jeffrey's throat.

This time, Carlo didn't hesitate. Moving to the edge of the bed, he gathered the child in his arms. Jeffrey went rigid for a moment before burying his face into Carlo's chest. His thin body shook with the strength of his sorrow.

"It's okay, it's okay," Carlo soothed in a thick voice as he rocked the boy back and forth.

His arms had grown stiff and his right leg had fallen asleep by the time Jeffrey's sobs faded away. The evenness of the child's breathing told him that Jeffrey had succumbed to exhaustion and was sleeping deeply.

In the morning, the boy would probably regret having let himself be so vulnerable in front of Carlo. In the morning, he would probably have rebuilt his walls and be as silent as ever. But for tonight he would sleep. And maybe some of what Carlo had said would take root and begin to grow.

Though his body cried out for him to change position, Carlo was loath to move. Tenderness swept through him as he gazed down at the sleeping child. Jeffrey's hair stood up in spiky clumps that tickled Carlo's chin. A smattering of freckles danced over a narrow nose and scattered across boy-ish cheeks.

Carlo's heart felt tight in his chest as impossible, irrational and totally impractical dreams chased around in his mind. Dreams of holding Jeffrey like this whenever the child needed comforting. Dreams of holding the boy's mother, and not just for comfort.

There was a song from a famous musical about daring to dream impossible dreams. Despite the optimism of the song, deep in his soul, Carlo knew he could not afford to dream those dreams. Because the cold, hard truth was, some dreams were simply unattainable.

Silent tears of grief, hope and gratitude streaming down her cheeks, Samantha stood in the shadows outside Jeffrey's open bedroom door and watched Carlo rocking her sleeping son. His left arm was wrapped securely around Jeffrey's body. He used his free right hand to make sweeping circles with the flat of his palm over her son's back.

It was the touch of that very palm against her forehead that had awakened her earlier. Though still groggy from sleep, she had been aware enough to realize he was checking her temperature, and she'd forced herself to lie still beneath his touch.

Sleep had nearly reclaimed her when he'd touched her a second time. This touch, the brushing of her hair from her cheek, had been far different, much more intimate, and heart-meltingly tender. It had shaken her to the core, and she'd suddenly found herself fighting an urge to reach up and cradle that hand to her cheek, to bring it to her mouth where she could press her lips against his open palm. Dismayed by the surge of longing that had swept through her, Samantha had feigned sleep until he'd left her room.

Why had he touched her like that? she'd wondered in those first few shatteringly vulnerable seconds after his departure. More importantly, why had she responded to that very touch so strongly? Was she so starved for a man's touch that she had nestled into it the way a spring bud opened and reached for the gentle rays of the sun?

Jeffrey's cries had interrupted her troubled thoughts. In her weakened state, it had taken her several minutes to climb from her bed and to reach with shaking hands for her robe. By then, the murmuring of a deep male voice had told her that Carlo had gotten to Jeffrey first.

With every step down the narrow hallway, she'd felt her strength returning. At the open door of her son's bedroom, she'd opened her mouth to interrupt, to tell Carlo she was well enough to comfort her son and that he could go back to bed. To tell him that, better yet, she was feeling so well he could go home, if he pleased.

But when she'd heard Jeffrey talking about his father, saying things to Carlo he'd never confided in her, she hadn't been able to utter a word. Her newfound strength seeping out of her, all she had been able to do was cling to the shadows and listen while her heart broke all over again.

What kind of mother was she that she hadn't been able to see the reason why her son had refused to confide in her? Had she been so wrapped up in her own pain and misery that she'd shut out her child?

Thank goodness Carlo had seen. Thank goodness he'd been strong enough to break through the walls Jeffrey had erected.

Carlo...

Samantha's heart thudded as she stared at him. In profile, his features seemed even more defined, more masculine. He wasn't wearing a shirt, and the bare skin of his broad shoulders and muscled arms gleamed invitingly in the room's soft light. What was even more inviting was the way his head bowed protectively over her son. Though she couldn't see the tenderness in his eyes, she sensed that it was there. It made her heart ache with yearning to look at him that way.

He was a very special man, she acknowledged. An insightful man who had managed to draw her son out in a way not even the professionals had been able to do. Was it because he had lived it, too? Because he, more than anyone else, understood?

Whatever the reason, she was so thankful she'd gone to him for help. She owed him a debt that could never be repaid. By the same token, she wanted him as far away from her as possible. How could she feel such conflicting emotions about one human being?

She didn't want to feel anything for Carlo Garibaldi. She didn't want to fall into the endless depths of his brown eyes. She didn't want to wonder how it would feel to have his full lips pressed against her own, or his strong arms wrapped tightly around her, the way they were her son. But most of all, she didn't want to care how he felt about her. She didn't want to wonder if, perhaps just a little, he was experiencing some of the same urges that she was.

It was the middle of the night. She was just recovering from a fever that had sapped her strength. Not to mention that, after witnessing the exchange between Carlo and her son, her emotions were in turmoil. In the morning, when she was feeling stronger, she would see things more clearly. In the morning, she'd be able to look at Carlo objectively and know that the feelings he aroused in her were purely physical and didn't mean a thing.

Even if she couldn't, it didn't matter. After tonight, the only time she would be seeing him was when he came for outings with her son. Surely, for those brief minutes of time, she should be able to control herself.

The important thing was that Jeffrey had finally reached out to someone. If she could get him to tell her the things he'd told Carlo, and keep him talking, maybe he'd find his

way back to her. She'd start the ball rolling by telling him
the plans she'd made in the event something happened to
her, so that he'd know he would never be alone.

Jeffrey's bed made an unexpected creak, and she jumped.
Moving back farther into the shadows, Samantha watched
while Carlo tenderly tucked her son beneath the covers. Before he could turn and see her, she silently made her way
back to her room.

Carlo was standing at the stove when Samantha walked
into the kitchen at eight o'clock the following morning. The
table had been set for three, with a bottle of syrup and a
stick of butter gracing its middle. Orange juice—freshly
squeezed, if she wasn't mistaken—filled three glasses to the
brim. The aroma of frying bacon was heavy on the air, and
Samantha's stomach rumbled at the delectable smell.

Even more delectable was the way he looked in the jeans
and rumpled cotton shirt he'd worn the day before. He
seemed at home behind the stove as he whistled along with
the music playing lightly on the radio. Too much at home.
Wasn't it every woman's fantasy to have a good-looking
man cook for her?

So much for her determination that her awareness of him
would fade away with the sunlight, she thought wryly.

He turned at the sound of her footsteps and smiled his
disarming smile. His eyes, she noted as her heart skipped a
beat, were framed by thick, black lashes. They were nice
eyes, the eyes of someone who had a good soul. The tiny
laugh lines that crinkled at their edges also spoke to a well-
formed sense of humor. Even if he did, at times, have trouble
taking a joke.

"How are you feeling?" he asked.

"I'll live."

Self-conscious in a way she hadn't been when she'd
greeted him at the door yesterday in her robe and pajamas,

Samantha smoothed a hand over hair that was still wet from her shower. She didn't care, she told herself, that she stood before him without any makeup on. She didn't care that she was wearing an old pair of jeans and an even older, shapeless Penn State sweatshirt.

"You look a lot better than you did yesterday."

She couldn't stop a smile at that. One thing was certain: she'd never get a swelled head while Carlo was around.

"Thank you. I hope I wasn't too much trouble last night."

"You weren't any trouble at all."

She'd made a decision while standing under the warm spray of the shower. She would keep her distance from him, treat him the way she would any stranger in her home, politely but impersonally.

"Still," she said, "it must have interfered with your plans."

"My plans were flexible," he replied lightly. "Besides, Jeffrey did most of the work. He insisted on it."

"He has been rather protective of me since James died."

"I'd say that was only natural, wouldn't you?"

"Yes, I suppose so." She looked over her shoulder to the empty den. Usually by this time on a Sunday morning, her son would be deep into cartoons. "Where is Jeffrey?"

"Still sleeping."

"Still? Usually he's up at the crack of dawn."

"He had a late night last night. He refused to leave your side. Poor kid finally conked out around eleven."

Carlo didn't say anything about the scene she'd witnessed in Jeffrey's bedroom, and she wondered why. She should thank him, she knew, but she wasn't ready to talk about it yet. If she tried, she'd get all emotional, and then where would her objectivity, her impersonality toward him, be? She'd thank him later, after he left, preferably over the safe distance the telephone provided. It was cowardly of her, but it was the safest way.

"Are you hungry?" he asked.

"A bit."

"I'm not surprised. You ate hardly anything yesterday. How about some French toast and bacon?"

"That sounds very nice. Thank you."

He tossed her a curious glance. "Coming right up." A minute later he set a plate loaded with more food than she normally ate for three meals in front of her.

"Aren't you going to join me?" she asked.

"I think I'll wait for Jeffrey, if you don't mind."

"Of course not."

She studiously avoided his gaze as she dug into the food on her plate. It was delicious, and she gulped it down with just a little more grace than a bear after a long winter hibernation.

"Seconds?" he asked when she'd cleaned her plate. She heard the amusement in his voice.

"If it's not too much trouble."

This time, when he placed her refilled plate in front of her, he didn't move away. "Is it something I said?"

The hand she'd extended for the syrup halted in midair. "I beg your pardon?"

He took a seat across from her, and she folded her hands in her lap.

"The way you're acting this morning. Like I was a door-to-door salesman you can't wait to get rid of. Did I say or do something wrong?"

Samantha stifled a sigh. She supposed it had been too much to hope he would let her behavior pass without comment. The failing in her reasoning was that, initially, she was the one who had gone to him for help, not vice versa. And he'd willingly—after some nudging on her part—given it. Truth to tell, she was being extremely ungracious, considering all he'd done for her and Jeffrey. Especially after last night. He deserved some sort of explanation from her, not her cold shoulder.

"No, Carlo," she said slowly. "You didn't say or do anything wrong." *You were just being you.*

"I haven't offended you in some way?"

"Of course not."

"It's just me then, is that what you're saying? There's something about me that's making you behave this way."

Her response was automatic and heartfelt. "Oh, yes, it's definitely you."

The flare of hurt in his eyes, quickly masked, told her exactly how thoughtless her remark had sounded. When she stepped into things, she thought ruefully, she always went the whole way. This time, she'd gone all the way up to her knees.

"Let me rephrase that." Unable to meet his gaze, she looked down at the full plate she no longer had any stomach for. "I'm treating you so abominably because I thought it would help. Me, that is. You see, you make me feel things I haven't felt in a long time."

"What things?" he asked softly.

She looked up then and found him gazing intently at her. She swallowed, and her heart pounded. "Man-woman things."

When he just sat there, absolutely still and obviously stunned, she smiled. "You didn't see that coming, did you?"

He inclined his head in agreement. "It came totally out of left field."

"Sorry."

"Don't be." He gave her a smoldering look that made her heart pound even harder. "I feel the same way, you know."

"I know." She drew a deep breath. "Before you say anything else, let me finish, please. I'm attracted to you, yes.

But I'm not going to do anything about it. I'm not going to get to know you better over drinks or dinner. I'm not going to have endless discussions with you, during which I'll discover that we both like product x and detest product y. In short, I'm not going to do any of the things that a woman usually does when she finds a man attractive. My son needs my undivided attention right now. Even if he didn't, I'm not ready for a relationship. I don't know if I'll ever be.''

"Because you're still in love with your husband."

"Yes."

He stood and moved back to the stove. She watched while he transferred several pieces of French toast to a platter he kept warming in the oven.

"You're right, of course," he said after he closed the oven door. "Now is not a good time for me, either."

"Because of the reason behind your leave of absence," she guessed.

"Yes."

"I'm glad we both feel the same way," she replied, though for some strange reason she didn't feel glad at all.

"Sure makes things easier all the way around," he agreed, his tone light.

For several minutes, the only sound in the room was the soft music playing on the radio. Samantha tried to think of something to say to bridge the silence that grew more awkward with every passing minute.

"Where'd you learn to cook?" she finally asked.

He shrugged. "When you come from a large family, you learn to pitch in wherever you're needed."

"How large is large?"

"Seven kids. Six boys and one girl. I'm second oldest."

"Your poor sister," she said. "How did she ever survive with all those brothers?"

His laughter was genuine. "You've got to be kidding. Kate was spoiled rotten, especially since she was the only girl, and the baby to boot. She's a lot like you, actually. Feisty. Independent. Determined to do it all on her own at all costs.''

It felt good to have the awkwardness gone between them. ''Wait a minute,'' she said. ''Your sister's name is Kate? As in Kate Garibaldi, the author of 'Straight Talk'?''

''The one and only.''

Samantha could hear the pride in his voice. And the love. ''I read her newspaper column every day. She has a way of getting to the heart of an issue and pushing all my buttons.''

''Yes, that would be Kate,'' he said indulgently. ''Button pusher extraordinaire. I'll tell her you said that. She'll be thrilled.''

Samantha carried her plate to the sink and scraped the uneaten food into the garbage disposal. ''Now I know why you're so good with Jeffrey. You had all that practice with your younger brothers.''

''You sound surprised.''

''Only that a single man would know his way around children so well.''

She turned and found herself close enough to him to feel the heat of his body, to smell his clean masculine scent. Moving quickly away, she said, ''Coming from a large family, I'm surprised you don't have a whole houseful yourself.''

She realized she was doing exactly what she said she wouldn't do: asking questions to get to know him better. Right now, though, it seemed safer than the charged silence that filled the room whenever they stopped talking. Plus she really wanted to know.

''I'm kind of surprised, too,'' Carlo replied. ''I always wanted a big family.''

She leaned back against the counter. ''What happened?''

''When I finally had the time to really devote to a relationship, I always made sure to avoid women like you.''

Surprised laughter bubbled from her throat. "What do you mean, women like me?"

"It's a compliment," he said.

"Is it? Sounds dull to me."

Eyes darkening with emotion, he said, "I don't think you're dull at all. I thought we'd already established that."

His words brought to mind things she would rather not think about. "The bacon's starting to burn," she said breathlessly.

He hurried to remove the sizzling pan from the burner, then busied himself placing strips of bacon on a paper towel to drain.

"So," she asked, trying to sound nonchalant, "why did you avoid women like me?"

"Because of my mother."

"Your mother?"

"Yes. She died when I was seventeen. For the next thirteen years I helped my dad raise the younger kids. I didn't have much time to get seriously involved with anyone."

"And when you did have the time?"

He turned to face her again. "I discovered I really didn't want to get involved. I guess, in a way, I felt like I'd already raised my family. It was almost as if I was trying to relive those lost years. Not," he added quickly, "that I begrudge devoting those years to my family. I don't. I'd do it all over again in a heartbeat. I guess I just wanted to play for a while."

"And you never played with women like me?" She didn't know why she couldn't leave the subject alone.

"No."

"Why not?"

"Because the only game you know how to play is house."

For some reason, the words rankled. "What makes you think I wouldn't have wanted to play anything else?"

"Well," he challenged, taking a step closer, "would you?"

She bit her lip in consternation. He was right, darn him. She'd never been a person who could dabble in casual relationships the way an artist dabbled in paints. But right now, with Carlo's forceful body so close to hers, with the heat of him enveloping her and seducing her with its warmth, she knew a reckless urge to throw all caution to the wind, to see what it would be like to have a wild, crazy, no-strings-attached affair with him. The strength of that urge scared the life out of her.

"No," she replied, stepping carefully around him. "No, I wouldn't."

"Guess you've answered your own question, then."

"Guess I have." She gave a shaky laugh.

"And I guess I'd better be going."

Relief flooded through her. "I thought you were waiting to eat breakfast with Jeffrey."

"Turns out I'm not as hungry as I thought. Besides, I think it would be better this way. For both of us. Tell Jeffrey I'll see him next Saturday at one o'clock. And wish him a happy Thanksgiving for me."

She caught up to him at the front door. "Thank you for staying last night, Carlo. I don't know how I would have managed without you."

"The pleasure," he replied, with a bow of his head, "was all mine."

Chapter 6

Face raised to the morning sun, and carrying the rakes he'd brought with him the day before, Carlo whistled as he walked home. The cool breeze that rustled through the trees like children whispering secrets felt wonderfully refreshing. Better yet, he felt refreshed, both inside and out.

For the first time in longer than he cared to remember, Carlo felt happy. Whole. Almost carefree. He knew if someone held up a mirror to his face, he'd find that his smile was as wide as the Grand Canyon. And it was all because Samantha had told him she was attracted to him. She wanted him as much as he wanted her.

Could the day get any better?

Oh, she'd said she wasn't ready, but he'd seen the way she trembled at his nearness. He'd felt her gaze on him when his back had been turned to her. He'd heard the soft catch of her breath when, by chance, his hand had brushed against hers. If he was patient, if he gave her time and didn't press, could he get her to change her mind?

A siren echoed in the distance. Like the warning it was meant to be, the sound reminded Carlo of everything he'd blocked from his mind since Samantha had made her unexpected announcement. It reminded him of the reason why, no matter how hard he wished otherwise, she would never be his.

His smile died, and with it, his happiness and his sense of hope. He recalled the way he'd flirted with her in her kitchen and tasted the bitter pill of self-loathing. What had he been thinking? Or, more specifically, what part of his anatomy had he allowed to do his thinking for him?

Before that morning he would have at least thought he'd have enough conscience not to take advantage of Samantha's vulnerability. Obviously he had no conscience at all.

Be realistic, he told himself. It was gratitude she felt for him, and nothing more. She had projected onto him all her hopes for her son. In her eyes, whether he deserved the honor or not—and in his mind he knew he didn't—he was the one who was going to give her back her son. Once Jeffrey was well again, she would no longer find him so…interesting. Given that she was still in love with her husband, she probably wouldn't look at him at all.

And his feelings for her? Were they simply the result of his guilt and his need to make things right for Samantha? Or were they something different entirely? Something far deeper and lasting. Something that only happened once in a lifetime.

In the end, it really didn't matter. He'd never get the chance to find out. Because, when Samantha learned the role he'd played in her husband's death—something Carlo would have to confess if, by some miracle, they actually became involved—her feelings for him would disappear faster than a tourist's wallet on a street crowded with pickpockets. It was far better to have her reluctant admiration and to do nothing to further it, than to indulge his feelings for her and wind up with her hatred.

He knew it was cowardly of him not to tell her the real truth about what had happened that day, but he already knew he was a coward. So what else was new?

Carlo heard the commotion before he saw it. When he turned the corner onto his street, he stopped dead in his tracks and swore out loud.

Could the day get any worse?

A squad car sat in front of his house, lights flashing. Behind it was a fire engine, the same engine, he supposed, responsible for the siren he'd heard a minute earlier. His brothers, all five of them, crowded his porch. Along with them, Carlo saw Lon Sumner, his deputy chief, and four firemen. From what he could gather from this distance, and from their gestures, they were trying to figure out the best way to break down his front door. If that wasn't bad enough, what seemed like the entire neighborhood had come out to watch the spectacle.

"Ask not for whom the siren blares," he murmured in grim amusement. "It blares for you."

With a sigh, he started down the street. Fifteen minutes later, relative peace and quiet had been restored to the neighborhood, and he was finally alone with his brothers. Without a word, he thrust his key into the front lock, gave it a vicious twist and, throwing the door wide, stalked inside. They caught up with him in the living room.

"Where the hell have you been?" Roberto demanded.

"We've been calling since last night," Antonio added. "You didn't answer your phone."

Carlo crossed his arms over his chest and braced his back against the fireplace mantle. His brothers stood just inside the doorway and were lined up according to age; Roberto first, then Marco, Bruno, Franco and, finally, Antonio. It was the formation they had always assumed when confronting a problem. The Garibaldi brothers against the world. Strength in numbers. More than a few bullies, not to mention several of his sister Kate's youthful suitors, had been known to flee when they'd seen that line-up. If he hadn't been so furious, Carlo might have laughed.

Instead, he silently counted to ten. When he spoke, his voice was deceptively calm.

"The reason I didn't answer my phone is because I wasn't home. Something you all should have figured out on your own."

Roberto stepped out from the pack. As the oldest, it was obvious he felt it his duty to take the lead.

"Where were you?"

"Helping a sick friend. Not that it's any of your business."

"What friend?" Bruno asked. "We called everyone you know. No one had seen you."

"It's someone new. Someone you haven't met."

"And this friend doesn't own a telephone?" Marco demanded. "You were too busy to call your family and let them know you were okay?"

This time, when Carlo counted to ten, it did little to take the edge off his temper. "Why should I have? I spoke to each of you yesterday morning. I even called you, Marco, to ask how to treat my friend's symptoms. Remember? You knew perfectly well I was okay."

He drew a deep, bracing breath. "What's going on here? I'm thirty-six years old, and all of a sudden the rest of you have decided I'm incapable of taking care of myself? You're driving me crazy. I can't turn around for stumbling over one of you."

"What's going on," Franco explained, "is that our brother, Carlo, the dependable one, the one who took over the responsibility of raising the rest of us when Mom died, has seemingly gone around the bend. You've taken a leave of absence from a job you love, and you won't tell us why. You seem distant, distracted all the time. You hardly ever smile. You won't talk to us.''

"Just what the hell is going on with you?'' Bruno burst in. "We think we have the right to know. If you're in trouble, we want to help.''

Carlo's irritation faded. If it had been one of his brothers acting the way he was, he would have called the fire department himself. He really couldn't blame them for being so upset.

"I'm sorry, guys. I didn't mean to worry you. As for what's going on with me, it's personal. It's not something you can help me with. I have to work through it myself.''

"It's not money trouble, is it?'' Franco asked. He was a financial analyst, and in his mind every problem boiled down to money. "'Cause if it's money you need, you know where to come.''

"I don't need any money, but thanks for the offer.''

"Are you sick?'' Marco asked.

"Not even a sniffle. And before you ask, I don't have cancer, or any other terminal illness. I'm perfectly healthy.''

"What about the law?'' Antonio, who was also a cop, asked.

"I'm not in trouble with the law, either. That's not why I've left the force.''

"I know,'' Roberto exclaimed. He clapped Carlo on the back. "It's a woman. You're having a wild, crazy affair, and you can't stand to be apart from her.''

"I am not having a wild, crazy affair.'' He wasn't even having a wild, crazy friendship. "Although why I should be admitting this to you, I have no idea.''

"And you wonder why we're worried.'' Bruno's exasperation was obvious. "You used to date a different woman every week. Do you know how many hearts you haven't broken lately? I hear talk that half the eligible women in town have taken to wearing black.''

Carlo had to smile. ''I think you're exaggerating things a bit.''

''No, he's right,'' Antonio said. ''Now that I think of it, it's been ages since I've seen you with a woman. What gives?''

''You ask me,'' Roberto said, ''you haven't been the same since the shooting.''

They were getting far too close to the truth for Carlo's comfort. ''If you'd come so close to death, I think you'd be changed, too,'' he said.

''Why can't you just tell us what's wrong?'' Marco asked. ''We're your family. There's nothing we can't face, if we do it together. Isn't that what you drilled into our heads the whole time we were growing up?''

It would be so easy to tell them, so wonderful to unload his burden. And it would destroy their faith in him. He didn't think he could bear to see that.

''There are some things even family can't help with,'' he told them. ''This is one of them. I wish I could make it easier for you, but I can't. You're just going to have to trust that I know what I'm doing. By the way, where's Kate? I'm surprised you didn't drag her along with you.''

''We tried,'' Roberto admitted. ''She told us to mind our own business and leave you alone, that you'd tell us what was bothering you when you were ready.''

Carlo's heart filled with gratitude. He could always rely on Kate to be the sensible one.

''I need to ask you guys a favor,'' he said. ''I need you to give me some breathing room here, no questions asked. That means no more calling every hour. And no more summoning the police and the fire department when you can't find me.''

"We're here for you anytime, day or night, if you need to talk," Antonio said.

"I know. Thanks." His gaze roved from face to face. "So, do I get that breathing room?"

"Sure, Carlo," Roberto said. "Anything you say. Right, guys?"

"Right," Marco, Bruno, Franco and Antonio replied in unison.

Carlo had a feeling it wasn't going to be that easy.

It wasn't. As promised, his brothers relaxed their vigil. However, to them, giving him some space meant that, instead of calling him every hour, they called him every two. Roberto had even sent a waiter from his restaurant with dinner that night. And Bruno had driven by in his squad car three times that Carlo had seen.

When Carlo's doorbell rang the following day just after noon, he heaved a resigned sigh. He didn't have to look out the peephole to know who he'd find standing there. He'd just returned from a long walk that he'd taken in an effort to clear his mind—not that it had helped—and he supposed he had been gone just long enough to arouse his brothers' anxiety. Any minute now he expected to hear the sirens that would announce the arrival of his deputy chief and the fire department.

The good news was, his brothers would only be able to cry wolf so many times before they were ignored entirely. He could only hope that time would arrive soon.

"Didn't we have this out yesterday?" he growled, wrapping his hand around the doorknob and throwing the door wide. "I thought you were going to give me some space. Why are…you…back…?"

Instead of his brothers, Samantha Underwood stood on his porch. Her cheeks were rosy from the cold air, and she looked as delectable as the cake she balanced in her hands.

"Why am I getting the strangest feeling of déjà vu?" she asked with a smile that made his heart skip a beat.

He smiled back at her. "Maybe because I yelled at you the last time you showed up unexpectedly at my door."

"Looks like I'm going to have to stop showing up unexpectedly, then."

"Please don't. You're welcome anytime." He was surprised at how much he truly meant it. "I'm sorry I yelled. I thought you were someone else. Again." He shrugged. "I'm going to have to stop doing that."

She tilted her head, and he saw a gleam of curiosity in her eyes. "Who exactly did you think I was?"

"My brothers."

She seemed surprised. "You don't like them dropping in on you?"

"It's not that. You see, lately they've taken it upon themselves to watch me closer than a bodyguard. It can be rather…well, trying."

"I can imagine. Why are they watching you so closely?"

"Because I've taken a leave of absence from my job."

"And?" she prompted.

Leave it to Samantha to realize his answer had been far from complete. "And I won't tell them why."

"Ahh." She nodded. "They're worried about you."

"Yes."

"Do they have anything to be worried about?"

The question meant she was wondering if maybe she'd asked a walking time bomb to help her with her son. Maybe she had. Walking time bomb or not, he knew he would never do anything to deliberately harm her or Jeffrey. But then, he'd never meant for anything to happen to James Underwood, either.

"I just need some time off."

"I can certainly understand that," she said. "There are days when all I do is yearn for a vacation. I would expect,

with the pressures of your job, that you would need one far
more often than me.''

His job, and the reasons for his ambivalence about it, were
subjects he definitely did not want to discuss with her. A
blast of frigid air reminded him that a cold front had roared
through, blowing the weekend's idyllic Indian summer
weather far to the east. She must be freezing. Remembering
his manners, he stood aside.

''Would you like to come in?''

''Thank you.''

A whiff of her perfume tickled his nose when she passed
by. The delicate scent reminded him of flowers and a
meadow in June.

Closing the door, he turned to face her, determined not to
let the sight or scent of her go to his head. It was a lost
cause, he realized. The briefest of glances her way was
enough to get his heart thundering. At least he could be the
perfect host, and not make her uncomfortable by letting her
see how she affected him.

''I suppose you're wondering why I'm here,'' she said.

Now it was his turn to feel the prickling sensation of déjà
vu. The last time he'd heard a variation of those words, the
mayor had spoken them, and they had marked a turning
point in his life. He didn't think he was ready for another
one.

''A little,'' he replied cautiously.

She moistened her lips with her tongue, and his apprehension was forgotten as he followed the movement with
fascination. *Get hold of yourself, Garibaldi!* he berated, giving himself a mental shake. He couldn't understand why it
was so difficult for him to ignore her allure. She was just
another pretty woman, wasn't she? He'd never had this problem before, and he was hardly inexperienced with the female
sex. Why could Samantha blow his composure to smither-
eens with just a flick of her tongue across her lips?

"I came by to apologize for being so rude to you yesterday," she said. "My behavior was uncalled for."

"You weren't rude," he felt compelled to say.

"Yes, Carlo," she corrected, "I was. After all you've done for me, and for Jeffrey, I'm ashamed of myself. I hope you'll accept my apology."

"Of course, although it really isn't necessary."

"I also baked you this cake as a token of my appreciation for taking care of me Saturday night. I don't know what I would have done if you hadn't stayed. Thank you." She offered the cake to him. "It's chocolate. I hope you like it."

"Chocolate cake is my favorite. Care to share a piece with me?"

"I'd like that very much," she agreed, to his surprise. "I only have a few minutes, though. I'm on my lunch hour."

He placed the cake on top of the old oak washstand that sat just inside his front door and helped her off with her coat. Beneath it, she wore a plain white uniform dress, white hose and white soft-soled shoes. Her hair had been folded into a neat, serviceable bun at the nape of her neck.

She should have looked prim and proper, and chastely untouchable. Instead, Carlo thought she looked sexy as hell. Florence Nightingale as portrayed by Gwyneth Paltrow. He couldn't decide whether she was an angel of mercy, or a temptress sent to claim what little was left of his soul.

She was trained to heal, and he needed to heal. Desperately. Could she give him the succor he craved? Could those long, slender fingers of hers soothe the ache in his heart? Could she give him an injection of her sweetness and light that would kill the regret and erase the memory of incompetence that haunted his every move? As the British would say: not bloody likely.

"The kitchen's this way," he said in a gruff voice as he bent to pick up the cake.

With every step he took, he was aware of her presence

behind him. He could hear the echo of her footfalls against the hardwood floor of the hallway. He could feel the heat of her body, so close to his. He could smell the fresh air on her skin, in addition to the light scent of her perfume.

Too late, he wondered if inviting her to share a piece of cake with him had been a smart idea. The way things were going, if his awareness of her didn't abate, before long he would be unable to resist the temptation she presented. When that happened, he was bound to make a fool of himself by doing something stupid, like reaching out to her. Samantha had made it abundantly clear that his attentions were unwelcome. Why couldn't he accept that and let it be?

Because he was a fool, that's why.

Unfortunately, he couldn't turn back now. He couldn't ask her to leave, at least not without an explanation. And Samantha befuddled him to the point where no ready excuse came to mind. The best thing to do was to cut the blasted cake, eat it as fast as he could chew, and shoo her out the door. In future, he'd be careful to keep his distance from her. It shouldn't be hard, since the only time he'd be seeing her was when he stopped by her house to pick up Jeffrey.

Relief filled him when he saw the carvings covering his kitchen table. He'd have to clear them away before they could eat, and the distraction would help take his mind off Samantha. First, though, he had to find a spot to set the cake down.

He opted for the counter beside the sink. When he turned, Samantha was bent over the table, examining the carvings. She raised her head and looked at him.

"Did you make these?"

"Yes."

"They're wonderful."

The admiration in her voice was real, and a shaft of pleasure pierced his heart. "Thank you."

"Can I touch one?"

''Of course. They're not fragile. They won't break.''

Gently, she picked up an eagle and turned it around in her hands.

''This is amazingly detailed. If you ever decide to leave police work, you'd have a promising future in wood carving.''

''It's something I've been giving a lot of thought lately,'' he admitted.

A look of amazement crossed her face. ''You'd actually consider leaving the force?''

''Spoken like a true cop's wife,'' he said without thinking. When the import of his words hit him, his smile died, and he felt stricken. Thanks to him, she wasn't a cop's wife anymore.

''I'm sorry, Samantha. I didn't mean to—''

She held up a hand. ''Don't apologize. People always apologize whenever they inadvertently speak of James, as if it hurts me to hear his name, to talk about him. What they don't understand is that I want to talk about him. I don't want to pretend he never existed.''

''Of course not,'' Carlo said stiffly.

Though he understood her feelings, he couldn't talk about James with her. He simply couldn't. And he didn't want to hear how blissfully happy they had been and how much she missed him. Guilt stabbed at him anew.

He cleared his throat. ''We'd better cut the cake so you're not late getting back to work. Give me a minute, and I'll move these out of the way.''

''Let me help.''

It took several trips to carry all the carvings into the dining room. On the last trip, his arms were so full of wooden animals, his head down to make certain he didn't drop any, that Carlo didn't see her coming through the doorway until it was too late. He ran full tilt into her.

Miraculously, he didn't drop any carvings. But that was

only because she reached out to steady him. The touch of her fingers against the bare skin of his arms sent a flame licking up his veins. Likewise, the soft pulsing of her breath against his cheek.

"Sorry," he muttered.

"No harm done," she replied in a low voice that sounded as strained as he felt. Releasing her grip on him, she stepped away.

He was still breathing hard when he reentered the kitchen a minute later. Walking immediately to one of the counters, he grabbed a knife from the cutlery drawer.

"Do you mind cutting the cake?" he asked. "If I do it, I'll just butcher it."

"I'd be happy to."

"Coffee or milk?" He placed two plates on the table and carefully avoided her gaze.

"Is the coffee already made?"

"No, but it'll just take a minute."

"In the interest of time, then, let's make it milk."

She sounded as eager to leave his kitchen as he was for her to go.

"Milk it is."

While she cut two generous slices, he poured the milk and tried to pretend the incident in his dining room hadn't happened. He realized that, other than his sister, Kate, he'd never had a woman in his kitchen. It was the one place he'd never invited his dates. He didn't know why that was so, but it was. Samantha Underwood looked good in his kitchen. Too damn good.

"I know it's none of my business," she said when they were seated across from each other, "but are you really thinking of leaving the force?"

The hand that had speared a piece of cake with his fork halted halfway to his mouth.

"You make it sound like a crime."

''For this community it would be. You're like a god to most people.''

What was he to her? he couldn't help wondering as he placed the fork back on his plate.

''Maybe the time has come for them to worship a new god.'' His voice sounded rougher than he'd intended.

She looked confused. ''What do you mean?''

He drew a deep breath. ''Nothing.''

''You didn't answer my question. Are you thinking about leaving the force? Is that why you've taken a leave of absence?''

''That's part of it,'' he admitted.

''But why?''

He shrugged. ''Things just haven't turned out the way I planned.'' Picking up his fork again, he took a bite of cake and chewed.

Her lips curved. ''Which means you don't want to talk about it.''

''No, I don't.''

''I understand. I think you should know I had another reason for coming here today. I wanted to thank you for comforting Jeffrey when he had his nightmare Saturday night.''

Carlo started. ''Jeffrey told you?''

''No. He hasn't said a word.''

''Then how did you know?''

''I saw you. I heard Jeffrey cry out. By the time I got to his room, you already had the situation in hand.''

So she'd watched him as he comforted her son. He wasn't certain how that made him feel.

''Why didn't you tell me?'' she asked.

Why hadn't he? Because he hadn't been sure that anything had really been accomplished. Jeffrey could have woken up the following morning and been just as withdrawn as ever. And because, if there really had been a breakthrough, he'd wanted Jeffrey to go to his mother of his own free will. After all she'd been through, Samantha deserved to take the credit for any progress Jeffrey made. Carlo deserved nothing at all.

"I didn't think there was anything to tell."

"You knew what to ask him," she said softly, regretfully. "I didn't. You even knew why he wasn't confiding in me. Because he didn't want to add to my burdens."

She shook her head, and pain filled her eyes. "I'm his mother. I know him better almost than I know myself. And still I didn't see it. How could that be?"

Carlo didn't know what to say. All he knew was that he couldn't bear her pain.

"I lost a parent at a young age. I just tried to remember what it was like."

"So did I, Carlo," she surprised him by saying. "My dad was a cop. He was killed in the line of duty when I was thirteen. And I still didn't have a clue as to why my son felt he couldn't confide in me."

Knowing about her father made matters doubly worse. "You were dealing with a lot of things you didn't have to deal with when you were a child. And boys aren't girls. They handle loss differently."

"Perhaps." She straightened her shoulders and made a physical effort to compose herself. "Now's not the time for regret anyway. Want to know why?"

"Why?"

"Because you were wrong about Jeffrey not making any strides. He has."

Carlo went still. "There's been a breakthrough?"

"Yes." A broad smile spread across her face, and her eyes positively glowed. "In school this morning. Jeffrey raised his hand in class. Can you believe it? His teacher called me the minute she dropped them off for gym. I think she was even more excited about it than me."

"That's wonderful, Samantha." He raised his glass of milk. "A toast. To Jeffrey and to baby steps. May there be many more."

"To Jeffrey and to baby steps," she echoed, clinking her glass against his.

"I guess this means you won't need me to act as Jeffrey's big brother anymore," he said as she took a bite of cake.

She chewed quickly and swallowed. "What do you mean?"

"You've gotten the breakthrough you've been praying for." He shrugged. "You don't need me anymore."

"Oh, yes, I do, Carlo," she said vehemently. "He raised his hand in class. That's all. He's still got a long way to go. If he confided in you once, I'm hopeful he'll do so again. I need you now more than ever. Jeffrey needs you. Please tell me you'll still be his buddy."

He didn't have the heart, or the right, to turn her down. "I'll be Jeffrey's buddy for as long as he needs me."

"Thank you."

She visibly relaxed, and they ate the remainder of their cake in silence.

"Thanksgiving's just three days away," he said, carrying their dirty dishes to the sink.

"Yes, it is."

"Do you have to work?"

"No, thank goodness."

"Big plans for the day?" he asked over the rush of water as he rinsed their plates and placed them in the dishwasher.

"Not really. Jeffrey and I are having a small celebration together."

"What about your mother?"

"What about her?"

"Aren't you having dinner with her?"

"She's away on a cruise."

"I just assumed she'd be back in time for Thanksgiving."

"Thanksgiving is the whole reason she went on the cruise."

"I don't understand."

"My father was killed on Thanksgiving day. Every year my mother goes on a cruise to get away from the memory."

To get away from it, Carlo wondered, or to steep herself in it? "How long has she been doing this?"

"Nineteen years. When we were little, she took my two older sisters and me with her."

So her mother had been grieving for nineteen years. How long would Samantha grieve for the man she had loved? Five years? Ten? Fifty? It had taken his own father well over ten years before he'd been ready to date again.

Drying his hands on a dish towel, he turned to face her. "Do your sisters live near here?"

"No. Bridget's in New York, and Colleen's in Los Angeles. They usually only make it home once or twice a year."

"And Thanksgiving's not one of those times."

"Not this year."

"Have dinner with me, then," he blurted impulsively.

She drew back in her chair. "I don't think that's such a good idea."

He gave himself a mental kick. "What I meant to say was, have Thanksgiving dinner with me and my family."

"The same family who's driving you crazy?" she asked dryly.

"The very one."

She shook her head. "That would be too much of an imposition."

"You wouldn't be imposing at all. It's a Garibaldi family tradition to share Thanksgiving dinner with those who would otherwise be eating alone. Last year there were a hundred and fifty of us."

Her eyebrows arched. "How could you possibly fit all those people into someone's home?"

"We don't. We have it at my brother Roberto's restaurant. It's on Mt. Washington, and has a beautiful view of the city. Please come. There will be a lot of children Jeffrey's age. Maybe he'll even take another baby step."

"Well…"

He leaned back against the counter and crossed one ankle over the other. "Tell me, Samantha, what were you going to make for this small celebration of yours?"

"Something simple." She shrugged. "Chicken, mashed potatoes, pumpkin pie."

"No turkey?"

"It seems a waste to cook a whole turkey for just two people. Jeffrey won't mind. He's not wild about turkey anyway."

"If you eat with us, he'll get to learn all about a traditional Italian Thanksgiving. Think of the educational benefits."

Her smile was slow and appreciative. "And just what is a traditional Italian Thanksgiving?"

"What is a traditional Italian Thanksgiving?" Carlo kissed his fingers and threw his hand wide in imitation of a gesture he'd seen his older brother make countless times. Roberto Garibaldi was serious about his food.

"A feast, Samantha. A veritable feast. Antipasto. Escarole soup. Italian bread. Lasagne. Turkey with all the trimmings, along with mashed potatoes, butternut squash, peas, corn, broccoli and cranberry sauce. And for dessert, apple or squash pie."

She laughed. "It sounds heavenly. But how could any one person possibly eat all that food?"

It was easy to smile back at her. "Simple. The meal takes several hours to eat by the time all the courses have been served. Say you'll come."

"How could I possibly turn that down? Not to mention

all the educational benefits. Thank you, Carlo. Jeffrey and I would love to come.''

''It's settled, then,'' he said quickly, before she could change her mind. ''I'll pick you both up at four.''

''I'm curious,'' she said. ''Why does your family do this?''

''My mother started it all over thirty years ago, when she asked our next-door neighbors to join our celebration. They'd just moved hundreds of miles from their families and were feeling lonely. We keep the tradition going in her memory. Every year, it gets a little bigger. One day we fully expect to have to rent out the convention center in downtown Pittsburgh just to accommodate everybody.''

''You loved your mother very much, didn't you?''

''Yes,'' he replied, his gaze on hers. ''I did. I still miss her.''

''Not many men would admit that, you know.''

He was genuinely puzzled. ''Why not?''

''Because it isn't…manly, I suppose. A man might think he'd look weak in someone else's eyes.''

''Loving someone doesn't make you weak, Samantha. It makes you strong.''

She stared at him for a long, tense minute before looking away. ''You're right, of course,'' she said softly, and Carlo knew she was thinking of her husband.

''It's late,'' she added, gathering up her purse and pushing her chair back. ''I'd better get back to work.''

Carlo pushed away from the sink. ''Thanks for the cake. It was delicious.''

''You're welcome.''

When they reached the front hallway, he helped her into her coat. At the door, she turned to him.

''I want to thank you again for all you've done for Jeffrey and me.''

She was too close, too beautiful, too tempting. ''All I did was give up a Saturday night.''

He said the words in a joking manner, to lighten the mood, and to take his mind off of how much he wanted to kiss her.

''No, Carlo. You did so much more than that.'' Her beautiful brown eyes gleamed earnestly. ''You gave my son the greatest gift of all. Peace of mind. For that, I'll never be able to repay you.''

The warmth in her eyes was his undoing. ''You're so lovely,'' he said unsteadily, and he could feel himself trembling.

She inhaled sharply. ''Carlo.'' The word was only half a protest.

Pressing a finger against her lips, he murmured, ''Shh. Don't speak. Don't think. Just feel.''

He still might have been able to resist her, but when she swayed toward him, he had no power against the urge that insisted he pull her into his arms. No power against the unrelenting demand that he lower his head and claim her mouth with his.

The kiss was heaven. She was heaven. After the briefest of hesitations, her slender body molded itself to his as if made just for him. Her lips were soft, incredibly soft. With a small sigh, she wrapped her arms around his neck. Her mouth parted, and he felt the wondrous thrust of her tongue against his.

Groaning, he pulled her closer. While his tongue tangled with hers and explored the inner recesses of her delectable mouth, he lost all sense of time and place, all sense of right or wrong. He was aware only of Samantha, of the feel of her breasts against his chest, of the thrust of her hips against his thighs.

A moment later, he felt bereft when she tore herself out of his arms.

Breathing hard, Samantha raised trembling fingers to her swollen lips. "I'm sorry. I'm not ready for this."

Carlo took a step back and fought for composure. "I know," he replied in a low voice.

She lowered her hand to her side. "Look, maybe it's not such a good idea for Jeffrey and me to come for Thanksgiving dinner."

Knowing that the day would feel empty if she wasn't there, he said, "Please don't change your mind. There will be so many people around, you won't have to spend any time with me if you don't want to."

To his relief, she gave a grudging nod. "Okay. So long as you accept that I don't want our relationship to become more personal."

"I promise not to extend my unwanted attentions your way without your permission."

"Very well, then. I'll see you Thursday."

"See you Thursday."

Carlo stood in the doorway and watched her drive away. Even though he knew he was torturing himself needlessly, he couldn't stop thinking about the way she'd felt in his arms. When he remembered her initial resistance to his embrace and, after that, the fervency with which she had returned his kiss, he couldn't suppress a sobering thought. Who exactly had Samantha been kissing? Carlo, or James?

Chapter 7

Samantha couldn't get the memory of Carlo's kiss out of her mind. No matter where she was, no matter who she was with and no matter what she was doing, it was constantly with her, replaying in vivid detail over and over and over again in a seemingly endless loop.

She would close her eyes to go to sleep at night, and she would see the way Carlo's eyes had darkened with emotion in the seconds before he'd bent his head toward hers. She'd take her first sip of coffee in the morning, and it wasn't the cup she'd feel against her lips, but the fullness of Carlo's mouth. She'd stand under the needles of the hottest shower spray she could endure, and she'd feel the heat of his strong arms around her. At work, she'd change an IV bag or make a notation in a patient's chart, and her breathing would grow ragged and her pulse rate would shoot up as she relived the uninhibited way she had responded to him.

Even now, three days later, as she stood at the floor-to-ceiling glass window fronting the main dining room of Café

Garibaldi, a window located high atop Mt. Washington and offering a breathtaking, panoramic view of downtown Pittsburgh at sunset, all she could think about was Carlo's kiss and how it had made her feel.

The edgy restlessness that filled her at the memory was driving her crazy. Where was her self-control? He was practically a stranger, after all. And it wasn't as if she hadn't been kissed before. So why couldn't she let it go?

Because kissing Carlo had been pure combustion. A lighted match to a puddle of gas. As a matter of fact, she was surprised she hadn't incinerated on the spot. She'd been married for ten years to a man she'd adored, and she had never experienced anything like Carlo's kiss.

It was amazing, she thought, what loneliness—and not a fair amount of desperation—could do to a person; how it could distort a little thing, like a mere kiss, way out of proportion until it assumed the size and shape of, oh, say, Texas. But that was exactly what had happened. It was the only plausible explanation.

Barring that one brief kiss, it had been over a year since a man had held her in his arms. If what Carlo had told her was true, and she had no reason to doubt him, it had been an equally long time since he'd held a woman. They were both lonely. They both had worries that were keeping them awake at night. Small wonder they'd put so much of themselves into that kiss.

He was a good man, like James. But he wasn't James. He never would be James. It would be wrong of her to use him to fill her loneliness.

Samantha licked her lips against the dryness that had overtaken her mouth and glanced around the large room filled with milling, chattering people. Thankfully, Carlo was nowhere in sight. Returning her gaze to the view, she acknowledged that, as big a mistake as it had been to respond to his kiss the way she had, it had been an even bigger mistake to come here, to have committed herself to sharing Thanksgiving dinner with his family and friends. Because that meant she'd be spending an entire evening in his company.

He'd promised he wouldn't kiss her again unless she asked him to, something she had no intention of doing. With any luck, he'd be sitting clear across the room from her, and she wouldn't even see him again until dinner was over and it was time for them to leave. There was nothing for her to worry about. Nothing at all.

Now, if only she could forget that kiss.

Closing her eyes, Samantha took several cleansing breaths and fought for composure. She'd never make it through the rest of the day if she couldn't control her thoughts. Forget the rest of the day. She wouldn't make it through the next ten minutes if she didn't get hold of herself.

Gradually, through an effort of will, she felt a blessed calm fill her. She also grew aware of the hum of voices surrounding her, and when she inhaled deeply, her mouth watered at the delicious aromas filling the room. She hadn't been eating much lately; she'd had no appetite. But right now, with the savory aromas of turkey, lasagne and apple pie floating on the air, she was suddenly, ravenously hungry.

Her stomach growled, and she came to a decision. This evening she would concentrate on the food, her surroundings and the people around her. She would ignore everything and anyone who threatened her newfound state of serenity. Surely it wouldn't be so hard.

"Enjoying the view?" Carlo asked from behind her.

Slowly, she turned to face him. One glance, and she knew the task she'd set herself would be one of the hardest she'd ever confronted. He looked so wonderful in a pair of black slacks and a white cable-knit sweater that stretched across what she now knew—thanks to the scene she'd witnessed the other night in her son's bedroom—were a phenomenal chest and spectacular shoulders, that her mouth watered even more than it had a minute earlier at the aromas swirling on the air. A burst of heat exploded in her midsection and radiated outward to warm the rest of her.

Was she enjoying the view? Oh, yes. Way, way too much. It had definitely been a mistake to come here.

"The view's…" She swallowed hard. "Quite something," she finished. Drawing a shaky breath, she reached inwardly for her rapidly fading composure and just barely managed to catch it and rewrap its tattered edges around her. "How's Jeffrey?"

"Fine. My nephew has taken him firmly in hand."

"He's responding to your nephew?" she asked in surprise. After raising his hand in class on Monday, there had been no further progress. Samantha was beginning to think that maybe Jeffrey's teacher had imagined the whole thing.

"Jeffrey's not talking," Carlo said. "But I clued Bobby in on the situation. He's a good kid. He'll stick by Jeffrey's side. Right now they're watching the latest Steel City Wrestling Alliance event that my brother taped from Pay-Per-View. Bobby's a big fan, too. Roberto has a big-screen television in his office, a ton of computer games and wall-to-wall munchies. Trust me, Jeffrey will be well entertained until the kids are brought up here for the main course."

"I know he'll be fine. Put my son in front of a Steel City Wrestling Alliance event, and he'll forget the rest of the world exists."

Carlo's eyes narrowed as he peered at her more closely. "Then what's wrong?"

Nothing, if you didn't take into consideration that she kept having the most inappropriate thoughts about him at the most inappropriate times.

"What on earth could be wrong?" Her voice came out a

squeak, and she cleared her throat. "Nothing's wrong, Carlo. Everything's perfectly fine."

He didn't look convinced. "You were pretty quiet on the ride over. And right now..." He shrugged. "You seem... distracted."

Distracted was as good a word as any for how she felt around him. And, excluding the small talk they'd exchanged on the ride over, she had been quiet. She hadn't known what to say to him. With Jeffrey being equally nonresponsive, the ride had been awkward, to say the least.

"I'm sorry. I guess I haven't been very good company."

"I didn't ask you here to be good company."

Suddenly, it was important for her to know. "Why did you ask me here?"

His response was immediate. "Because it's a Garibaldi family tradition—"

"To share Thanksgiving dinner with those who would otherwise be spending it alone," she interrupted. "Yes, yes, I know."

"Yes."

"And that's the only reason?"

Carlo seemed to go still. When he spoke, there was an intensity in his lowered voice that caught her off guard and sent her pulse galloping.

"Do you want there to be another reason?"

What was wrong with her? Samantha wondered desperately. Why was she trying to goad Carlo into admitting that maybe his motive for inviting her here was less than altruistic? She didn't want him to have nonaltruistic feelings for her, so why was she deliberately bringing them to the forefront? She didn't know. All she knew was that she always felt off balance around him. Maybe challenging him like this was her way of trying to maintain control.

She drew a ragged breath. She'd made a resolution to concentrate on the food and her surroundings, and she was determined to stick to it. That meant not goading Carlo into admitting something she didn't want to hear or face.

"Do you want there to be another reason, Samantha?" he repeated.

Somehow, she managed to find her voice. "Of course not. I'm sorry, Carlo. I don't know why I'm in such a combative mood today." That was the truth, at least.

"You sure you're not still worried about Jeffrey?"

It shamed her to admit that her son had been far from her thoughts. But if it took Carlo's focus off of her, she was willing to admit to anything.

"A little, I suppose."

"He'd be bored to tears if we forced him to sit with the adults the entire time."

"I know."

"I'll take you down to see him, if you'd like. We still have some time before the meal gets underway."

"No, Carlo." She squared her shoulders with sudden determination. "That won't be necessary. You see, I think I've been part of the problem."

His brow furrowed. "Why would you think that?"

Over the past months, she'd given the matter a lot of thought. "Since his father died, I've hovered protectively over him. Hard as it will be for me, Jeffrey won't be able to get better if I don't take a step back and give him some room."

Carlo's smile was understanding. "Under the circumstances, it's only natural you would want to shield him from further pain. Don't beat yourself up about it."

"I know. Thanks." She forced herself to smile back at him. "Anyway, enough time has passed. Jeffrey needs to move on."

"What about you?"

Once again, with one softly worded question, he had caught her off guard. "What about me?"

"Isn't it time for you to move on, too?"

"I have moved on, Carlo. I had no choice."

"Have you?" he challenged. "Have you really?"

"Yes," she replied with all the firmness she could muster. "I have. I'm standing alone, when I used to stand as one of a pair. I never thought I'd be standing this way, and I don't like it much, but I've accepted it as my reality."

He took a step closer to her, crowding her, making her aware of the heat of his body and his strength. "You don't have to stand alone, you know."

The way his eyes had grown dark and heavy-lidded told her he was remembering the kiss they'd shared. Her heart thudded and her breathing grew shallow. For long seconds, she was powerless to do anything more than fix her gaze on the sensuous mouth that had kissed her with such devastating thoroughness.

Samantha nearly groaned out loud. Now *he* was goading *her*. And she didn't know how to respond. Not here. Not now. Not with all these people around, some of whom, she realized as her gaze darted desperately around the room, were staring at them with open curiosity.

"You promised, Carlo," she warned.

Disappointment flashed in his eyes in the second before they went blank. "I'm sorry. You're absolutely right. I did promise. And you've made your position more than clear."

The smile that now curved his lips was polite and decidedly impersonal, as was his voice, when he spoke. "Can I get you something to drink?"

She shook her head. "I'm fine, thanks. But I would like to offer my thanks to our host, if that's possible."

Anything to take her mind off the man whose nearness she found so disturbing. And whose questions were even more so.

His shoulders lifted in a careless shrug. "Certainly. Follow me."

*   *   *

The huge kitchen was filled with gleaming stainless steel counters and appliances. Pots and pans hung overhead as well as covering almost every available surface. Around the room, at least a dozen people in white coats peered into ovens and pulled the lids off of steaming pans to stir their contents. At the center of the chaos, Samantha saw a tall man calmly issuing directions.

"Roberto," Carlo called.

The tall man turned and, after offering one more instruction over his shoulder, rushed toward them with a beaming smile. Samantha needed only one glance to know he had to be one of Carlo's brothers. The resemblance was unmistakable.

"Carlo!" Roberto cuffed his brother on the shoulder. "It's about time you showed up. We could use your help."

"In a minute," Carlo replied. "First, if you could spare a second, one of our guests would like to meet you."

"I always have time to meet a guest." Roberto trained his laughing eyes on Samantha before cupping both of her hands between his. "Especially when she is as lovely as a summer breeze."

Samantha couldn't help smiling at the line that was older than both of their ages put together. Thank goodness, handsome as he was, when this particular Garibaldi turned his charm on her, her heartbeat remained utterly steady. It was a relief not to have to be on her guard with him.

"Samantha," Carlo said, his tone wry, "I'd like you to meet my older brother, Roberto, owner of Café Garibaldi and an incorrigible flirt. Roberto, this is my guest, Samantha Underwood."

"I am not an incorrigible flirt," Roberto protested. Leaning toward Samantha, he confided in a stage whisper, "It's my wife, you see. A very possessive woman. She watches me like a hawk."

"I heard that," a smiling woman who was busily basting a turkey called.

Roberto laughed and blew the woman a kiss. "You know that I only have eyes for you, my love."

"That's because I'll cut them out if I ever do catch you looking at another woman," she retorted.

Roberto's eyes twinkled with merriment. "She would, too," he told Samantha.

"In a heartbeat," his wife confirmed.

"Isn't she the loveliest thing you've ever seen?"

The woman in question was small and round, her eyes blue, her face flushed with the heat from the oven. She was indeed lovely. And if the way she was looking at her husband was any indication, she was also very much in love. Samantha couldn't stop the pang that squeezed her heart. Without a second thought, she pushed it away. She'd had her time; she wouldn't begrudge others theirs.

"Yes," she agreed. "She's very lovely."

You don't have to stand alone, you know. The words Carlo had uttered mere minutes ago echoed in her ears. The offer, and the unspoken promise behind it—that if she would let him, he would stand by her side—were more seductive than he would ever know. But it was too soon. She wasn't ready. And she'd promised herself she wouldn't use Carlo, or any other man, to ease her loneliness. It wouldn't be fair.

Besides, even if he did stand by her, it would only be for a little while. As he himself had said, he didn't play house. Samantha, as they'd both acknowledged, didn't know how to play any other game. When, and if, she did open up her heart again to someone, it would be to a man who could offer her something besides a temporary arrangement. Banishing Carlo's words from her mind, and the traitorous flutter of hope from her heart, Samantha concentrated on her host.

"You're a very lucky man, Mr. Garibaldi."

Letting go of her hands, Roberto smiled his agreement.

"Welcome to Café Garibaldi, Samantha," he said, without a hint of flirtation in either voice or demeanor. "I can call you Samantha, can't I? And you must call me Roberto."

Nodding, she said, "Thank you for including me in the festivities."

"No thanks are necessary. We're delighted to have you share our feast with us." He waved a hand. "The More The Merrier is the Garibaldi family motto. So, have you met the rest of the crew? No? Come with me."

Carlo looked as if he wanted to protest, but before he could say a word, Roberto had taken her by the elbow and was ushering her around the room. Bemused, Samantha had no choice but to follow.

Roberto introduced her to his wife, Louise, who was in charge of the turkeys. She met Marco Garibaldi, who was overseeing the lasagne; Bruno and Franco, who were responsible for dishing up all the pies; Antonio, who worked busily over pan after pan of simmering vegetables; and Kate and her handsome husband, Steve Gallagher, who were putting the finishing touches on the antipasto platters.

By the time they'd circuited the room, Samantha felt her head spinning. She might not be able to put a name to every face twenty minutes from now, but she would always remember one thing: the love she felt in that room. That these people not only cared for each other, but that they also took great enjoyment in the feast they had selflessly prepared at their own expense was readily apparent.

"Your family does all the cooking?" she asked Roberto.

"Of course. It's Thanksgiving."

"I just assumed your employees would help out."

"Only if they volunteer. Thanksgiving is a time for family and friends, not for work. We cook the food together, and we sit down to eat it together. Afterwards, we do all the cleaning up together. Everyone has a job."

"What's your job?" she asked Carlo, who had finally caught up with them.

"Carlo helped bake pies yesterday and spent all morning stuffing turkeys," Roberto said. "That's why I gave him the afternoon off. Don't worry, he'll make up for it later. He gets to scrub the pots and pans."

Carlo gave a theatrical groan. "Again?"

"Can't let all those muscles go to waste," Roberto told him. "I need someone with brawn to keep my pots and pans sparkling."

Samantha was still trying to come to terms with a mental picture of Carlo up to his muscular forearms in piecrust and turkey stuffing when Roberto said, "There's one more person I'd like you to meet."

He directed her toward an older man who was quickly and expertly slicing loaves of Italian bread. "This is my father, Lorenzo Garibaldi. He comes all the way from Florida to be with us every year."

The words were said softly, and with obvious love and respect.

Samantha eyed the elder Garibaldi, a trim, tanned man who didn't look a day over fifty although he had to be at least ten years past that milestone, and knew exactly what Carlo would look like in thirty years. Refined. Dignified. Distinguished. And definitely devilish.

She didn't know why the image disturbed her so.

"It's a pleasure to meet you, Mr. Garibaldi."

Lorenzo put down the knife and wiped his hands on his white jacket. "You're Carlo's date?" he asked.

It was only then that, aghast, Samantha realized they all thought she was Carlo's date. That was why Roberto had flirted with her so outrageously. That was why he had taken pains to introduce her to everyone in the room. A quick glance at the smiling, expectant faces aimed her way confirmed that impression. No wonder Carlo hadn't wanted her to be introduced around.

"Yes—er, no."

She waited for Carlo to correct the misimpression, to tell them all that he and Samantha were just acquaintances, but he seemed to be as at a loss for words as she was.

"I came here this evening at Carlo's invitation," she said weakly.

"That son of mine behaving himself?"

"Dad," Carlo interjected. Finally.

"Shh!" the elder Garibaldi ordered. "I'm talking to Samantha."

"He's been a perfect gentleman," she assured him.

Lorenzo patted her on the arm. "It's good to know I raised him right. You let me know if he gets out of line."

"Dad."

This time Carlo's voice sounded as desperate as Samantha was beginning to feel. Turning to Roberto, she tried to change the subject by saying brightly, "Tell me, is that a hint of sage I smell?"

"You like to cook?" Roberto asked, his excitement evident.

Relief coursed through her. For the time being, at least, she and Carlo were out of the hot seat.

"Very much. Baking is my specialty."

"Ah, baking," Roberto said with relish.

"Down, darling," Louise chided, laughter in her voice. To Samantha she added, "I'm sorry to interrupt, but you don't want to get my husband started on food right now, or we'll never sit down to eat."

"What can I do to help?" Samantha asked.

Louise nodded at the heaping trays of antipasto. "You can carry one of those out to the dining room."

"Speaking of which," Roberto said, glancing at his watch, "it's time for the first course. Places please."

There was a flurry of activity as everyone shed their white coats, revealing the dress clothes they wore underneath. In turn, they each picked up a tray of antipasto and lined up at the swinging doors while Roberto dimmed the lights in the dining room, signaling everyone to take a seat.

"I'm sorry," Samantha whispered to Carlo as they passed through the swinging doors.

"For what?" he whispered back.

"They think I'm your date."

"Is that so awful?" He sounded irritated.

"It's just…it puts you in an awkward position."

"How?"

He was being deliberately obtuse. "You'll have to explain the truth to them later."

Impatience flared in his eyes. "Why should I have to explain anything? I'm a grown man. My personal life is my own business. When they never see you again, they'll just assume we didn't hit it off. End of discussion. No harm, no foul."

When he stopped at a table to their right and placed the antipasto tray in the center, Samantha took the opportunity to scurry to a table at the rear of the room. Thankfully, there were two seats left. One for her, and one for Jeffrey when he arrived later.

"Is this seat taken?" a deep voice asked from behind her.

Samantha looked up into Carlo's face. "But…what about Jeffrey?"

The mocking light in his eyes told her he knew she'd run from him, and why. "We'll make room for him when the time comes." He leaned down so that only Samantha could hear him and added, "Don't worry. I won't bite."

To her mortification, she felt a flush redden her cheeks. "I never thought you would," she lied.

Thankfully, he chose not to challenge her comment.

After taking the seat next to her, Carlo proceeded to

charm everyone at their table. Everyone, that is, except Samantha, who, after introducing her to their tablemates, he basically ignored. Perversely, she found his behavior more exasperating than if he had centered all of his unwanted attention her way.

Despite her annoyance, as the first course progressed she couldn't help studying him out of the corner of one eye. She'd never seen him this way, so relaxed and carefree. His smiles came easily, and his laughter was hearty. She found herself wishing she'd brought her camera with her. She'd love to capture his image, and the image of everyone else in the room, on film. He had the most marvelous bone structure. And his profile: he could have been the prototype for the head molded to a Roman coin.

Laughing at a remark one of the other guests had made, Carlo turned that well-sculpted head her way, and their gazes collided. Samantha swallowed hard at the jolt of awareness that shot through her. Unable to look away, she watched with fascination as his laughter faded and his eyes grew darker than midnight. Her heart thudded. Low in her abdomen, she felt a gathering heat.

"Enjoying yourself?" he asked in a husky voice.

"Yes," she replied, surprised at what a good time she truly was having. There was definitely something to be said for good food, good company and good conversation. "Thank you for inviting me."

"Thank you for coming."

"A toast," Roberto announced from the center table.

Samantha managed to tear her gaze from Carlo's as a hush settled over the room. Roberto pushed back his chair and stood.

"At this time of year," he said, "we always pause to reflect on our many blessings. I am especially grateful this Thanksgiving, because my brother, Carlo, who could not be with us at our feast last year, but who insisted we carry on without him, is with us today. Stand up, Carlo, so everyone can see how well you have recovered.''

Looking uncomfortable, Carlo complied. As applause erupted around the room, Samantha gazed up at him and remembered how close he had come to losing his life that awful day a year ago. Somehow, amid all the conflicting emotions he aroused in her, she'd forgotten that. She'd also forgotten that he'd received his injuries trying to save her husband.

A lump formed in her throat as she realized she owed him a wealth of gratitude; not only for what he was doing for her now with Jeffrey, but for the sacrifices he had made for her husband in the past. She would try not to forget again.

The applause died down, and Roberto raised his glass. Everyone else followed suit.

"To friends, old and new. May your blessings be many and your troubles few."

"To friends," Samantha echoed. As she clinked her glass against Carlo's and those of her tablemates, she recalled the blessings she did have. Despite the heartache of the past year, she had much to be thankful for. Her son, who had just been settled across the room at a special kids' table and who was the joy of her life. Her mother. Her friends. And Carlo, the man sitting at her side, who disturbed her in more ways than she could count, and who just might turn out to be the biggest blessing of all.

When she was a child, Samantha had adored leaning back in her chair until it was balanced only on two legs. Hardly a dinner went by that her mother didn't caution her to keep all four legs firmly on the floor. The thrill had come from rejecting that safety and in embracing the delicious fear that she might fall flat on her back. This evening, as she gazed at Carlo, she felt the very same way. The question was, which way would she fall? Would she land squarely on her feet? Or would she fall flat on her back?

Chapter 8

It had been a mistake to invite Samantha here, Carlo reflected as he rinsed a pot and handed it to Marco.

Raising one arm, he swiped at the beads of perspiration dotting his brow. The scalding hot water was making him sweat, and the heavy protective gloves he wore only made him hotter. To make matters worse, his back was beginning to ache from bending over the stainless steel sink. Unfortunately, a quick glance at the stack of pots and pans that still needed cleaning told him the mountain was as high as ever.

And a quick glance across the room told him that Samantha was as beautiful as ever. Oh, yes, it had definitely been a mistake to invite her here.

"So that's your sick friend," Marco said.

"Who?" Carlo replied, feigning ignorance, as he scrubbed viciously at the caked-on food stubbornly clinging to a saucepan.

"Cinderella," Marco quipped sarcastically before jerking

his head in the direction of where Samantha was packaging up leftovers with their sister, Kate. "Who else? Her."

"She has a name. It's Samantha."

"And a nice name it is, too. She is your sick friend, isn't she?"

Carlo stifled a sigh. Sometimes—hell, almost all the time lately—he cursed coming from a large, nosy family. And it wasn't because he had to wash all these pots and pans.

"Yes, Marco, she's my sick friend."

"You stayed at her house last Saturday night?"

"Yes. I helped take care of her and her son."

"All night?"

"All night. What's your point?"

"I thought you said you weren't having a wild, crazy affair."

"I'm not."

Marco gave a disbelieving laugh. "You expect me to swallow that?"

Carlo shoved the now-gleaming pot into his brother's hands. "Why shouldn't you?"

"You brought her with you today, Carlo."

"So?"

Marco spread his arms wide, causing the wet pan to drip water across the tile floor. "So, how many times have you brought a woman to Thanksgiving dinner?"

Carlo busied himself with another pot. He knew the answer, but he wasn't about to give his brother the satisfaction.

"I haven't kept count."

"Well, I have. Want me to enlighten you?"

"I'm sure you'll have your say, regardless of my wishes. So you might as well spit it out."

"Exactly zero," Marco responded with gloating satisfaction. "Interesting, don't you think, considering the number of women you've dated over the years? Samantha is the first woman you've ever brought to Thanksgiving dinner. Even more interesting is that you brought her out to the kitchen to meet the family.''

Carlo gritted his teeth. ''She wanted to pay her respects. Is that a crime?''

Marco shot a glance across the room. ''Look at her.''

Carlo did, and his heart lurched straight up into his throat. It was her dress, he decided. Half covered by the apron she wore to protect it, it was still lethal. The charcoal gray wool not only clung to her breasts and hips like a lover's hands, it also exposed an amazing length of slim, shapely leg to his view.

If Carlo thought he'd been hot before, just looking at Samantha had him practically steaming. His belly was full of turkey and lasagne, and yet he was suddenly ravenous. For her. He'd never wanted a woman the way he wanted her.

Which explained why he couldn't stop thinking about her. And why he had goaded her the way he had earlier. It also explained why he had tried to make her admit she was having as much difficulty as he was ignoring the tug of attraction between them.

Talk about hormones overriding common sense.

Three days ago, he would have chalked his lingering fascination with her up to guilt, and nothing more. But three days ago, he hadn't held her in his arms. Three days ago, he hadn't felt the softness of her lips beneath his and the warmth of her embrace. No, it was more than just guilt. The truth was, he wanted her. He wanted her so badly, he ached with the need. And he couldn't have her. It was driving him crazy.

Even if he had something to offer her, even if the secret he kept from her didn't exist, she'd told him his attentions were unwelcome. If he had half a brain, he'd just let it, and her, go. He planned on doing exactly that, just as soon as enough blood returned to his brain to enable him to think clearly.

"I'm looking at her, Marco," he said roughly. "Satisfied?"

"And what do you feel when you look at her? Not that you need to tell me. It's written all over your face."

Tearing his gaze from Samantha, Carlo grabbed a pot from the pile and submerged it into the scalding water. "She's just a friend."

Marco's eyebrows arched. "Since when have you been just friends with a woman?"

"Lay off, will you?" he groused, unable to hide his irritation. "She's James Underwood's widow."

"So?"

"So, she's not ready for a relationship."

"You ask me, whether she's ready or not, you're falling in love with her."

The words hit Carlo like a sucker punch to the gut, and for a minute he could do little more than gulp in needed air. "I am *not* falling in love with her," he finally managed to say.

"I don't believe it." Marco took a step back, a look of amazement spreading over his face.

"What?"

"You're blushing."

Carlo felt his face grow even hotter. "I am not blushing. If my face is red, it's from the hot water."

"Sure it is."

Marco snagged Antonio, who was passing by with an armload of soiled table linens. "Look at him, Tonio. Isn't he blushing?"

"Damned if he isn't," Antonio replied in wonder. "What did you say to him?"

"Only that it looked like he was falling in love with his lady friend."

"That'd do it," Antonio agreed.

"Aren't you supposed to be vacuuming the dining room?" Carlo all but snarled.

"I'm going, I'm going," Antonio said with a good-natured smile. "Sheesh. I thought love was supposed to gentle the beast, not make him even more grouchy."

"For the last time," Carlo said with exaggerated patience, "I'm not in love. With anyone. Capiche?"

"Well, I, for one, hope you are having an affair with her," Marco said when Antonio was out of earshot.

Carlo knew he should keep his mouth shut, but the word escaped before he could swallow it back. "Why?"

"Because, if you are, it would mean you haven't totally withdrawn from everything. Like the way you've shut your family out—"

"Marco," Carlo warned.

Marco waved a hand. "I know, I know. You need your space. I'm not prying. I was just making an observation. For what it's worth, it's my considered opinion that you should have a no-holds-barred, wild, crazy affair with Samantha Underwood. And if, in the process, you two fell in love, well, what would it hurt?"

What would it hurt? If only Marco knew, he'd never make such an outrageous suggestion.

Carlo couldn't help stealing one more glance at Samantha. He wanted her. Lord, how he wanted her. He felt protective of her and wanted to help her and her son. He felt an incredible amount of guilt for the part he'd played in her husband's death. But the one thing he didn't feel for her was love.

That would be beyond stupid.

Samantha spooned leftover stuffing into a plastic container and tried to pretend she wasn't stealing glances at the man bent over the sink across the room. Carlo should have looked ridiculous in that starched white apron and the yellow rubber gloves that traveled past his elbows to encase his upper arms. Instead, he looked incredibly virile.

"How are you holding up?" his sister, Kate, asked. "You look a little stunned. I should have warned you what you were in for, when you volunteered to help."

Samantha felt a rush of relief that Kate chalked her distraction up to the task at hand, and not to Carlo's presence in the same, albeit huge, room. "I'll survive."

Kate grinned at her. "A lot of people find us overwhelming at first. My husband certainly did. Don't worry, you'll get used to us."

"That's good to know," was all Samantha could think to reply. After all, she could hardly tell Carlo's sister that the last thing she planned on doing was getting used to them. That, after tonight, it was exceedingly unlikely she'd ever see them again.

Determinedly, she turned her attention away from Carlo. When she saw how enthusiastically the younger woman was carving one of the remaining turkeys, Samantha felt her lips twitch.

"You really enjoy this, don't you?"

"Oh, yes," Kate replied, her eyes shining. "This whole day really gets me in the spirit of the upcoming holiday season."

"It was fun," Samantha said. "And the food was wonderful."

"I'm glad you had a good time. That's the whole point."

Samantha tilted her head to one side. "Do you have a favorite year? Or do they all pretty much blend together?"

"Not at all. Every year something memorable happens. For instance, this year I met you. Then there was the last Thanksgiving my mother celebrated with us. I was nine years old, and Roberto proposed to Louise in the middle of dessert. That caused quite a stir."

"I bet it did." Samantha chuckled.

"But I'd have to say my favorite Thanksgiving was the year I met my husband. Steve and my brother Bruno were rookies together on the Pittsburgh police force. Since Steve had no family to share Thanksgiving with, Bruno brought him here."

A dreamy expression crossed Kate's face. "It was love at first sight. Of course, it took us two tries at marriage to get it right. But it all worked out in the end."

"No wonder you love this day so much," Samantha said. "All those wonderful memories."

Kate nodded. "Exactly. Who knows, maybe you'll even join us again next year and help us make some more."

The open speculation in Kate's eyes had Samantha suppressing a groan. "Maybe," she hedged. Then, to change the subject she asked, "What do you do with all the leftovers?"

"Send as much as we can home with guests, and donate the rest to a local homeless shelter." Kate dumped the now denuded turkey carcass into a trash compactor. Curiosity still gleaming in her eyes, she asked, "So, do you live in Bridgeton?"

"Yes. We moved here two and a half years ago."

"We?"

"My husband, my son and I."

"Oh."

There was a wealth of disappointment in that one little word.

"Is something wrong?" Samantha asked.

The other woman shook her head. "No. I just could have sworn…"

"What?"

Kate flashed her a brilliant smile. "Nothing. So you moved here two and a half years ago?"

"Yes. When my husband filled an opening on the Bridgeton police force. Before that, we lived in Philadelphia."

She didn't know why she was being so talkative. Something about Kate inspired confidence.

"Was your husband on the force in Philadelphia?"

"For seven years."

"Must have been quite a difference for him, coming from a big city police force to a much smaller one."

"Actually, it was ideal for both of us. It gave James more time to spend with our son, and it allowed me to move close to my widowed mother. The town I grew up in is just five miles from Bridgeton."

Kate reached for another turkey and began carving. "Where is your husband today? Is he on duty?"

It had never occurred to Samantha that Carlo's family might not know who she was. She'd just assumed everyone knew, that Carlo would have explained.

"No. I'm a widow, Kate. My husband was killed a year ago."

Kate looked stricken. "Oh, my goodness. I didn't know. I just never associated your name with...I'm so sorry, Samantha."

"It's okay," she said, and surprisingly it was. For some reason the familiar pain didn't squeeze her heart at the mention of James.

"How well do you know my brother?" Kate's tone was cautious.

Samantha busied herself scraping out the contents of a tall pot. "Not well. We're just...friends."

"Nothing more?"

This time, there was no disguising the curiosity in the other woman's voice. "No, nothing more."

Kate leaned closer and spoke in a confidential tone. "I have to tell you, woman to woman, it's been over a year since I've seen him with a date. He hasn't been the same since the shooting."

Consternation flooded Kate's eyes, and she bit her lip.

"Damn! I've gone and done it again. I'm sorry, that was thoughtless of me."

"No, no, that's okay," Samantha demurred. "I want to know. Why hasn't he been the same?"

Kate's sigh was heartfelt. "No one really knows. His emotions used to be out there for all of us to see. Now he just keeps everything bottled up inside."

"Like Jeffrey," Samantha murmured.

"Who?"

"My son. He's withdrawn from everyone since his father's death. That's why I'm here today with Carlo, actually. He's helping me with Jeffrey. I went to the mayor with my concerns about my son, and he suggested I go to Carlo. Carlo's agreed to be a buddy to Jeffrey, and to hopefully coax him out of his shell."

"Sometimes I could throttle the mayor," Kate muttered as she stabbed at the turkey.

"I beg your pardon?"

"I'm sorry." Kate shot her a rueful look. "It's not your fault. It's just…Carlo takes on too much. He thinks he can save the world single-handedly. After my mother died, he put his life on hold for thirteen years to raise the rest of us. As police chief, he devotes an untold number of hours to our community. And now, when the mayor asks him to head another of his pet projects, he agrees. He never does anything for himself."

Kate drew a ragged breath. "When he took his leave of absence, I was the only one happy about it, because he was finally doing something that was just for him. Of course, it drives my other brothers crazy that he won't talk to them about it. We're a family of talkers, in case you haven't noticed."

"I noticed," Samantha said wryly.

"Me, I think Carlo's earned his right to be silent for a while. I just wish the others would leave him alone."

And Samantha? Did Kate wish she'd leave Carlo alone, too? She felt a flash of guilt. Was she asking too much of him that he be her son's buddy? A part of her felt that it was only right she should go to him and tell him he was off the hook, that she'd find someone else to help her with Jeffrey. But the other part, the part without a conscience, said no.

The only person Jeffrey seemed to be responding to was Carlo. She couldn't give Carlo an out now. If that was selfish of her, so be it. She'd just have to live with it. All she was asking was that he spend a couple of hours with her son every week. Surely that wasn't too much.

"So," Kate said in a hearty voice, "what do you think of my macho brothers? Handsome as sin, aren't they?"

Samantha made a noncommittal sound in the back of her throat. The Garibaldi men were definitely handsome. And definitely macho. But only one of them had the power to make her go weak-kneed with just a glance from his dark brown eyes.

"Hard to believe, isn't it," Kate went on, "that only Roberto's married?"

"Maybe they're just not ready to settle down," Samantha volunteered.

Kate chuckled. "That's always a possibility. However, I think their single status might have more to do with the fact that, good looks and charm aside, they've all been blessed with more than a healthy dose of testosterone. Someone a little less charitable than I am might even at times be moved to call them male chauvinist pigs. I, however, prefer to think of them as forceful."

Forceful definitely described Carlo, Samantha thought. "I'm sure they'll all eventually find a woman who enjoys that forcefulness."

"It's an event I pray for nightly," Kate said fervently. "That, and the peace it would give me."

"Peace?"

"Yes. If they were busy with families of their own, they wouldn't have time to meddle in mine."

"According to Carlo," Samantha said, "they've been meddling a lot in his lately."

"They're worried about him," Kate said simply. "So am I."

Samantha felt confused. "I thought you said he'd earned his silence."

"He has. But that doesn't mean I'm not worried sick about him. When a Garibaldi man gets quiet, there's definitely something wrong. And when he takes a leave of absence from a job he adores, it only makes things worse."

For a minute, Samantha allowed herself to wonder what demons were driving Carlo. Was there something wrong? Was whatever it was that was bothering him somehow, in a way she couldn't figure, tied to the day James died? Kate had said he hadn't been the same since that day. But what person could remain unaffected after seeing what Carlo had seen, after living through what he had?

"He almost died, Kate. It seems only natural to me that he would be changed after such an experience."

"He went back to work against the advice of his physician," Kate told her. "Did you know that?"

No, she hadn't. Truth to tell, there was a whole lot about the day of the shooting, and its aftermath, that she didn't know. However, given what she'd learned about Carlo, she wasn't surprised.

"Well, there you have it," she told Kate. "Maybe he realized his physician was right, and he took a leave of absence to get stronger."

"Maybe."

Compassion for Carlo welled within her, and Samantha pushed it aside. If she was to keep her distance from him, and his family, she couldn't involve herself in their troubles.

To speculate any further about what was bothering him would take the subject out of the realm of idle concern. It would make it personal. It would mean that she cared. And she didn't. Couldn't.

"I'm sure he'll be fine," she said. "He seems okay whenever he's with me."

"Speaking of which," Kate observed, sliding Samantha a sidelong glance, "an enterprising young woman just might be able to snap him up. That is, if she had a mind to."

"Is that so?" Although her heart was beating a furious rhythm, Samantha kept her voice deliberately bland.

"That was a hint, in case you didn't recognize it."

Oh, she'd recognized it, all right. In her own way, Kate meddled in her brothers' lives as much as they did in hers.

Samantha forced herself to meet and hold the other woman's gaze. "Carlo and I are just friends, Kate. That's all. I'm not ready for a relationship. Truth is, I don't know if I'll ever be."

"Oh." The light in Kate's eyes died. "Then I have only one thing to say. And please, take it in the spirit in which it is meant. I think you're a very nice person, Samantha, but I love my brother. With all my heart. I've seen the way he looks at you. Please don't hurt him. He's been through enough. I don't think he can take any more."

Dismayed, Samantha looked away. Surely Kate was wrong. Yes, Carlo had admitted his attraction to her, but things hadn't progressed to the point where she could cause him any pain. Had they?

Because she didn't know what to say that would reassure both Kate and herself, Samantha did the only thing she could in this situation. She busied herself with her work and pretended she hadn't heard Kate Garibaldi's warning.

The night sky was black and starless as Carlo steered his car through the silent streets of Mt. Washington. The pulse of the heater made the interior warm and toasty. So why did he feel a lingering chill?

A glance at the woman in the passenger seat gave him his answer. Subdued, Samantha huddled against the passenger door, hunched so deeply into her coat that the upraised collar brushed the top of her cheekbones. Her golden hair fell forward to hide her face from Carlo's view.

It was painfully obvious that she was putting as much space between them, both physically and mentally, as she could. So obvious, in fact, that he knew if he were to stretch his arm across the top of the seat, she'd probably find a way to wedge her body into the small space between the edge of the seat and the door.

Glancing in the rearview mirror, he saw that Jeffrey was asleep in the back seat. No help there. Not that anyone could ever accuse the child of being a chatterbox. Still, it would have been nice to have someone to talk to.

In police work, silence could often be a useful tool to wear down the resistance of an uncooperative suspect. Over the years, Carlo had become quite skilled at its use. But tonight, when the source of the silence was the woman at his side, and when all it served to do was to allow his mind to wander into dangerous territory—specifically, the conversation he'd had with Marco—silence was the last thing he wanted or needed.

He reached out and switched on the radio. Barbra Streisand's rendition of ''Jingle Bells'' filled the air.

''Can you believe it?'' he asked, shaking his head ruefully when the song ended and a commercial came on. ''Christmas carols already. Of course, the mall started putting up their decorations right after Halloween, so I guess I shouldn't be surprised.''

Samantha thrust her hands deeply into her coat pockets. ''I guess not.''

Okay, so that conversational road was a dead end. Deciding to try another route, he patted his still full stomach with one hand.

"After all that food today, I don't think I'll be able to eat for a week."

"Uh-huh."

He'd never seen her so distracted. "Is something wrong?"

"What?"

She blinked and turned her face toward him. In the passing light of a streetlamp, he saw that her features were remote, withdrawn.

"Oh...no...no...everything's fine." She turned away again. "Thank you for asking."

That settled it. Something was definitely bothering her. Now that he thought about it, she'd been unusually quiet since helping Kate out in the kitchen.

"Did my sister say something to upset you?"

Her laughter sounded forced. "Why would you think that?"

The evasiveness of her reply was quite revealing. If not Kate, something that had happened tonight had definitely upset her. But what? He wished he knew. However, to press her on the matter, when she obviously didn't want to share, would only drive her deeper into her shell, something he definitely didn't want.

Shrugging, he said, "Just checking."

She stared straight out the windshield, refusing to meet his gaze. "I'm just tired, Carlo. It's been a long day. After all that work, I would think you'd be tired, too."

If only that were so. Unfortunately, and to his eternal dismay, he felt energized simply by the sight of her.

"It must have been all that coffee I drank," he lied. "I'm wide awake." He waited a beat. "Good thing, too, since I'm driving."

When he chanced a glance at her, she wasn't smiling.

Trying again, he drummed his hands against the steering wheel.

"Bada-bing," he said, resorting to the now-universal, thanks to a popular television show, announcement that a joke had been offered up for enjoyment.

Still no response.

"That was a joke, Samantha."

"I know."

He drew a long breath and blew it out slowly. He really hated this feeling of awkwardness. He hadn't felt so inadequate in a female's presence since the tenth grade, when he'd asked Bridget Hanlon, the most popular girl in school and a senior to boot, out on a date. That Bridget had said yes to his request didn't do a thing for his confidence at this moment. Try as he might, there was just no figuring Samantha Underwood out.

"I think Jeffrey enjoyed himself today," he finally ventured.

She nodded. "I think so, too."

"Did you?"

"Very much, thank you."

"Get enough to eat?"

"More than enough." She yawned.

This took small talk to an all-time low, he realized wryly. If only his brothers could see him now. They'd be rolling on the floor in hysteria at his lame attempts to engage Samantha in conversation. Much more of this scintillating talk and, wide awake as he was, even he would fall asleep.

"So, what do you think of my family?"

That, at least, elicited a smile from her.

"They're...interesting."

A chuckle rumbled deep in his throat. "Interesting is definitely a diplomatic way of describing them."

Her smile turned into an answering chuckle, and he felt a jolt of triumph when she withdrew her hands from her coat pockets and turned in her seat to face him. He'd finally managed to pique her interest enough to break through her distraction.

"Okay, they're a bunch of characters," she allowed. "Nice characters, though. Particularly Roberto."

Now they were getting somewhere. "So you liked them?"

"Very much."

"They liked you, too."

"What was it like, growing up with so many siblings?"

He grinned at her. "Noisy."

"And?" she prompted.

"Hectic, crazy, chaotic. Aggravating. Fun. There was always something going on, always someone coming or going. Mom used to say that whenever things got quiet around the house, it meant we were either all in school, sedated, or someone was up to no good."

She laughed softly. To Carlo, the sound was like a soothing balm on an open wound. He wanted to hear it again. And again. And—

"Were you ever up to no good?" she asked.

A surge of nostalgia accompanied the memories that washed over him. "Constantly."

"I don't believe it."

"Why not?"

"I don't know." She shrugged. "Kate told me how you were always the responsible one."

He wasn't exactly sure why, but the remark rankled. "And responsible people never get into any trouble?"

"Not usually."

"You make me sound so...virtuous."

"Is that a terrible crime?" She seemed amused.

"When you're ten years old, it is," he said. "I was seventeen when my mother died, plenty old enough to have finally achieved a minimum level of responsibility. Maybe even of maturity. Believe it or not, though, I was also a kid once, too. I got into my fair share of scrapes.''

"Tell me about them."

Carlo's heart slammed in his chest. Was there anything more seductive than a woman who gazed at you out of wide, interested eyes and asked you to talk about yourself? Especially when that woman had no idea how seductive she really was.

"I don't think so," he said carefully, trying to school his emotions so they wouldn't show on his face. Now that she'd opened up to him, he didn't want to chase her back inside herself by letting her see how much she affected him.

"Why not?" she challenged. "Scared?"

He laughed. "Terrified. If I told you even half of the trouble I caused, you'd probably have second thoughts about leaving me alone with Jeffrey."

"That bad, huh?"

"I was what my mother called mischievous. Let's just say I've reformed, and leave it at that."

"Definitely that bad," she agreed. There was a playful lilt to her voice when she added, "Since you're not going to tell me, I guess I'm just going to have to use my imagination."

She closed her eyes.

"What are you doing?"

"Using my imagination." Her lips curved in a way he found highly seductive. "I can just picture you now."

His heart skipped a beat. "You can?"

"Uh-huh."

He was almost afraid to ask. "What do you see?"

"A young boy with scraped knees, dirt under his fingernails and dark hair in need of a good combing. He's telling his friends to go long as he draws his arm back to throw a football. Unfortunately, the throw goes wide and crashes through a window."

Carlo felt his lips curve. "After the window breaks, does the boy stay, or run?"

She thought for a moment, then opened her eyes. "The boys he's with scatter, and at first he runs, too. But then he returns to face the music. And he offers to pay for the broken window."

He nodded his approval. "Very good."

"My picture was accurate?"

"Dead-on. I'm impressed."

"You forget, I have a son of my own. It wasn't that hard."

He couldn't resist. "When you were ten years old, would you have liked that boy you just described?"

There was a long pause before she said, "When I was ten years old, I thought all boys had cooties."

"When did they stop having cooties?"

She held up a hand. "Don't, Carlo."

"Don't what?"

"Don't flirt with me."

"I was just teasing," he chided gently. But he wasn't. Not really.

Samantha, being Samantha, chose to call him on it.

"It sounded like flirting to me."

Ignoring the warning voice that kept repeating every reason why he should keep his big mouth shut, he said, "Okay, so I was flirting with you. Would it be so terrible if we indulged in a little harmless flirtation?"

He brought the car to a halt at a red light and turned to face her. When his heated gaze locked on hers, he heard her give a quiet gasp and watched while her throat worked convulsively. In the dim light, her eyes looked wide and melting. Pleading.

Desire hit him, hard, fast and hot, and a pulsing warmth centered in his groin. A man could get willingly lost in those beautiful eyes, he realized. As for the parted lips that were so tantalizingly near, why, if a man had half a mind to, he could spend years exploring their softness.

Carlo's mouth went dry with want. "Well," he pressed in a low voice. "Would it?"

A shutter came down over her eyes, and she looked away. Despite the tremor he'd seen on her lips, and despite the gasp of awareness that had escaped her throat, her voice was flat and unemotional when she spoke.

"A flirtation is only harmless when the participants engaged in it know that nothing will come of it. That there will be no kisses. No caresses. No intimacy. But when you flirt with me, Carlo, it feels highly intimate. And right now we both have issues that prohibit such intimacy. So yes, it would be, to use your words, so terrible for us to engage in a harmless flirtation. One, if not both of us, could get hurt. Correct me, please, if I'm wrong."

A car horn blared behind him, making him aware that the light had changed. His fingers tightened around the steering wheel as his foot pressed against the gas pedal. She was right, damn it.

The ever-familiar guilt surged over him, leaving a bitter taste in his mouth. Once again, even though he'd known better, he'd lost control. Once again, he'd pressed her to give him something she couldn't give, something he had no right to ask for. It was time, once and for all, to place a lid on his fanciful, impossible thoughts. And his attention squarely back on the road, where it belonged.

"No," he said slowly, "you're not wrong."

"I didn't think so."

Silence stretched between them.

"This may sound crazy," Samantha finally said, "but I wish Jeffrey would get into trouble again, the way you did when you were a kid."

He heard the wistfulness in her voice and understood perfectly. If Jeffrey would do something that would result in a reprimand or a temporary grounding, it would mean he was well on the road to being his old self again.

Carlo negotiated a sharp turn. "It doesn't sound crazy at all."

She looked down at her lap. "Thanks. For everything. Sometimes I feel so alone. It's nice to be with someone who understands."

Warmth filled him. He might not be able to erase the past, but at least he could give her this. He could offer her comfort, for as long as she would take it from him.

"You can call me, anytime you need to talk. I hope you know that, Samantha."

She raised her head and flashed him a smile. "I do. It means a lot."

"It means a lot to me, too."

She seemed to hesitate, then said, "Can I ask you something personal?"

After a similar hesitation, he nodded.

"Does the reason you took a leave of absence from police work have something to do with the day James was killed?"

Chapter 9

The unexpectedness of Samantha's question knocked him for such a loop that Carlo almost ran a red light. Reeling, he jammed his foot on the brake and strove for emotional control.

"I'm sorry," she said, bracing her right hand against the dashboard as they jerked to a stop. "I shouldn't have asked you that."

A quick look in the rearview mirror assured him that, miraculously, Jeffrey was still asleep. "Why did you?"

He knew he sounded defensive, evasive, the way she had when he'd asked if Kate had said something to upset her. He couldn't help it. He needed to know.

"I'm not sure. Probably because your sister said you haven't been the same since that day. It made me wonder if your injuries had played a part in your decision to take a leave of absence."

Carlo almost sagged with relief. So she hadn't figured out his guilty secret. Yet.

The light changed, and he carefully stepped on the accelerator.

"What else did my sister say?" To his ears, his voice sounded hoarse, unnatural.

"You really want to know?"

"I wouldn't ask if I didn't."

"She said you take on too much responsibility, that she'd—no offense to me—like to ring the mayor's neck for talking you into being Jeffrey's buddy, and that you went back to work way too early and over your doctor's protests."

He shot her a glance. "You and Kate seem to have talked a lot."

She shrugged. "It passed the time."

Which told him nothing about whether Samantha had been the one asking questions about him, or whether Kate had simply offered the information without any prodding on Samantha's part. Since Samantha had made it clear that he would never be anything more than a friend, did it really matter?

When he looked over at her again, the play of darkness and light across her face made her seem otherworldly and mysterious. He knew he should probably drop the subject, but his sister's comment intrigued him. Besides, his need to know if Kate had said anything else about him, and that day, that might unwittingly tip Samantha off to the truth made the risk acceptable.

"How does Kate think I'm different?"

"She said you're too quiet. Like Jeffrey."

He was nothing like Jeffrey. Jeffrey was an innocent. Carlo was far from innocent. He had blood on his hands. Jeffrey's father's blood. And it wouldn't wash away, no matter how hard he scrubbed.

"To my family," he said, "a person is quiet if he doesn't

relate his entire life story to everyone he meets. By that definition, I suppose I am too quiet."

"I see."

He wondered what exactly she did see, and if it was far too much.

"Do I seem overly quiet to you, Samantha?"

"No."

The way she said the word, with just a hint of doubt, made his lips twist wryly.

"Why do I distinctly hear the word 'but' ringing in my ears?"

She seemed to hesitate. "There's just something… I don't know how to explain it, other than to say you seem to hold yourself at a distance from everyone around you."

And she didn't? To challenge her on that, however, would be to take the subject into extremely dangerous territory.

"Does that include you? Do I hold myself at a distance from you, too?"

"Of course."

"What about my abortive attempts to flirt with you?" he asked. "Were they impersonal? Were they distant?"

"No." The admission was grudging. No hint of a "but" there.

"Yet you still agree with my sister that I'm not the man I was a year ago," he pressed.

"I have no way of telling," she replied coolly, "since I didn't know you then."

Even though he no longer harbored any illusions about himself, Carlo still felt amazed and sickened that he could stoop so low as to try to turn Samantha's words around on her. Unlike the times when he couldn't control his impulse to get a rise—a sexual rise—out of her, he knew exactly what he was doing. If he kept her on the defensive, he hoped she'd forget all about the question that had made him so uncomfortable. If he made her angry enough, she wouldn't waste a second thinking about him, or her conversation with Kate, and would thus never put two and two together.

A wave of self-disgust washed through him. Was there no end to the damage he would inflict on her? Just how low would he sink to protect his precious pride?

For one insane moment, Carlo toyed with the idea of telling Samantha the truth about the day her husband died. It would feel so good to tell someone, to take the huge weight off his shoulders. He might even be able to sleep again at night.

Reason intervened before he could open his mouth. If he really needed to talk to someone, he could always go to a priest. Or a good psychiatrist. The last person he could unburden his conscience to, however, was the one person who, by his actions, he'd harmed the most. It would only cause her more pain. The temporary relief he would feel wouldn't be worth it. It wouldn't solve anything. It wouldn't change what he'd done. It wouldn't give Samantha her husband back.

Not to mention that, forever after, she would look at him with condemnation in her eyes. If she looked at him at all.

"I'm sorry, Samantha. My behavior was uncalled for. I guess I'm a little touchy on that subject."

That, at least, was the truth.

She still wouldn't look at him. "That's okay. I was being far too personal."

Therein lay the problem. He wanted her to be personal. He wanted to get personal with her in return. She'd run screaming for the hills if she knew exactly how personal.

More than getting personal with her, though, he wanted her to be happy. He hated seeing her so alone, so vulnerable, so cut off from the world around her. So mired in the past and so in love with a man who would never return. If not Carlo himself—and it never would be him—he'd like to see her ready to involve herself with someone. Because that would mean she was ready to return to the land of the living.

"What Kate said about me being different," he began. "I suppose she's right. When you come that close to dying, it changes your outlook on a lot of things."

He spoke carefully, measuring his words so as to stick as closely to the truth as possible without giving anything away. "It changes the way you look at the world and other people."

And the way you look at yourself. Especially the way you look at yourself.

"That's what I told your sister," she surprised him by saying.

"Out of curiosity," he asked, "did you and Kate talk about anything besides me?"

It was too dark for him to be sure, but he thought she blushed.

"We may have managed to discuss the weather and the state of the world for a second or two," she said dryly.

"Ouch." He flashed her a grin.

She didn't grin back. "How many times were you shot, Carlo?"

He blinked in surprise. "You don't know?"

"No. I...avoided the newspaper and news accounts of the shooting. I couldn't bear it."

It made sense. She wouldn't have been concerned with his injuries anyway, only with what had happened to her husband.

"Four times."

"Where?"

She, above anyone else, had a right to know. But if she asked him further details about the events of that afternoon, what would he say? He had no idea.

"In my right shoulder, my right thigh, my right lung and my abdomen."

"You must have been in the hospital for a long time."

He pulled up at a stop sign and looked in all directions for approaching vehicles. "Three weeks in intensive care. Three more weeks in a regular hospital room. And six months at a rehabilitation center."

"I had no idea," she said softly. "Why were you at the rehabilitation center for so long?"

"The bullet in my abdomen was pressing against my spinal cord. They had a tricky job removing it. For a while, I was paralyzed. They didn't think I'd be able to walk again."

"But you proved them wrong."

He didn't like to think of the long hours he'd spent, sweating and in incredible pain, while he'd tried to get his reluctant legs to obey the commands he'd willed his brain to send to them. Worse, though, had been the way his family had hovered protectively over him the entire time, treating him like the hero he was not. And the flowers and cards people had sent telling him how proud they were of him and how they were praying for his full recovery.

"Yes, I suppose I did."

He knew he should feel a sense of satisfaction in his accomplishment, but all he felt was hollow inside. Empty. A yearning for completeness filled him. Would he ever feel whole once more? Would he ever look at the world again and feel confident about his place in it?

"To look at you now, no one would ever guess the extent of your injuries," Samantha said.

"I worked hard to get my strength back." Until his leave of absence, he'd spent two hours a day at the gym.

"It shows," she replied.

"Thank you."

"You're welcome."

Several silent moments passed before Samantha asked, "Did you really go back to work against the advice of your doctor, the way Kate said?"

He'd still been on crutches when they'd released him from the rehab center. His doctor had expected him to take another two months to heal completely, and his insurance company had reluctantly agreed to continue paying benefits for that length of time. But Carlo had been determined it would be otherwise. Four weeks later, he'd abandoned his crutches and was back at work, as well as working out regularly at the gym.

"Yes," he said.

"Why?"

"I couldn't stand the idleness." It had given him too much time to think.

"Yet you took a leave of absence not long after you returned to work."

Three months later, to be exact. "Yes. I guess the doctor was right, after all. I wasn't ready."

And, now that he had all the time in the world to think again, to try to work through his problems, he refused to do so.

"Was the job too demanding physically?"

Once again, she was getting uncomfortably close to the truth.

"Yes," he lied, then held his breath and prayed she wouldn't ask more. After all, she'd just watched him lift and wash a ton of heavy pots without keeling over. Surely that would indicate to her that his stamina wasn't as low as he'd like her to believe.

"I hope you're feeling up to going back to work soon," she said.

He let out a silent sigh of relief. "Thank you. I hope so, too."

Her driveway loomed ahead, and he pulled the car to a halt in front of the garage. After opening the passenger door, he waited for Samantha to climb out of the car.

"Don't wake him," he said when she leaned into the back

seat and gently called Jeffrey's name. "I'll carry him inside."

She straightened and turned to face him. "There's no need. He can make it on his own steam."

"I know he can. But he's had a long day. It would be a shame to wake him. Look at him. He's out like a light."

Samantha did as Carlo suggested, and her face softened with tenderness. "You're right. I'll carry him inside."

"Please, Samantha. Let me."

"But your injuries…"

"Are healed enough for me to carry one small boy."

"Look," she said, "it's cold, it's late and I'm tired. I really don't have the energy to argue about this."

"Then why," he interrupted, "don't you just give in gracefully and let me carry Jeffrey inside? If you recall, I was strong enough to carry you to bed once."

She stepped aside and looked away from him. "Put that way, how can I refuse?"

"That's why I put it that way."

Moving around her, he leaned into the back seat and gathered the child into his arms. Jeffrey's eyes opened for a fraction of a second before fluttering closed again.

"Your sister was right," he heard Samantha say from behind him.

"About what?" he asked, backing out of the car.

"The whole lot of you Garibaldi men are as macho as they come."

Knowing Kate, she hadn't been paying them a compliment.

"Something else you and my sister discussed," he murmured as he settled Jeffrey onto his shoulder.

"You'd be surprised by what your sister had to say to me," Samantha muttered.

The odd note in her voice had him focused on her rigid back as he followed her to her front door. The way she rattled her keys and made a show of opening the door told him she didn't want to pursue the subject further. Truth to tell, he'd had his fill of uncomfortable discussions this evening. He was just as willing as she was to let it go.

"Are you okay?" she asked when they'd stepped into the foyer. Her gaze ran over his face as if searching for signs of strain. "He's not too heavy?"

Her concern touched him at the same time that it sent a flare of guilt through him. Another sin he'd have to atone for when the time came.

"I'm fine, Samantha."

"In that case, I'll go turn down Jeffrey's bed."

Flicking on lights as she went, she hurried up the stairs.

Carlo followed at a slower pace, enjoying the feel of the child in his arms. As he leaned over Jeffrey's bed and slowly lowered the sleeping child to the waiting mattress, he felt an odd reluctance to let go. While he carefully removed Jeffrey's coat, Samantha slipped off the boy's shoes and unbuckled and removed his belt. She reached for the pajamas that lay folded on a chair, then dropped her hand.

"I suppose it wouldn't hurt to let him sleep in his clothes for one night," she said.

"It never hurt me," he replied, reaching for the covers Samantha had neatly folded back.

The tenderness Carlo felt as he tucked the blankets snugly under Jeffrey's chin told him his feelings for the boy had undergone an abrupt about-face. No longer was he suffering Jeffrey's company out of a sense of guilt and obligation. Far from it. From agreeing to be Jeffrey's buddy to assuage his conscience, he'd moved on to wanting to help Jeffrey for Jeffrey's sake alone. He wanted to see Jeffrey laugh and run and play and rejoice in life again. And his reasons for wanting all that had nothing to do with guilt. They were much more personal. He was growing to love the child.

After smoothing a tender hand across the top of Jeffrey's

head, Carlo straightened and turned to find Samantha watching him from the foot of the bed. He froze when he realized what had escaped his notice until that moment. She'd taken off her coat. With no apron to mask the way the gray dress clung to the lines of her body, she stood before him in all her glory. The sight took his breath away.

But it wasn't just her curves that beckoned him. Or the weary look in her beautiful brown eyes that begged him to smooth the hair off her forehead the way he had her son's. It was more, much more, than her physical allure that drew him to her, that made his heart thunder in his chest so hard he feared it might burst free at any moment.

It was the way she'd joked with him when she'd been burning up with fever. The way she'd sublimated her pride by approaching a total stranger for help with her son. The way she, in the midst of her own pain and loss, could still find it in herself to care for another person's—his—perceived weaknesses. Samantha Underwood was the most caring person he'd ever met.

Carlo felt something tighten in his chest as the truth he'd been avoiding from practically the moment he met her hit him squarely between the eyes. Marco was right. He was falling in love with her. Hard.

He should have known it all along. That was why he had no self-control whenever he was near her. That was why he kept trying to get a rise out of her. To see if she was feeling the same things he was.

It was wrong, all wrong. It was a love she wouldn't accept, even if he were free to give it. But he couldn't halt the feelings washing over him with the strength of a tidal wave any more than a wad of chewing gum could plug a leak in the Hoover Dam. Heaven help him.

The look on his face terrified her. It wasn't so much the desire burning in his dark brown eyes that threw her for such a loop, but the intensity of the yearning Samantha saw there. A yearning that seemed to emanate from the depths of his soul.

I've seen the way he looks at you, his sister had said. And now, for the first time, Samantha saw, too.

Please don't hurt him. He's been through enough. I don't think he can take anymore.

The words that had echoed over and over in her ears during the drive home replayed themselves once more. Unfortunately, if what she saw in Carlo's eyes was real, and not a trick of the light, the only thing she could offer him was pain. Because she was determined not to respond to the open invitation she could read there.

For ten years, all her plans, all her hopes, and all her dreams had centered around the life she and James had built together. He'd been gone for little over a year. To consider a future that didn't include him, to consider allowing another man into her heart, seemed traitorous and wrong. It was too soon. Much too soon. Whether what she was feeling was simply desire—and that was all it really could be, she told herself—or something else, she couldn't indulge it. No matter how sorely tempted she was to do just that.

Some of her ambivalence must have shown on her face, because, throat working, Carlo took a step toward her.

"Samantha?" he queried huskily.

Balling her hands into fists at her sides, she tore her gaze away and deliberately hardened her heart against the naked appeal in his eyes. She had to remain strong. For both their sakes.

"Thank you for today," she said stiffly. "And for carrying Jeffrey upstairs."

"He's a great kid."

He cared for Jeffrey, too, which, in addition to her loneliness, only enhanced his appeal. She'd seen it in the gentle way he'd placed her son on the bed, and in the way he'd tucked the covers securely around her sleeping child's body. The path to a man's heart might be through his stomach, but the path to a woman's was definitely through her children.

Drawing a ragged breath, Samantha willed him to go, to leave her in peace, before she lost what little self-control she had left.

"Yes, he is."

"You've done a good job with him."

"Thank you." She waited a beat, then added, "It's been a long day, Carlo."

He took the hint. "I guess I'd better be going."

Sweet relief coursed through her. "It is getting late."

They didn't speak as she escorted him down the stairs. With every careful step, Samantha was conscious of the man behind her, of his gaze on her back, of the heat radiating from his strong, male body, of how safe and protected and whole she'd felt the last time he'd wrapped his arms around her.

She clasped the front door handle with the desperation of a drowning person grabbing for a life preserver. One more minute, and he'd be gone. One more minute, and she'd be away from his overpowering, seductive influence. One more minute, and she'd be safe. She would no longer be unduly tempted to betray her husband's memory. And she would make certain that, in the future, they'd spend as little time together as possible.

When she opened the door, the sight that greeted her eyes made her catch her breath. In the silence of the night, the first snowfall of the season spiraled softly to the ground. Because the air was unnaturally still for November, without even the hint of a breeze, the flakes floated down to earth in straight lines, like thousands of tiny soldiers at stiff attention.

"What is it?" Carlo asked at her shoulder.

"It's snowing."

He moved to stand beside her in the doorway. For untold minutes they watched in silence while the snow coated tree limbs and carpeted the grass.

"Isn't it beautiful?" she finally asked.

"You like snow?"

"I love it. Especially the first snowfall. It always makes me think of my father."

He glanced over at her. "Why is that?"

The memory made her smile. "Dad had this ritual he insisted we perform every year in honor of the first snowfall. He called it our snow dance. We'd go outside and twirl around with our arms outstretched while the snow fell down around us."

"Sounds like fun."

"It was. I remember one year, he woke my sisters and me up at three in the morning, and we went outside in our nightgowns and slippers. It was a night just like this, still and not too cold. My mother thought we were crazy, but we loved it." She gave a soft sigh. "I didn't realize before tonight how much I miss doing it."

"Let's do it now, then."

She shot him a quick look. Leave it to Carlo. Whenever she least expected it, he always managed to catch her off guard.

"You're kidding."

He spread his arms. "Do I look like I'm kidding? Let's do the snow dance, Samantha."

She didn't want to delve too deeply into how he really looked, and how those looks affected her. "No."

"You're the one who said she missed it. Let's do it. You and me. Together."

Did he know how suggestive his words sounded, or was it just her overstimulated imagination and her overstretched nerves finding hidden meanings in every word he spoke?

She leaned back against the door, as if the hardness of the wood at her back would help stiffen her resolve.

"I don't think so."

He looked disappointed in her. "Why not? It would be a fitting way to end a day filled with thanks, to give thanks for the snow. Don't you agree?"

She did agree. And she should be grateful that, for whatever reason, he'd abandoned his earlier seriousness and adopted this playful, carefree mood. She just didn't feel carefree enough to do the snow dance with him.

"I'm not a kid anymore, Carlo."

"What does being a kid have to do with doing the snow dance? Your father did it, didn't he, and he wasn't a kid."

"But the neighbors..." she protested, even though there wasn't a neighbor in sight and all the windows of the adjoining homes were black.

"Are all in bed, by the looks of things," he retorted. "Besides, I didn't think appearances mattered so much to you."

She knew he was referring to the remark she'd made when he'd insisted on staying with her the weekend she was sick.

"They don't."

"Then what's the problem?"

He was, but to tell him that would only encourage him, and she didn't want to lead him on.

"I don't have my coat on, Carlo."

"So? As you already said, the night is mild. And that dress seems warmer than the nightgowns you and your sisters used to dance in." He held out his hand to her. "Don't be an old fuddy-duddy, Samantha. Let's dance."

"Fuddy-duddy? You're calling *me* a fuddy-duddy?"

"If the name fits..." he teased.

Against her better judgment, she allowed him to draw her out onto the front porch and down the steps to the yard, to draw her into the game he was playing.

His smile was pure devilment and lethal to her heart rate. At least he wasn't looking at her in that way of his that was lethal to her soul.

In the center of the yard, he dropped her hand. "Okay, I'm ready to dance. Tell me what to do." Fat snowflakes gleamed in his hair and on his eyelashes.

She rolled her eyes. "This is so silly."

"Want me to go home?" he taunted. "Tell me what to do."

"Stretch out your arms." She waited for him to do as instructed. "Now tilt your head up to the sky, stick out your tongue, close your eyes, and turn around in a circle. Go slow at first, though, or you'll get really dizzy and fall down. The trick is to be the last one standing."

He turned once, then looked over his shoulder at her. "You're just going to stand there and let me look like a fool all by myself?"

Samantha couldn't suppress the laughter that bubbled in her throat. After giving a rueful shake of her head, she succumbed to the inevitable and stretched out her arms and her tongue. For the next few minutes as, eyes closed, she performed the dance that symbolized many of her happiest childhood memories, she forgot her self-consciousness, her tension and the man at her side. She twirled around in the darkness feeling more lighthearted than she had in ages, and the only cold she felt was not the air around her, but the taste of melting snow on her outstretched tongue.

The dance ended abruptly when she collided with a hard body. Carlo's hard body. Dizzily, she clutched at the shoulders of his leather jacket so she wouldn't fall.

"Sorry about that," she said, laughing, while the world still spun crazily around her. "Looks like I should have taken…my own…advice…"

The world suddenly righted itself, and she saw the naked hunger blazing in Carlo's eyes. Her heart faltered.

"Samantha." He said her name thickly, his hands closing around her upper arms and pulling her toward him.

The sudden change in his mood caught her with her defenses down. Unable to move, her breathing shallow from her exertion and the way he was looking at her, she stood motionless in front of him. Caught up in the haze of desire that encircled them like a warm, protective cloak, she gazed at his face, memorizing every feature. Her heart thundered in her ears and a purely carnal need uncurled in her belly, heating her from within.

"I want to kiss you," he said.

The part of her consciousness that still had the ability to form coherent thought wondered why he'd announced his intention instead of simply carrying it out. Then she remembered. He'd promised he wouldn't kiss her without her permission. He was an honorable man; he wouldn't break his promise. It was up to her now. All she had to do was take a step back, and his hands would drop from her arms. She could walk away, and the moment would end. It was that simple. And that complicated.

He was standing too close. She couldn't think properly. The need to escape—from him and from the feelings he aroused in her—was strong. Overpowering, however, was the consuming need to feel, just one more time, his arms around her. To feel, just one more time, the wonder of his kiss.

She'd been alone for so long. She wanted his strength. She needed his comfort. She ached for his warmth. Would it really be so wrong?

As if they had a will of their own, her arms wound their way around his shoulders. Latching her fingers at the base of his neck, she pulled his head down to hers.

"So go ahead and kiss me," she murmured and heard him groan when she pressed her mouth to his.

His embrace was everything and more than she'd hoped,

and dreaded, it would be. With his arms tightly around her and his mouth on hers, for the first time in a long time Samantha felt she was where she belonged.

The contrast between the cold night air and the heat of Carlo's body and mouth was delicious. Equally delicious was the raspy feel of his beard against her skin.

His mouth was gentle at first, then, as she responded, it hardened to a fierce demand. Her lips parted beneath that demand, her tongue tangling with his in a dance far more erotic than the snow dance was ever intended to be.

The strength of her response took her by surprise. She had no control over the way she ran her hands over him and pressed her body shamelessly against his, trying to get as close as the restriction of their clothing would allow. No control over the small sounds escaping her throat when his mouth moved to nuzzle her neck and the incredibly sensitive skin of her earlobe. No control over the way she cried out his name with hoarse delight when his hand closed around one swollen breast and stroked her hardened nipple through the fabric of her dress.

Restlessly, urgently, she raised her hands to cup his cheeks and bring his hot mouth back to hers. She felt lost in a sensual fog, a thick, impenetrable, sensual fog, and she never wanted it to clear.

"Samantha," Carlo said against her mouth what could have been minutes, hours, even days later, so lost was she in the sensations coursing through her. "Samantha."

Blinking, she pulled her mouth from his to gaze unseeingly at him. "What?"

"You're shivering," he said gently. "Don't you think we should go inside before you freeze?"

Freeze? She wasn't anywhere near freezing. On the contrary, she was hot. Burning hot. For him. She wasn't shivering from the cold, she was trembling from need.

It was the pressure of his arousal against her thigh, a pressure that felt devastatingly intimate despite the fabric of both his pants and her dress separating their skin, that brought Samantha to her senses. A wave of shame washed over her. Another couple of minutes, and she would have willingly made love with Carlo right there on her front lawn, the snow, the freezing temperatures and the neighbors be damned.

Carlo was right about one thing, she thought as she tore herself from his embrace. They needed to go inside. But not to get out of the cold. They needed to talk. And she needed to set the record straight.

She felt him behind her as she stumbled up the walk and into her front hallway. After closing the door, his hands settled on her shoulders and gently turned her to face him.

"Now," he said, his eyes ablaze with a flame that seared her skin and threatened to weaken her resolve. "Where were we?"

"No, Carlo," she said firmly as he pulled her toward him. He stilled. "No?"

She remained stony in his embrace, and he dropped his arms to his sides.

"No," she repeated, taking a step back and ignoring the regret that pierced her at the loss of his touch.

His gaze searched her face. "What's wrong?"

"What's wrong," she explained, thrusting unsteady fingers through her hair, "is us. I'm sorry. This whole situation is entirely my fault, but I can't do this, Carlo. I can't use you like this. I can't use you to fill my loneliness."

He didn't speak for a long moment. "Is that what you're doing?" he finally said in a low voice. "Using me?"

"What else could it be?"

His lips twisted wryly. "I was kind of hoping it would have something to do with me."

"It can't have anything to do with you." She heard the desperation in her voice and drew a calming breath.

"Why not?" he asked.

"Because I still love my husband."

Emotion flared in his eyes. She couldn't tell whether it was anger or pain.

"When I kissed you, you weren't responding to your husband, Samantha. You were responding to *me*. You called out *my* name, not his. Doesn't that tell you something?"

It certainly did. It told her that she was a lot lonelier than she'd thought, a lot more susceptible than she'd ever imagined to an attractive man's charms.

"Don't get me wrong. I'm grateful, Carlo, for all you've done for Jeffrey and me. More grateful than you'll ever know. But if I let those feelings, well, get out of hand, and gave you the wrong impression, I apologize."

A nerve pulsed in his cheek. "So what you're trying to tell me is that you kissed me the way you did to thank me for helping you out with Jeffrey."

She nodded. "Exactly."

"Liar."

The accusation was all the more effective for the lack of heat in his voice. She knew the source of her response to him: loneliness. But did he, she wondered, really know what was motivating his response to her?

"Can't you see what you're doing?" she asked.

"What *I'm* doing?"

"Yes, Carlo. What *you're* doing. You're using me to forget your problems."

His indrawn breath was audible. "You really believe that?"

Her eyes pleaded with his for understanding. "I really do. I also believe that as long as you're…focused…on me, you don't have to pay attention to the reason why you took your leave of absence."

He looked away. "I told you why I took that leave. I'm not strong enough physically to go back to work."

"Yet you can carry a fifty-pound child up a flight of stairs, not to mention me. And you can't meet my eyes when you tell me a lie."

His gaze flew back to hers, and she added, "I'm not a fool, Carlo. I know there's something else at work here. Something you don't want to talk about. Something personal. That's okay. Just do us both a favor and don't lie to yourself about it."

His eyes gleamed with a cynicism that pierced her heart. "So now you're a psychiatrist, in addition to being a nurse?"

"You don't have to be a psychiatrist to see the obvious."

"You're certainly right there." Leaning back against the door, he thrust his hands into his coat pockets. "Speaking of the obvious, what about you?"

She blinked, taken aback at his sudden attack. "What about me?"

"You do know that you're using your late husband to keep from getting involved with me."

She crossed her arms over her chest and stared at him mutinously. "And why would I do that?" Her voice was icy.

"So you don't have to risk falling in love again. So you don't have to risk getting hurt."

His gaze pinned hers with a force that wouldn't allow her to look away. "What I really think is that it wasn't as easy for you to ignore what's between us as you thought it would be. Maybe you've been thinking about our earlier kiss a lot and wishing it would happen again. Maybe, tonight, when the opportunity arose, you jumped at the chance to kiss me again, the way I jumped at the chance to kiss you."

"That's some theory," she said in a shaky voice.

"Yes, it is. So, tell me. Is it anywhere close to the mark?"

She didn't—couldn't—answer.

"Then," he said, "I guess the question becomes, do you

plan on spending the rest of your life pining for a dead man?''

She was trembling again. With rage and impotence and the hopelessness of it all.

"You don't understand, Carlo."

"Then maybe you should explain it to me."

"I'll try." She sat down at the foot of the stairs and braced her hands against her knees for support.

"When someone dies, you don't lose them all at once. That would be too kind. What happens is, you lose them a little bit at a time. First, there are reminders everywhere you look. The pants he left hanging over a bedroom chair. His favorite coffee mug sitting in the kitchen sink. His scent on the bedsheets."

She swallowed the lump of pain in her throat, and her voice thickened with emotion. "But you try to be strong, for your son. And you finally get the courage to give your husband's clothes away, to wash that favorite coffee mug and the bedsheets. Unfortunately, it doesn't end there. Just when you think you're finally handling things, and that you just might make it through the day without losing it, you turn on the answering machine and you hear his voice, or you see a picture of him that you forgot to put away, and you fall apart all over again."

Her voice lowered until it was almost a whisper. "What I'm trying so clumsily to say, Carlo, is that I'm afraid if I stop loving James, he'll really be gone. And I'm not ready to let him go. Can you understand that?"

His shoulders slumped, and he turned away from her. "Yes," he said quietly. "I suppose I can."

"I'm sorry," she said softly. "I never meant to hurt you."

"I know."

"From now on, I think your dealings should be with Jeffrey only. It will spare us both further...discomfort."

"As you wish."

He placed a hand on the doorknob, then turned back to face her, his dark eyes intent, the lines of his face serious. "I just have one more thing to say to you, Samantha. No one should be as alone as you are."

She could bear anything but his pity. "What about you, Carlo? Aren't you equally alone?"

"Guess that makes us two of a kind. Good night, Mrs. Underwood."

He pulled the door open and walked out into the still-falling snow.

Chapter 10

Carlo had hoped to be able to build a snowman with Jeffrey. But when Saturday arrived, all that remained of that first, miraculous snowfall were a few quickly melting patches of slush and the memory of Samantha's face, the feel of her in his arms, the taste of their shared kiss, and the sting of her ultimate rejection.

It wasn't at all surprising that the snow had melted. The temperature had risen well above freezing, and the ground wasn't frozen solid yet. The way Samantha's heart was. The way Carlo wished his own heart could be.

After a frosty greeting from Samantha, during which both of them had gone to great pains to avoid eye contact, Carlo took Jeffrey to the gym. Most members must have been home, watching the big college football game on TV, because, except for two other people, he and Jeffrey had the place to themselves.

Which gave them ample opportunity to talk. Unfortunately, neither one of them seemed disposed to conversation.

Samantha had looked pale and drawn, Carlo reflected as he spotted Jeffrey on the bench press. Even though he knew better, he'd wanted to reach out to her, to gather her close and comfort her. Did she look that way because of him? Because of what had happened the other night? Did it really matter?

He'd come to the conclusion sometime during the past two days that it really was for the best to keep their personal contact to a minimum. No matter how much it stung. There could be no happily ever after where he and Samantha Underwood were concerned. He'd been a fool to try and delude himself otherwise. If she looked so distressed after a mere kiss, he could only imagine how she would look if he told her the truth about the day her husband died.

She was probably right, anyway. He *was* using his attraction to her to keep his problems at bay. By pretending to himself that he was falling in love with her, he was successfully avoiding making a decision about his future. It was distracting him from what was important.

The solution was to help Jeffrey take that final step, to draw him out of his shell to the point where he was interacting normally with his peers again, and to rid him of any thoughts of revenge. Afterward, time, counseling and his mother's love would do the rest. Once Jeffrey took that final step, they could all make a clean break.

And once the tie was severed, maybe Carlo could decide what he was going to do with the rest of his life. Before someone else—namely the mayor—made that decision for him.

He waited until Jeffrey had finished his third set of repetitions and was sitting up on the bench to ask, "Are you still plotting revenge against the man who shot your father?"

Jeffrey gave him a "get real" look.

"Why?"

"He killed my dad," the boy said matter-of-factly. "He needs to pay."

Jeffrey walked over to the leg curl machine. Carlo followed and watched in silence while the boy adjusted the weights and sat down.

"He is paying," Carlo said. "He's in jail for the rest of his life."

Jeffrey completed a set of presses before replying. "That's not enough."

Carlo went down on his haunches beside the machine. "What *would* be enough?" he asked quietly.

"For him to die, too."

How well Carlo remembered the simple logic of a child. Everything was either black or white, good or bad. There were no in-betweens, no shades of gray. Unfortunately, too many children grew to adulthood with their logic stunted firmly in childhood. He didn't want that to be the case for Jeffrey.

"An eye for an eye, you mean?"

Jeffrey nodded.

"He's in jail, Jeffrey. How do you plan on carrying out your revenge? You'll never get a weapon past the visitor checkpoint. Even if you did, they'd never let you close enough to harm him. In maximum security, there's a Plexiglas wall between you and the person you want to see. You have to talk to each other on a telephone."

"There are other ways."

Carlo felt a chill race up his spine. "What do you mean?"

"I saw this television show, where a guy paid some other guy, who was already in jail, to kill someone for him."

"So you plan on paying someone else to do your dirty work for you?"

"If I have to."

A part of Carlo couldn't believe he was having this conversation with an eight-year-old boy. But there you had it.

Loss, especially loss resulting from violence, did unexpected things to people. Perhaps addressing the method of revenge wasn't the best route to go. Maybe he should address Jeffrey's need for revenge directly.

"Why did your dad became a cop?"

The boy didn't hesitate. "To uphold the law. That's what he always said when anyone asked him."

"What do you think he meant by upholding the law?"

"He wanted to make sure people did what was right."

"And if they didn't?"

"He made sure they were punished."

So far, so good, Carlo thought. "How did he do that?"

"He arrested them."

"And after he arrested them? Did he decide what their punishment would be?"

"No. They went to trial, and a judge gave them their sentence."

"Does the judge get to decide what sentence to give?"

Jeffrey shook his head. "No. The law tells him that."

"And who makes the law?"

"We do."

Carlo drew a deep breath. This was it. He either made his case or lost it totally here.

"You do know, don't you, that if you try to kill this man, you'll be breaking the law?"

Wariness crept into Jeffrey's eyes. "Yes."

"That in the eyes of the law, the law your father respected above all else, you'll be just as guilty as his killer is?" Carlo pressed.

"Yes."

"That's okay with you?"

"In this case it is."

"I see. I have another question for you, and I want you to think for a minute before you answer. What do you think would happen if each person who thought he'd been wronged by someone else took the law into his hands and decided to carry out his own brand of justice? What do you think would happen then?''

Jeffrey's chin jutted out stubbornly. "I don't know."

"Yes, you do," Carlo chided gently. "The world would become a very dangerous place, not to mention that a lot of people, many of them probably innocent of the crimes they'd supposedly committed, would get hurt. Or worse. It would be the opposite of everything your dad worked for."

"Maybe," was all Jeffrey would allow.

"That's one of the reasons we have the law. To protect us, no matter whether we're guilty or innocent, from injustice."

The boy remained silent.

Carlo had saved the toughest questions for last. He asked them now.

"Do you think your dad would want you to break the law? Ever? Would he be proud of you if you did?"

Jeffrey bit his lip and looked away. "No."

"Would he want you entertaining thoughts of revenge?"

"No."

"Think about it, will you?"

The boy gave a slight nod.

"Good." Carlo clapped the child on the back and moved over to the free weights stacked against the far wall.

They were on their second set of bicep curls when Jeffrey asked, "What do you remember about your mom?"

Smiling, Carlo met the boy's gaze in the full-length mirror that lined the wall. "I remember her laughter. I remember that she loved chocolate, hated peas and always cried when she peeled onions and watched sad movies. I remember how she always pretended to get mad when my brothers and I would wrestle in the living room."

"When did she die?"

"Almost twenty years ago."

"And you still remember all that?"

Carlo nodded. "That, and a whole lot more. Why?"

Jeffrey shrugged and looked away. "I was just wondering."

The boy's actions told Carlo that he was doing a lot more than wondering. "Is this about your dad?"

Jeffrey hesitated. Then, a desperate look in his eyes, he blurted, "I think I'm forgetting him. I don't want to do that."

Carlo placed his weights on the rack and turned to the boy. "You'll never forget him, Jeffrey. *Never.* I promise you that."

"Really?" Jeffrey demanded, a sheen of tears coating his eyes. He blinked them back and added, "Then why, except when I look at a picture, can't I remember what he looked like?"

"What was his favorite color?" Carlo asked.

"Blue," Jeffrey answered promptly.

"His favorite sport?"

"Baseball."

"Favorite food?"

"Pork chops."

"Was he right-or left-handed?"

"Right."

"See?" Carlo said gently. "You're not forgetting him. Not what was important about him. Your dad will always be a part of you." He touched Jeffrey's chest at heart level. "In here."

Using his upper arm, the boy swiped at a lone tear. "I really miss him."

Once again, the weight of his guilt filled Carlo with despair. Ruthlessly, he shoved the feeling away. He couldn't give in to his misery and help Jeffrey at the same time.

"I know you do," he said.

Jeffrey let out a shuddering breath. "Mom says we should be thankful to have had him for as long as we did."

Though Carlo wanted badly to reach out to the child, to wrap his arm around the boy's shoulders and offer comfort, he held his arms rigidly at his sides. To reach out would be to invite an intimacy he couldn't afford to cultivate. When Carlo exited Jeffrey's life, he didn't want the boy to feel he'd abandoned him. Jeffrey had already suffered too much loss. Carlo didn't want to add to the child's misery. He'd already caused him enough pain.

"She's right you know," he said huskily.

Clearing his throat, he sat down on an exercise mat and patted the space next to him. He waited until Jeffrey had taken a seat beside him to say, "Can I ask you something?"

Jeffrey forced a smile. "Sure."

"I hear you raised your hand in class last week."

"Uh-huh."

"But you haven't raised it since."

There was a pause. "No."

"Is it because you didn't know any of the answers to the questions your teacher asked?"

"No."

Carlo let that go for now. "Have you asked any of your friends to play on the playground?"

Jeffrey looked down at his lap. "No."

"I thought you weren't going to pull away from people anymore."

"I don't want to, but..."

"But what?"

Frustration lit the eyes Jeffrey raised to Carlo. "It's not that easy. The other kids don't talk to me. I don't think they like me anymore."

Carlo's heart ached for the child. Pity, however, wasn't going to help Jeffrey heal the breach with his friends.

''The first move is going to have to come from you, Jeffrey,'' he said gently.

Jeffrey bit his lip. ''I don't know if I can.''

''It's scary, I admit it. But you can do it. My mother always said that if you do one little thing that terrifies you each day, pretty soon you won't be afraid of anything.''

Good advice, Carlo reflected. But what were *his* fears? That he was a gutless, useless coward? That Samantha and Jeffrey would hate him if they learned the truth? How did he face that?

He'd face his problems later. Right now, he was going to help Jeffrey face his.

''Who was your best friend?''

''Matt.''

''Okay. Here's what you're going to do. On Monday, you go to Matt and tell him you're sorry for ignoring him for so long. Then you ask if you can be friends again.''

Jeffrey didn't look convinced. ''What if he says no?''

''You understand that his feelings are hurt and that it might take a while for him to forgive you. Don't give up on him, though. Try again later. And again, for as long as it takes. In the meantime, go to someone else.''

''You mean I keep trying until I get someone to play with me?''

''Yes.''

''Even if it's a girl?''

Carlo felt his lips twitch. ''Even then. Think you can do it?''

''I...I'm not sure.''

''Come with me.'' Carlo climbed to his feet.

''Where are we going?''

''To face a fear.''

Thirty minutes later, they'd showered and changed and were walking through downtown Bridgeton. A feeling of triumph filled Carlo when he saw a group of boys about Jeffrey's age engaged in an impromptu touch football game in the park.

"Do you know any of these kids?" Carlo asked as they approached.

"No," Jeffrey replied.

"Great. It'll make it easier."

"It'll make what easier?"

Instead of answering, Carlo asked, "Would you like to play football?"

The longing in Jeffrey's eyes was plain to see. "I suppose so."

Carlo inclined his head toward the group. "Then go ask if you can join them."

The boy held back. "I can't."

"Why not?"

Jeffrey toed the ground. "What if they say no?"

Carlo tossed the question back at the child. "What if they do?"

"I'd feel stupid."

"So you'd feel stupid." Carlo shrugged. "Big deal. You don't know these kids. Would it really matter?"

"I guess not."

"Would your heart stop beating if they said no?"

"No."

"Would the world come to an end?"

"No."

"Would a sign reading Loser pop up above your head for everyone to see?"

A smile tugged at the corners of Jeffrey's mouth. "No."

"Then what's the problem?" Giving an encouraging smile, Carlo said, "Look at it this way. If you can get these kids to accept you, think how easy it'll be to get back together with your *real* friends."

Jeffrey squared his shoulders. "Okay, I'll try."

Carlo's heart swelled with pride. "That's the attitude."

Jeffrey took a step, then looked back. "You're not going anywhere, are you?"

"I'll be right here," Carlo promised.

Heart thumping, he held his breath as Jeffrey approached the group, then let it out in a long sigh of relief when the leader nodded for Jeffrey to go out in the field. A minute later he was cheering lustily when Jeffrey threw a pass that was caught for a touchdown.

"Hey, mithter."

Carlo turned to see a gap-toothed, freckle-faced girl sitting on a set of bleachers about ten feet away. She didn't look more than six years old.

"Hey," he said.

"Want to thit down?"

"I think I will." He took a seat beside her. "Are you watching the game?"

"Yeth." She held a bag of candy out to him. "Want a pieth?"

Carlo took a caramel. "Thanks. You a football fan?"

"No."

He shot her a curious look. "Then why are you watching?"

The girl nodded at the boy who had agreed to let Jeffrey play. "Becauth *heth's* playing."

"Ah," Carlo said knowingly. "An older man, eh?"

"Ithn't he wonderful?" The girl sighed. "He doethn't know it, but I'm going to marry him thomeday."

With determination like that, Carlo didn't doubt it for a minute. Jeffrey got the ball again and ran it for a few yards before a touch on his back forced him to give it up. Carlo cheered the boy's progress.

"Ith that your thon?" the little girl asked.

His heart gave a painful jolt at the innocent question. "No," he said softly, sadly. "He's just a friend."

* * *

Two hours after Jeffrey left with Carlo, Samantha's mother breezed through the front door. Maxine Miller looked radiant: rested, tanned and about ten years younger. The hug she gave her daughter was fierce, and, for just a minute, Samantha allowed herself to cling to the embrace the way she had as a child.

"You look wonderful," she told her mother when she pulled away.

"I feel wonderful," Maxine replied with a carefree laugh. She ran a measured gaze over Samantha. "You, on the other hand, look in need of a long vacation."

Trust her mother not to pussyfoot around the truth, or to ignore the dark circles under her eyes, Samantha thought wryly.

"Just a little bout of insomnia," she said quickly, to keep her mother from probing further. "It'll pass. Come on into the den, and I'll get us both a cup of coffee. I want to hear all about your trip."

Five minutes later, they were sitting companionably together on the sofa, steaming mugs of hot liquid cradled in their hands.

"Not that I need to ask," Samantha said after taking a bracing sip, "but how was the cruise?"

Maxine gave a long, satisfied sigh. "Wonderful. Simply wonderful. And you, dear? How was your Thanksgiving?"

Samantha didn't want to think about Thanksgiving, because it reminded her of the kiss she'd shared with Carlo, and its aftermath. She could still see vividly the hurt look in Carlo's eyes when he'd arrived earlier to pick up Jeffrey.

"We muddled through." She gave her mother what she hoped was a brilliant smile. "I'm so glad you're home. We missed you."

"I missed you and Jeffrey, too." Maxine cast a glance around the room. "Where is he? I have a gift for him."

Carefully avoiding her mother's gaze, Samantha opened

the small drawer in the coffee table and pulled out two coasters. After placing her mug on one of them, she offered the other to Maxine.

"He's out with Carlo."

"How's that going?"

"Well." Samantha ran a finger around the rim of her mug. "Jeffrey seems to be responding."

"That is good news, honey."

"Yes, it is." Samantha heard the lack of enthusiasm in her voice and could have kicked herself.

Apparently Maxine heard it, too, because she asked, "Is something wrong?"

"No." She drew a deep breath. "Everything's exactly as it should be. I'm just tired. A full night's sleep, and I'll be good as new."

Maxine set her coffee mug down on the coaster. "In that case, I'd like to take Jeffrey home with me tonight. Give you a break. Maybe even kick that insomnia of yours."

Samantha forced a smile. She really didn't want to be alone tonight, with nothing to do but think. But she couldn't deprive her mother, or Jeffrey, of time together.

"That would be lovely." She rose. "He should be back any minute. I'll just go toss a few things into a bag for him."

"Sam," her mother called after her.

An odd note in Maxine's voice alerted Samantha that all was not as it should be.

"Yes?"

"I have to tell you something."

Slowly, Samantha pivoted to face the older woman, who now stood behind the coffee table. "What is it?"

"It's…about the cruise."

Samantha's chest went tight with apprehension. "Is something wrong? Are you all right?"

Maxine waved a hand at her. "I'm fine. It's just…I met someone."

Samantha caught her breath. "You met someone?"

"A man. Actually, when I say I met someone, I didn't mean on the cruise. It's Seamus McCracken. He went with me."

Seamus McCracken was her mother's next-door neighbor. Five years earlier, he'd been widowed when his wife died of cancer.

"I see," Samantha said carefully.

"We stayed on separate decks, of course. You don't mind, do you?"

Did she mind? This was a major milestone her mother had passed. To take a companion with her meant that the sense of loss that compelled her, once a year, to flee the house she'd shared with her husband was fading.

What was wrong with her? Samantha thought in sudden consternation. This was fantastic news!

"Of course I don't mind," she said sincerely. Crossing the room, she gave her mother another hug. "I think it's wonderful. I always hated the thought of you being alone over the holiday."

"With hundreds of people aboard ship, I was hardly alone."

"You know what I mean." Samantha's gaze sharpened on the older woman. "So you and Seamus are an item."

A light flush covered Maxine's cheeks. "I suppose you could say that."

"Seamus McCracken is a lovely man."

Maxine's flush deepened, and her eyes lit up. "He is, isn't he?" After a pause, she asked, "You're really not upset about this?"

"Why should I be?"

"Your father…"

"Has been gone a long time," Samantha said gently. "He wouldn't begrudge you a little happiness."

"To tell you the truth," Maxine said, "I wish I'd done this years ago. I've wasted so much time."

"You were mourning dad. You weren't ready until now."

Tenderly, Maxine reached out to brush a lock of hair from Samantha's face before gathering both of Samantha's hands between hers.

"No, honey. I wasn't mourning. I was denying reality. I spent nineteen years waiting for your father to walk back through the front door. Nineteen years refusing to believe that he was really gone, and that everything we'd hoped and planned and dreamed for our life together had changed. But he is gone. He's not coming back. And I'm still here. Like it or not, life goes on. I know that now. Take my advice. Don't wait nineteen years to search for your own happiness."

Filled with a restlessness that wouldn't let her sit still, Samantha roamed the silent rooms of her house. Three hours had passed since Carlo had returned Jeffrey to her. One hundred and eighty endless minutes, since Jeffrey had left with her mother.

Darkness had fallen, and the only notice she had given it was to switch on a lamp here and there in passing. Dinnertime had come and gone, unheeded. She was too wound up to eat, too wound up to watch television or read, and definitely too wound up to sleep. For once in her life, she was even too wound up to bake. All she could do was pace, while snatches of past conversations, with her mother and with Carlo, echoed in her ears.

I spent nineteen years waiting for your father to walk back through the front door. Nineteen years refusing to believe that he was really gone, and that everything we'd hoped and planned and dreamed for our life together had changed.

When I kissed you, you weren't responding to your hus-

band, Samantha. You were responding to me. You called out my name, not his.

Take my advice, honey. Don't wait nineteen years to search for your own happiness.

You do know, don't you, that you're using your late husband to keep from getting involved with me.

Were they both right? Was she living in denial, the way her mother had? Was she thrusting Carlo away from her so that she wouldn't experience any more pain? Did she want to wait nineteen years, or even one more minute, without Carlo's arms around her?

When her pacing took her past the guest bedroom, she went inside and pulled out the photograph of James she kept at the bottom of her sweater drawer. Sitting on the edge of the bed, she traced a finger over the smiling face that, for so long, had been dearest to her heart. How odd, she thought, that her yearning for Carlo seemed to mix so completely with her grief for James, until she could barely distinguish one emotion from the other.

She wanted Carlo. In her arms and in her bed. Today and tomorrow and… She bit her lip. Was wanting and needing him this way a betrayal of everything she and James had shared? Was it a betrayal of James's love?

Finally, after months of avoiding it, she asked herself the one question she hadn't allowed herself to ask since James's death. If she was the one who had died, would she have wanted James to mourn forever? Would she have wanted him to be alone? Of course not.

But it's only been a little over a year, her inner voice chided. *It's too soon. It's wrong to feel this way.*

As had happened often during those early, dark months when she was first alone, Samantha felt a presence beside her. A loving, supportive presence. It was almost as if the unseen specter was reaching out to her, offering comfort. She was probably deluding herself, but she liked to believe that it was James's presence she felt. If she concentrated hard enough, she sometimes imagined she could hear her husband's voice.

"We had a good life together, didn't we?" she whispered.

Yes, James's voice echoed in her brain, strong and warm and loving. *We did.*

A tear rolled down her cheek. "But it's over now."

In this time and in this place.

"I loved you, you know."

I know you loved me, Sam. I've always known that. No one can ever take that from us. But I never wanted you to be alone. Do you understand?

And, finally, she did. "You're not coming back, are you?"

You don't need me anymore. You're strong enough to face whatever you need to face. Be happy, Sam.

As quickly as it had appeared, the presence was gone.

Just as quickly, the pain and guilt Samantha had felt for so long fell away. She understood now. The measure of her love for James was not how long she grieved for him, now that he was gone. The measure of her love for him was the love she'd expressed while he was alive. Her mother was right. James was gone; he wasn't coming back. No matter how much she wished that could be so. And he wouldn't want her to spend the rest of her life alone.

Before she lost her courage, she set the picture aside and picked up the telephone receiver.

"It's me, Samantha," she said when Carlo answered. "Could you come over in an hour? There's something important we need to discuss."

When she hung up the phone, her heart thundered and her body trembled with anticipation. After taking a deep breath, she began humming low in her throat as she pulled clothes out of her dresser drawers and closet and carried them back to the master bedroom.

Chapter 11

His mind in turmoil, and the brisk night air stinging his cheeks, Carlo roamed the dark streets of Bridgeton. There could be only one reason for Samantha's unexpected invitation. She'd had time to think since their confrontation two evenings before, time to decide that it wasn't enough to have him out of her life. She wanted him out of Jeffrey's, too.

When he reached the foot of the path leading to her front door, he saw that the porch light had been turned on in anticipation of his arrival. For a long moment, he simply stared at the light. Then, drawing a deep breath, he marched up the path.

What Samantha didn't know was that he'd come to some decisions of his own. She might think she was going to get rid of him, but he wasn't about to make it easy for her. As a matter of fact, he planned on fighting her, tooth and nail, every inch of the way.

The irony of the situation wasn't lost on him. He was the one who'd been dragged, kicking and screaming, into being

Jeffrey's buddy, and now he was going to do some kicking and screaming of his own in order to continue being that buddy.

"You have to let me keep seeing Jeffrey," he announced without preamble when she opened her door to him.

"Carlo."

He didn't hear. "I told you I'd stay away from you, and I'll keep my word. But Jeffrey and I have come too far, made too much progress, to stop now, regardless of your feelings for me. So if that's what you've summoned me here for, you can forget it."

"Carlo."

He threw a hand wide. "Do you know what he plans on doing Monday? Do you? You, if anyone, should understand what a major step that is."

"Carlo."

This time, the soft, patient way in which she uttered his name penetrated the heat of the passion coursing through him.

"What?" he asked slowly, warily.

Amusement flickered in her eyes. "First it was every time you opened your door to me. Now it's when I open my door to you. Tell me. Do you always jump to conclusions this way?"

Only with her, it seemed. Only with her.

He blinked. "I don't understand."

"Maybe this will help. I didn't summon you here, as you put it, to ask you to stop seeing Jeffrey. Far from it. If that was all I wanted, I could have easily told you over the phone."

"Oh."

He didn't know which emotion ran stronger, the relief that left him weak, or the embarrassment that heated his cheeks. One thing was certain: he'd just made a colossal fool of himself. Still, if she didn't want him to stop being Jeffrey's buddy, why had she asked him to come? Whatever the reason, it had to be bad. But if that were the case, why was she smiling? Why was she looking at him in a way that made his blood pound hotly?

"Is Jeffrey okay?" he asked, just to be sure.

"Jeffrey's fine."

"You?"

"I'm fine, too." She stood back from the door. "It's dark and it's cold. Would you like to come inside?"

He filed past her and was immediately filled with warmth: the warmth of her home, and the warmth that was Samantha herself. The truth of the matter was, inside, with her and with Jeffrey, was the only place on earth he wanted to be.

"What exactly does Jeffrey plan on doing Monday?" she asked, closing the door and then securing the dead bolt.

His gaze fastened on the locked door, Carlo's brain whirled with a thousand implications. Why had she thrown the dead bolt? She'd never done so on any of his previous visits. In all likelihood, after she'd told him whatever it was she had to say, he would be leaving, and she would have to go to the bother of unbolting it.

Because he didn't want to jump to yet another conclusion, he decided that habit, and the need for safety, were the only logical explanations. After all, it was past 9:00 p.m., and she was a woman alone in the world. It only made sense that she would be security conscious. She'd certainly made it more than clear that she didn't want to be alone with him.

"First thing Monday morning, Jeffrey's going to go to Matt and tell him he's sorry he's neglected him for so long. Then he's going to ask if they can be friends again. After that, he's going to repeat the process with all of his other friends."

Along with a hint of tears, gratitude glimmered in her eyes. "Oh, Carlo." Her hands flew to her heart. "That's the best news I've had all week. You really are making strides with him. Thank you.''

Despite his earlier assurance that he'd keep his hands off her, if she kept looking at him that way, as if he was a medieval knight who'd just presented her with the Holy Grail, he wasn't sure he could be held responsible for his actions.

"I'm not doing anything," he felt bound to say. "Jeffrey's doing it all himself. I just happened to be around when he was ready.''

"If you say so.''

Her tone of voice told him she believed otherwise, and he was honest enough to acknowledge that he liked having her gratitude aimed his way. However large or small his true role in Jeffrey's recovery, it felt good to have her look at him with appreciation in her eyes. It sure felt a damn sight better than her rejection.

Clearing his throat, he said, "What's so urgent you couldn't tell me over the phone?''

"First things first. Can I take your coat?''

She seemed suddenly nervous, and he got the distinct impression that she was buying time in order to build up her courage for whatever it was she had to say. In addition, he noticed that her color was high and that her eyes were overly bright. During an interrogation, many a suspect had looked the same way—their one last show of bravado, so to speak—before breaking down and confessing to their crimes. But what crime could Samantha have possibly committed? What subject could be so difficult for her to broach?

"That's better.'' She nodded with approval at his faded jeans and turtleneck sweater once she'd helped him slip his leather jacket from his shoulders.

His growing concern couldn't stop him from doing some assessing of his own. It couldn't keep his breathing from growing erratic as he drank in the way her eyes and mouth smiled at him, the way her small, upright breasts pushed against her navy blue sweater, and the way her hips gently rounded the fabric of her gray wool pants.

Damn. Even after she'd told him she was still in love with her husband and planned on staying in love with him for what bordered on forever, even after she'd admitted that she'd only been using him to fight her loneliness and hell would have to freeze over before she would let another man into her heart, he still wanted her. With a ferocity that made him shake.

Balling his hands into fists at his sides, and gritting his teeth against his need, Carlo willed himself to stay in control. He would get through this. Somehow. And, when she'd had her say, he would beat a hasty retreat before the remaining shreds of his pride crumbled at the feet of his continued need of her. Before he reached out, pulled her close, and refused to ever let go.

After hanging his coat in the closet, she turned and, still smiling, took a step toward him. Then, like the suspects he'd interrogated, she came to an abrupt halt. Her bravado faded and, along with it, her smile. Uncertainty etched itself across every feature of her face.

"I—" she began, then stopped.

"What?" he asked, allowing the urgency he felt to vibrate in his voice. "What is it, Samantha? Why did you ask me here? What's wrong?"

"Nothing's wrong," she said quickly. Biting her lip, she added, "I'm sorry. I'm handling this badly, I know. It's just…well, I didn't think it would be so hard."

He could feel the tension rolling off her, see it in the set of her shoulders and the way she looked at him, her eyes seeming to beg him for some sort of understanding. She was scaring the pants off him.

"For heaven's sake, just spit it out. Say whatever you have to say, and be done with it."

To his amazed disbelief, she burst out laughing. Totally confused, all he could do was stare at her while she rollicked with mirth.

"What's so funny?" he finally demanded.

"You are." Another gust of laughter shook her, and she held onto her sides. "Spit it out, he says. Spit it out. Spoken just like a man."

His frustration edged up a notch. "What did you expect? I am a man."

Her laughter subsided, and she wiped a tear from the corner of one eye. "Yes, Carlo, I know. Believe me, I know. Thank you. I needed that."

"You did ask me here to tell me something?" he prompted.

Where a minute ago she'd seemed unsure of herself, now she was the picture of confidence. The smile she aimed at him was purely feminine and one hundred percent lethal to his heartbeat.

"I've been doing a lot of thinking these past couple of days. About what you said the other night. How I was afraid to risk caring for someone again. And I've come to a decision. You were right."

"I was?" he said hoarsely, barely able to hear his words, his heart was thundering so loudly in his ears.

"Yes, you were."

"About what?"

"Do I really have to spell it out to you?" she asked softly.

"Yes, Samantha, you do. I don't want to jump to any more conclusions where you and I are concerned."

She nodded her understanding. "Then let me make this perfectly clear. I asked you here because I want you to do what we've both wanted from the moment we met. I want you to make love to me. Now. Here. Tonight."

He was instantly, painfully, irrevocably aroused.

"You do want me, don't you, Carlo?"

More than the air he needed to breathe. "I thought you said I was only using you to forget my troubles."

"A self-defense mechanism," she explained.

"You also said you were only using me to fill your loneliness."

"The same self-defense mechanism."

"So now you're saying it was all a lie?"

She drew a deep breath. "I'm saying that I want you, Carlo. I don't want you to stay away from me. I want you to take me in your arms, hold me, kiss me, make love to me."

He'd never seen her like this, so bold, so open, so damn beautiful and alluring he didn't think he could take it if it was all a game.

"Don't tease me, Samantha," he pleaded. "Not about this."

There wasn't even a hint of playfulness in the eyes she leveled on him.

"I'm not teasing you, Carlo. I've never been more serious about anything in my life."

It was the answer to his every dream, and he was terrified of trusting that it really could come true.

"But James…"

"Is gone," she said. "He's not coming back. I know that now. I accept it."

"And Jeffrey…"

"Is at his grandmother's." She waited a beat before adding meaningfully, "Until tomorrow afternoon."

This time, there could be only one answer to the implications charging around in his brain. Incredible as it seemed, Samantha had invited him here this evening to share her bed. It wasn't a declaration of love, or for that matter, a declaration that love might come in the future. But it was a declaration of desire, and that was more than he had ever allowed himself to hope for.

His conscience chose that moment to rear its ugly head. If all he wanted was to make love to her, he could do as she asked without a second thought. But if he ever wanted a chance for things to go beyond the lovemaking stage, he had to tell her what had happened that awful day. He had to tell her the part he'd played in her husband's death. Of course, once he did, there would be no lovemaking. And there would be no love. Ever.

"There's something I should tell you," he began.

She placed a finger against his lips. "Shh. Not now. We'll have plenty of time to talk. Later. Much later."

"But—"

She shook her head at him. "No buts. I don't want to think about the future. I don't want to think about the past. I just want to think about now. This minute. You and me. Together. How's that sound?"

"Like heaven on earth."

Her eyes glittered with promise. "I don't know where this is headed, or if it's heading anywhere at all. But for tonight, I just want to go along for the ride."

She held out her hand to him. "Come with me?"

He was too weak. And far too cowardly. Desire had him in its exquisite grip and refused to let go. If she was giving him this one night, he didn't think he had the strength to resist her.

"I don't have anything to offer you, Samantha." The admission was a last stab at doing what was right.

"Oh, yes, Carlo," she contradicted, "you do. You make me feel alive again. I want to revel in that feeling for as long as it lasts."

Trembling, he pushed his doubts and fears aside. He took the hand she offered and pressed it to his lips. "And you make me feel whole again."

She led him up the stairs. When they reached the guest bedroom, he stopped, expecting her to take him inside. A tug on his hand carried him forward until they came to the closed door of the master bedroom.

"Are you sure?" he asked.

She nodded. "I moved back in this evening."

When he still hesitated, she said, "It's just a room, Carlo. That's all."

The bedroom was softly lit by dozens of candles, and the bedcovers had been carefully turned down. This evening had, he realized, been choreographed to the last detail, including the champagne chilling in a silver bucket and the package of condoms on the bedside table that had him doing a double take.

"You worked hard," he said.

"Even though it didn't go exactly the way I planned, it was a very calculated seduction," she admitted. "Do you mind?"

Did he mind? It was the fulfillment of his every fantasy.

"Not in the least." He spread his arms in open invitation. "Seduce away."

Her playful smile was back. "It'll be my pleasure."

She was wrong. It would be his.

"You'll have to forgive me," she said, taking hold of the bottom of his sweater and tugging it up over his head, "if I'm a little clumsy at this. But it's been a long time for me."

"It's been a long time for me, too," he said, catching his breath as she ran her hands from his chest to his abdomen.

He captured her hands and pulled them to his heart. "I don't need fancy words, Samantha. I don't need smooth, I've-done-this-a-thousand-times-before moves. I sure as hell don't need contortionistic poses. All I need is you. Being here with you, like this, is enough. More than enough."

Gratitude joined the desire blazing in her eyes. "It's enough for me, too." She smiled at him in a way that was both teasing and sexy as hell. "Now, where was I?"

"Sure you don't want me to take the lead?" he offered.

She stilled. "Do you need to take the lead?"

"This is your dance," he said, and felt her relax. "I'm perfectly content to follow, if that's what you want."

"It's what I want."

He pressed her hands to his chest and smoothed them down to his abdomen. "In that case, I believe you were right about here."

Her fingers traced lightly over the skin of his stomach before inching lower, exquisite in their torture. When they brushed against the brass buckle of his belt, he felt his muscles tense.

"Ah, yes," she teased. "Now I remember."

Slowly, deliberately, her hands touching him so intimately that his groans of pleasure seemed pulled from the depths of his soul, Samantha removed the rest of his clothing. It was all he could do not to reach out and touch her the way she was touching him, especially when she began removing her own clothes. By the time she stood naked before him in the flickering candlelight, Carlo was so aroused he feared that one more touch from her would set him off.

"You are the most beautiful thing I've ever seen," he said, breathing hard.

Her eyes darkened as she wound her arms around his neck and affixed her body to his. "And you have the most self-control of any man I've met."

Somehow, despite the sensations exploding inside him at the feel of her naked form so closely aligned to his, he managed to hang on to that control. Barely.

"Trust me, it's fading fast."

"Good," she said with evident satisfaction.

"Does that mean you want me to take the lead now?"

"It means," she said moving her hips suggestively against his, "that I want us both to do whatever gives us pleasure."

Thank God. He didn't think he'd be able to stand much more.

"Since I have your permission, it will give me the greatest pleasure to do this."

Lowering his head, his mouth plundered hers. One arm closed around the nape of her neck, pulling her close. With his other hand, he kneaded and caressed one breast, teasing her nipple until it felt as hard as he did.

"You feel so good," he groaned, leaning his forehead against hers. "If this is all a dream, I don't ever want to wake up."

"It's not a dream, Carlo. Does a dream feel like this?"

She ran her hands down his arms.

"Taste like this?"

She traced her tongue over his lips.

"Burn like this?"

Her hand closed around his erection, and he nearly lost his mind with the pleasure of it.

"No," he managed to say. "This is all very real."

She led him to the bed and pulled him down beside her.

"Make love to me, Carlo," she demanded. "Make love to me now."

He needed no further invitation. After protecting himself, he joined his body to hers and lost himself in the sensation of her tightness and heat.

He'd never felt this way with a woman before, as if each touch, each caress were more spiritual than physical. He'd certainly never trembled like a mighty oak before the force of a hurricane at a mere glance from her, at a whisper in his ear of the delights to come.

She touched his skin, his hair, her body sheathed his arousal and responded to his every thrust, her cries filled his ears, but it was his heart that responded to each stimulus. It was his heart that bloomed and swelled until he thought it would burst. Afterwards, when the ultimate peak had been reached and crested, and they lay spent and breathless in each other's arms, it was his soul that felt a deep and utter contentment. A contentment that lulled him into a deep sleep.

"Too late," Carlo cried, thrashing against the bonds holding him. "Too late, too late, too late."

"Shh," a voice soothed, and he felt something cool and soft against his forehead. "Shh."

His eyes flew open, and he bolted upright. Staring wildly into the darkness, his breath coming in tortured gasps and his heart thundering in his ears, he tried to gain his bearings. Where was he?

"It's okay," the soothing voice said. Samantha's voice.

He turned his head toward the sound and saw her sitting beside him. Though the outline of her body was shadowy in the darkness, he could tell that she was naked.

"It's okay," she repeated. "It was just a dream."

Memory returned, and he tensed. They'd made love. Wild, sweet, wonderful love. And afterward he'd fallen asleep with his arms around her. He'd let his guard down, and the dream had returned.

The candles must have burned out, he realized as his eyes grew accustomed to the darkness. Either that, or Samantha had blown them out. The bonds he'd been thrashing against were the bed sheets that his tossing and turning had twisted around his body. And the something soft he'd felt against his forehead had been the brush of Samantha's fingertips.

The luminous dial on the bedside clock read 2:00 a.m. He'd been asleep for nearly three hours. A record, really, since the dream, when it chose to taunt him, usually claimed him shortly after he closed his eyes.

"I guess I fell asleep," he said, because he didn't know what else to say.

"We both did," Samantha replied.

"I hope I didn't frighten you."

"You didn't."

He glanced at the clock again. "It's late. Maybe I should go."

She placed one hand against his arm. "I want you to stay, Carlo. And I want you to tell me about your dream."

It wasn't a dream, he wanted to shout. It was a waking nightmare. A monument to his criminal incompetence.

His shoulders bowed beneath the crushing weight of his guilt. He'd let her seduce him without telling her the truth. He'd selfishly imbibed the sweetness of her body like a drunk with a fresh bottle, recklessly ignoring the consequences of his actions, and in so doing had ruined any chance—slim though it might have been—that they had of a future together.

A groan of despair ripped from his throat and echoed in the silence. Leaning forward, he cupped his head between his hands.

"You've had the dream before, haven't you?" Samantha asked, her voice gentle and understanding.

"Yes," he said thickly. "Yes."

"Tell me about it," she said. "Maybe it will help."

"I can't," he moaned.

"Tell me, Carlo. Please. Let me help. What are you too late for?"

At her gentle probing, the words refused to stay locked inside him any longer. He needed to tell someone the horrible truth he'd kept bottled up for so long. He needed to tell her. He owed it to her.

"That day," he said.

"What day?"

"The day James died."

"What about it?"

He raised anguished eyes to hers. "My fault. It was all my fault."

Even in the dark, he could see the confusion on her face. "What was your fault?"

He had to look away from her, or he'd never have the courage to go on. "I wanted to tell you before, but I was too much of a coward."

Haltingly at first, then the words picking up speed and nearly tripping over themselves in their eagerness to be heard, he related every detail of what had happened that day. When he finished, when he'd emptied out all the regret, the sorrow and the guilt, he felt more spent than he had after the most demanding of workouts. Staring down at the hands he repeatedly clasped and unclasped in his lap, he braced himself for Samantha's revulsion, for her hatred. For her utter and complete rejection.

The bed gave, and he felt her leave his side. So it was to be that way, he thought. She couldn't even stand to look at him. His throat worked, and he swallowed the lump that had lodged there. Head bowed, he waited for her icy voice to order him to leave. He knew that, this time, he wouldn't fight her decision to banish him from both her and Jeffrey's lives.

Instead of angry words, though, he heard the sound of a match being struck. The sound was followed by the odor of phosphorous, and then a wavering light filled the room. The bed gave again when Samantha returned to his side.

"Is that why you took a leave of absence from the force? Because you blamed yourself for what happened?"

"Yes," he said, his gaze still on his hands. "When they gave me that commendation, I realized what a fraud I was. I also realized I had no business putting anybody else's life at stake."

"Carlo," she said softly. "Look at me."

Incredibly, when he gazed into her eyes, all he saw was compassion. At first, he didn't understand. How could she not blame him?

He must have spoken his thoughts aloud, because she said, "You were on a crowded street. There were women and children there. You did nothing criminal. If you had, the investigation afterward would have surely found that. For all you know, your caution saved lives by giving the innocent bystanders time to get out of the way, before the shooting started."

"But it wasn't enough," he protested. "James still died. It's still my fault."

"Why?"

"Because I didn't react quickly enough. Because I didn't immobilize Gary Pierce when I had the chance."

"Because you didn't anticipate Fred Bishop doing something stupid, like running out of his house waving a gun?"

"Yes," he agreed with a nod.

"Using your reasoning," she said softly, "I'm the one responsible for James's death."

He started. "That's ridiculous."

"Is it? I was the one who persuaded him to move back to Pittsburgh so we could be closer to my mother. If we'd stayed in Philadelphia, James would still be alive now."

"You have no way of knowing that," he protested. "Anything could have happened. Why he could have—"

The triumphant look she shot him stopped him midspeech.

"Exactly," she said. "By the same token, you have no way of knowing whether, if you had done anything differently that day, the outcome would have changed. You didn't kill James, Carlo. Gary Pierce did. And he's sitting in jail for the rest of his natural life to pay for his crime. I think it's time you lifted your self-imposed sentence."

She reached out and brushed the hair back from his forehead. "I also think it's time you forgave yourself for not being perfect."

Even though he was the one in the wrong, even though he had no right to feel anything other than shame, he couldn't stem the defensiveness that arose inside him at her words.

"I never thought I was perfect," he said stiffly.

"No," she replied. "But you try to be."

"What does that mean?"

"It means that you demand more from yourself than from anyone else. Like when your mother died, and you were determined to be both mother and father to your brothers and your sister. Like when you took on being Jeffrey's big brother at a time when you didn't have the emotional resources, or the heart to do so, just because the mayor asked you to. Because I asked you to."

He fixed his gaze on the shadows flitting across one wall. "I just want to do what's right."

"We all do, Carlo. Well, most of us, anyway. Sometimes, though, when things go wrong, we have to cut ourselves some slack."

His gaze flew back to hers. "Even when a man's life is at stake? Even when your actions lead to his death?"

"Gary Pierce's actions led to James's death. All you did was try to generate hope in an already hopeless situation."

"Not to my way of thinking," he maintained.

"Can you leap tall buildings with a single bound?" she demanded, and for the first time he heard a hint of frustration in her voice.

"Of course not."

"Do you have X-ray vision?"

"No."

"Then you're not a superhero." She spread her arms. "You're just a man, Carlo. A good man, but a man nonetheless. You can't save the world from all its ills. No matter how much it galls you to admit it. Tell me something. If your positions had been reversed, if you were the one being held at gunpoint and James was the one coming to your rescue, would he have acted any differently than you did?"

It was a question he'd never thought to ask himself. Had, in truth, been afraid to ask. Now that he did, the answer seemed so clear, he couldn't believe he'd missed it.

"No, I don't believe he would have."

"I don't believe so, either," she replied softly.

"I just wish James hadn't died," he said in a low voice.

"We all do." Samantha smiled gently at him. "Were you listening when you spoke to my son, the night you comforted him when he had his nightmare?"

"Of course."

"Then you should know that every word you said to Jeffrey applies to you, too. And to me, only I didn't realize it until today. You told him that death touches everyone, and that when it does, we can't let the pain of it force us to withdraw from the people who love us most. When we do that, all we do is hurt ourselves. Don't hurt yourself anymore, Carlo. For your sake."

"But I haven't withdrawn," he protested. "Not the way Jeffrey has."

"Haven't you?" she challenged. "What would you call taking a leave of absence? What would you call avoiding your brothers?"

He grimaced. "Withdrawal."

Once again, her fingertips brushed soothingly across his brow. "You need to give yourself time to heal. Once you do, you'll be able to look at what happened without blaming yourself. Trust me on this. I'm right. You know I am."

He reached out a hand to gently cup her chin. Samantha turned her face into the embrace, kissing his palm. Then, pulling away, she pressed her lips briefly to his right shoulder. From there she lowered her head and kissed his chest just below the area of his heart. A third kiss was placed to the side of his abdomen. Finally, her gaze firmly on his, she pressed a soft kiss against his right thigh.

Carlo's heart contracted when he realized what she was

doing. She was kissing the scars he'd received that awful day.

"You amaze me," he said thickly.

She seemed surprised. "Why?"

"Your strength. After everything you've been through, all the pain and loss, you can still reach out so selflessly to others. To me. It's incredible."

"Is it so wrong for me to want to help you?"

"That's the point. I thought I was the one who was supposed to help *you*."

"Maybe," she said, closing her arms around him and resting her head against his collarbone, "we can help each other."

For the first time since he'd awakened, he grew aware of their nakedness and was filled with the wonder of the act they'd shared earlier. Needing no memory, just the feel of her supple skin, his body responded to her closeness. Within seconds he was fully aroused.

Rolling her onto her back, Carlo smiled down at her. "Maybe," he said, brushing his hand across one breast and thrilling to her swiftly indrawn breath, "we can."

"I think," she replied, slanting him a wicked smile as her hands did some exploring of their own, "we at least owe it to ourselves to try."

A rush of gratitude and desire filled him. He wanted to tell her that he loved her, but he knew he had no right. His future was still very much up in the air, and until it got resolved, one way or another, he had nothing to offer her. That she'd forgiven him for the role he'd played in her husband's death was a wonderful gift, perhaps the best gift, other than the feel of her in his arms, that he'd ever received. But it didn't absolve his guilt. It didn't make things miraculously right. He didn't know what would.

For now, though, he was content merely to hold her, to

caress her, to hear her soft cries of pleasure, to make love to her. He was content to relish a sense of inner peace he hadn't felt in longer than he could remember, and to let tomorrow take care of itself. Tomorrow.

Chapter 12

If there was a more hellish place on earth than a shopping mall during the last two weeks before Christmas, Carlo had yet to go there.

Dismay filled him as he gazed at the teeming throng milling through the department store that anchored one end of the local mall. In her haste to get to the latest sale, a woman rushed by and nearly elbowed him in the kidneys. Christmas carols blared from unseen speakers, causing him to look longingly toward a pair of earmuffs on a nearby table. Maybe they would muffle the sound to the point where his ears didn't ring and his head didn't ache.

It wasn't that he hated Christmas. On the contrary. He loved it. He loved everything about it. He'd even been known, from time to time, to don a red suit and play Santa Claus when the occasion called for it.

What he hated was shopping. Any kind of shopping. The simple act of pulling into a mall parking lot was enough to give him the heebie-jeebies. Add the holiday season to the mix, and he felt like a condemned man who'd been denied his last meal.

The endless crowds made him claustrophobic. The unceasing noise made him yearn for the peace and quiet of solitary confinement. And the total lack of Christmas spirit, as shoppers shoved one another out of the way in their fervor to fill their Christmas lists before the shelves had been picked bare, made him despair for the future of a holiday that, before being ruined by crass commercialization, had been designed to bring joy, not foul tempers.

He wouldn't have stepped within a mile of the mall, had in fact been thrilled that all his time spent whittling meant he wouldn't have to buy any gifts this year, if it hadn't been for Jeffrey. But when he'd asked the child how he would like to spend their time together this Saturday afternoon, Jeffrey had said he wanted Carlo to help him do his Christmas shopping. So here they were, in the middle of a crowded department store, searching for the perfect gift for Samantha.

It hadn't taken long for Jeffrey to select a gift for his grandmother and his teacher. But when it came to Samantha, the boy had grown markedly choosy. Thirty minutes had come and gone, and he had yet to decide on his mother's gift.

"What about this?" Carlo held up a colorful scarf.

"Uh-uh." Jeffrey shook his head. "She hates scarves."

"How about this, then?" Moving over to another table, Carlo picked up a leather belt.

"No. Mom has lots of belts."

"There's a carousel of earrings over there that looks promising."

"I don't think so. She doesn't wear much jewelry."

"Do you have any idea what you're looking for?" Carlo could hear the desperation in his voice.

"I'll know when I see it," the boy replied with youthful logic. "It has to be just perfect."

It was beyond Carlo what the perfect gift could be, when you were eight years old and only had ten dollars to spend.

Just then Jeffrey's eyes lit up. Carlo followed the boy's gaze to a table full of porcelain figurines. His heart fell. He was no judge of prices, but even he could tell at a glance that they had to cost more than ten dollars. Probably a whole lot more.

"This is it," Jeffrey said, picking up the figurine of a nurse and turning it over reverently in his hands. "She looks just like mom. Isn't she beautiful?"

A salesclerk, who had been straightening the merchandise on an adjacent table, smiled at Jeffrey and said, "She's one of our top-selling items. You've made a very wise choice."

Carlo knew the second the boy saw the price tag, because his smile faded, his shoulders drooped and he placed the figurine carefully back on the table.

"How much is it?" he asked.

"Thirty dollars." Dejection filled Jeffrey's voice. "That's twenty dollars more than I have."

How should he handle this? Carlo wondered. He could offer Jeffrey the twenty dollars, but he was pretty certain the boy would turn him down. Jeffrey had a lot of pride, not to mention that, on the drive to the mall, he'd told Carlo how long he had saved up so he'd have his own money to buy his mother a gift.

Jeffrey was right, Carlo thought, glancing at the figurine again. It did look like his mother. Samantha would love it. It was the perfect gift. Even if it wasn't, Carlo didn't think he could take another thirty minutes until Jeffrey found another perfect gift.

"Let's go," Jeffrey said dully, turning away. "We'll have to look somewhere else."

"Okay."

Carlo eyed the salesclerk, who was staring at Jeffrey with obvious compassion. Feigning a coughing fit, he reached into his pants pocket and pulled out a twenty-dollar bill along with his handkerchief. With the handkerchief as a shield, he dropped the bill on the floor at the salesclerk's feet. Inclining his head toward the dropped bill, he nodded at her and prayed she got the message.

She did, or at least he thought she did when she stooped to pick it up. For all he knew, she could be pocketing it for herself, and he'd just thrown away twenty dollars.

His faith in his fellow human held true when, a second later, she gave him a conspiratorial wink before exclaiming, "Wait a minute! Does that price tag say thirty dollars?"

Carlo picked up the figurine. "Sure does."

"I can't believe it." She shook her head and acted indignant. "That's what I get for sending someone else to do my job. All of these figurines have been specially marked down for Christmas. That price tag should read ten dollars."

Jeffrey slowly turned around. "Really?" he asked, as if afraid to hope.

"Really," she assured him with a smile.

"That means I can buy it for my mom." Excitement filled his voice.

"Looks that way," Carlo said.

"Would you like me to wrap it for you?" the clerk asked.

Five minutes later, the package wrapped and snug in a bag, Carlo and Jeffrey reentered the main mall and headed for the entrance they'd used earlier. Just when he thought they were about to make good their escape, Jeffrey tugged on his arm.

"There's Santa. Can I go see him?"

Carlo looked in the direction of Jeffrey's pointed finger and suppressed a groan. From where they were standing, the line to sit on Santa's lap seemed at least ten miles long. Poor Santa was starting to look less than jolly. His ho-ho-ho sounded forced, and if the expression on his face was anything to go by, his knees were feeling the strain of bouncing so many children.

Determined to give both Santa and himself a break, Carlo turned back to Jeffrey and tried to think of a way to talk the child out of his planned visitation. He'd even resort to bribery, thereby risking Samantha's ire, if that was what it took. He was that desperate.

The words he'd formed stuck in his throat when he saw the hope, and the belief, shining in the boy's eyes. If, after everything he'd been through, Jeffrey still believed, Carlo didn't have the heart to deny him. Not even if he had to wait ten hours in line and have his ears assaulted by the unending blare of Christmas carols.

"Why not?" he said, and was rewarded with a bright smile.

The line inched along at a snail's pace.

"How are things going at school?" Carlo asked.

Jeffrey shrugged. "Good."

"You volunteering in class?"

"Uh-huh."

"You and Matt doing okay?"

"Uh-huh."

"Playing together at lunch?"

"Uh-huh."

"Going over to each other's houses after school?"

"Uh-huh."

"What about your other friends?"

"Joey's still holding out, but I think he'll come around."

"I'm sure he will. You just keep plugging away at him."

"I will."

Carlo gazed thoughtfully at the child. "Was it as hard as you thought it would be, going to your friends and asking for forgiveness?"

The line moved ahead an inch or two, while Jeffrey formulated his answer.

214   *Dad in Blue*

"At first I was scared. Real scared. But when I made myself talk to Matt, it wasn't bad at all. After that, the rest was pretty easy."

"It is amazing," Carlo said, nodding in agreement and thinking about how long and hard he'd agonized over telling Samantha the truth about the events of the day James Underwood died. "We build things up in our minds, and then reality rarely matches the terrors we imagined."

"Mom says the same thing all the time, whenever I get scared of something," Jeffrey replied.

"She's right, you know."

"I know." Jeffrey turned solemn eyes up to Carlo. "Know what I thought Matt would do when I went up to him?"

"What?"

"I thought he'd punch me in the stomach really hard."

"Did he?"

"Nope."

"What did he do?"

Jeffrey grinned. "He punched me in the arm."

"Is that different?" Carlo asked.

Jeffrey gave him a "get with it" look. "'Course it is. It meant we were friends again."

"I see." Carlo suppressed a grin.

A speculative gleam lit Jeffrey's eyes. He opened his mouth as if to say something, then shut it abruptly and looked away, shuffling his feet across the floor.

"What is it?" Carlo said. "Is there something you want to ask me?"

Jeffrey seemed to mull it over for a minute before returning his gaze to Carlo's.

"You always tell the truth, right?"

"I try to."

"If I ask you a question, will you give me an honest answer?"

"If I can."

Jeffrey nodded. "Okay, then. Do you like my mom?"

"Of course I do," Carlo responded promptly. "She's a nice lady."

Jeffrey shook his head impatiently. "No. That's not what I meant. Do you *like* my mom? You know, the way a boy likes a girl."

Carlo hadn't been expecting this and didn't know what to say. "Oh."

As if by unspoken agreement, he and Samantha hadn't announced the change in their relationship to anyone. Nor had Carlo spoken to Samantha about where the relationship might be headed. Not because he didn't want to, but because he knew he had no right to broach the subject, at least not until he got his life back in order. Samantha, who had every right to ask, had remained mum.

The one thing she had said to him was that she didn't want him sleeping over when Jeffrey was home. Jeffrey was too young and impressionable to be exposed to an intimate relationship between his mother and another man, especially a relationship that might not have a future. It was one thing for Jeffrey to think of Carlo as a buddy. It was a far different thing for him to think of Carlo as the man in his mother's life. She wouldn't, under any circumstances, put her son's emotional welfare at risk that way. Had they been strangers who had just started to date, she never would have dreamed of introducing him to Jeffrey until she was certain the relationship had a future.

Though her words had made his heart ache, Carlo understood her caution. Jeffrey had been through enough. Until Carlo figured out what the future held for him, until both he and Samantha were certain that their feelings for each other were of a permanent nature as opposed to purely chemistry, it was best they kept their relationship a secret.

With that in mind, for the last two weeks they'd chosen

their private moments together carefully. Samantha had taken to dropping by his house during her lunch hour, or when her mother had taken Jeffrey for an hour or two. Carlo would visit her in her home after he was certain that Jeffrey was asleep. She'd invited him over for dinner a couple of times each week. On those occasions, with Jeffrey present, they'd been careful to behave formally with each other.

And, except for their lovemaking, they kept things light, teasing. They avoided any mention of the future. They rarely spoke of the past. They had each been scrupulous in their care to keep their conversation rooted firmly in the present.

Somehow, though, as careful as they had been, Jeffrey must have picked up on the undercurrents between them.

Which left Carlo with something of a dilemma. Did he tell Jeffrey the truth, or did he lie to him? Recalling the promise he'd made to the boy weeks ago, he knew there was really only one thing he could do. If he lied, and if he lost Jeffrey's trust, it wouldn't be easy to win it back. Samantha might not welcome his decision, but he really had no other choice.

"Yes, Jeffrey," he finally said. "I like your mother the way a boy likes a girl. I like her very much."

"I thought so," Jeffrey replied. "I think she likes you, too."

"Does that bother you?"

Again, Jeffrey seemed to give the question a lot of thought. When he spoke, there was a reflective tone in his voice that was far more mature than his eight years. But then, it wasn't surprising, given all the child had been through.

"I want my mom to smile again. She smiles when she's with you."

"She makes me smile, too," Carlo said.

Jeffrey tilted his head to one side. "Are you going to marry her?"

Carlo's heart raced at the thought. "It's too soon to know. Way too soon. Not all people who like each other the way your mom and I do end up getting married, you know. In fact, very few do."

He reached out and ruffled the boy's hair. "Why don't you let us take things one step at a time, and we'll see what happens. Okay?"

"Okay," Jeffrey agreed. "Can I ask one more thing?"

"Sure."

"Even if you don't marry my mom, can we still be friends?"

Until that moment, Carlo hadn't realized that Jeffrey was as attached to him as he was to Jeffrey. While it wasn't the love of a father for a son, it was more than just the affection of one buddy for another. And it would grow deeper, stronger, the more time they spent together.

Relationships were funny things, Carlo realized. You entered into one, determined to keep your distance, do what you had to do and put in whatever time necessary before getting out, but before you knew it you were involved up to your eyeballs. You were no longer counting the hours it took you away from what you really wanted to do, because it was what you really wanted to do.

Was it ever possible to touch another person's life while remaining at a distance? Was it possible to remain untouched when that person reached out to you? It certainly wasn't for Carlo where Jeffrey was concerned. It most definitely wasn't possible where Samantha was concerned.

With all that in mind, Carlo had to wonder if he was playing with fire. When Jeffrey lost his father, it had almost destroyed him. If the relationship between Carlo and Samantha, for whatever reason, never came to fruition, how would it affect Jeffrey? Would the child withdraw inside himself again? If so, would anyone be able to draw him back out?

Carlo knew one thing. He had enough guilt on his conscience. He'd never forgive himself if he caused Jeffrey any harm.

"I promise you, Jeffrey," he said, his voice husky with emotion and his hand pressed to his heart in a pledge, "that no matter what, you and I will always be friends."

"Someone is certainly in a good mood," Eve Carpenter, one of Samantha's fellow nurses, commented.

Distracted from the paperwork she'd been busily filling out, Samantha looked up from her seat in the middle of the curved nurse's station. Eve, a petite brunette, was standing at the far end of the station, an open patient's chart in her hands.

"Who?" Samantha asked.

"You," Eve replied with a laugh.

"Me?"

"Yes, you. You were whistling, weren't you?"

Samantha blinked. "I was whistling?"

"Yes. Didn't you know?"

"I guess I wasn't paying attention. Sorry if I disturbed you."

"You've been whistling for two weeks now," Eve said. "Nonstop. The hospital grapevine is buzzing madly about it. Everyone wants to know why you're so happy."

It was because of Carlo. Because of the way he made Samantha feel. Even though she cautioned herself not to get her hopes up too high, just the thought of him was enough to make her heart sing. And when she actually saw him and touched him...

"It must be the Christmas season," she told Eve. "This time of year always puts me in a good mood."

"Must be. Monica told me you didn't even flinch when Mr. Johnson pinched your behind yesterday afternoon."

Cyrus Johnson was the bane of the cardiac wing's existence. No nurse's posterior was safe whenever he was in residence.

Samantha laughed. ''Mr. Johnson is just a lonely old man who gets himself admitted periodically, because it's the one place where he gets some attention. Trust me. A few soothing words, and he'll turn to putty in your hands.''

''You really are full of the Christmas spirit,'' Eve said wryly. ''Care to pass some my way?''

''Sure. I'll bottle it up, and we'll sell it in the gift shop. We'll make a fortune, and then you and I can retire and live the rest of our lives in the lap of luxury.''

''Deal,'' Eve said, laughing.

A light blinked on the console. Mrs. Cavanaugh's room. Mr. Johnson might be an old lecher who played fast and free with his pinching fingers, but Mrs. Cavanaugh made Oscar the Grouch look sweet-tempered. The woman never had a kind word to say, no matter how hard they worked to make her comfortable. Both Samantha and Eve groaned.

''Want me to get it?'' Samantha asked.

Eve heaved a weary sigh. ''No. I'm already up. I'll get it. Just promise me one thing, will you? Get that stuff bottled ASAP. I need to slip a huge dose into Mrs. Cavanaugh's IV.''

''Just as soon as I finish this paperwork,'' Samantha promised.

''We all know when that will be,'' Eve said, rolling her eyes. ''When hell freezes over.''

''That's the Christmas spirit,'' Samantha teased.

Still chuckling, she buried her head back in her paperwork. A minute later, a deep male voice interrupted her.

''Can anyone tell me where I might find the most beautiful nurse on the cardiac ward?''

When Samantha looked up, she saw a huge bouquet of roses. The roses moved to one side to reveal Carlo's face.

Her heart thumped the way it always did whenever she saw him.

"Oh, Carlo, they're beautiful."

"You like them?" He placed the arrangement on top of the curved counter.

"Of course I like them. But you shouldn't have. They must have cost a fortune."

"They were worth every penny to see the look on your face."

She gazed enquiringly at him. He'd never come to her place of work before, and she wasn't sure how she felt about it. She knew one thing. The hospital grapevine would have a field day if they got wind of this.

"Was there some special reason, other than the roses, that you stopped by?"

"Yes, as a matter of fact, there was." He waited expectantly.

"Aren't you going to tell me?"

"I was kind of hoping you'd figure it out by yourself."

Her eyes went round when she noticed what had at first been obscured by the roses, and later by her preoccupation with his presence.

"Oh, my goodness," she murmured with awe. "Your beard's gone. You shaved."

His fingers stroked his now-smooth cheeks. "You like?"

"You have cheekbones," she accused.

"Is that good or bad?"

"Put it this way, they're more sculpted than mine."

He spread his arms and gave her an impudent grin. "I am as Mother Nature designed me."

Mother Nature had done a magnificent job, Samantha conceded. With or without a beard, Carlo Garibaldi was one handsome devil. And he was hers, her inner voice prompted, bringing her a rush of pleasure. At least for now.

"Notice anything else?" he prompted.

Her eyes went round again. He was wearing his uniform.

"You're going back to work," she said softly.

"Yes," he confirmed.

"When did you decide this?"

"It was the oddest thing," he said. "I got up this morning, and without consciously thinking about it, pulled my uniform out of the closet. I looked in the bathroom mirror, picked up my razor, and knew I was ready."

"Oh, Carlo, that's wonderful. I'm so happy for you."

"It's because of you," he said, the look in his eyes giving her a thrill. "I wouldn't have gotten to this point without your support and encouragement."

She held her breath. "Does this mean you've accepted that you're not responsible for James's death?"

"It means, Samantha, I've accepted that I did my best."

"That's not the same thing," she pointed out.

"No," he said seriously, "it isn't. I will always feel regret over my actions that day. But I'm willing to concede that I might not be entirely responsible. That other factors were in play."

"Well, it's about time," she said with satisfaction.

"You do know," he said, "that this means we'll have some other things to talk about."

"You mean about us," she said slowly.

"Yes."

"So there is an us."

"I think there's a good chance there will be. At least as far as I'm concerned."

"I think so, too," she admitted.

The happiness in his eyes melted her heart.

"There's no rush, Samantha. I know our relationship is still in the early stages. Whenever you're ready to talk about the future, just let me know."

"I will."

"Good."

A light blinked on the console in front of her. Mr. Johnson was paging a nurse.

"I'm sorry," she apologized, pushing back her chair and climbing to her feet, "but I have to go. A patient needs assistance, and we're short-staffed today."

"I don't want to keep you from your work," he said. "I was hoping, though, that you and Jeffrey would be free to have dinner with me tonight, in celebration of my going back to work. I thought we'd let Jeffrey choose the place."

"If you give him the option, he'll probably pick McDonald's."

She knew he wouldn't kiss her. Not here, where people could see. Yet she suddenly discovered that she needed his kiss desperately. For some reason, she needed his reassurance.

"I don't care where we eat," he said. "I just want to spend the evening with you two."

It was all the reassurance she needed. "Why don't you pick us up at six, then? I've really got to go, Carlo. Have a good first day back at work."

"See you tonight."

"See you."

She hurried down the hall without a backward look. When she emerged from Mr. Johnson's room five minutes later, the roses were the first thing to catch her eye. At the sight, a sense of foreboding filled her, and a shiver raced up her spine. Shaking off the disquieting feeling, she went back to work.

The feeling of foreboding didn't leave. If anything, over the next week, it intensified.

Samantha couldn't understand it. It made no sense. Christmas was just a week away. She'd spent many a happy hour baking cookies and pies, wrapping presents and addressing cards. Her son was making great strides, and she had a wonderful man in her life. A man who had been through a rough patch of his own, and who seemed to be on track once more. A man who was everything she'd ever wanted and more, and whom she was planning to tell Christmas morning that she was ready for their talk. So why, when everything was going so well, was she so certain that something terrible was about to happen?

The answer came late that afternoon. Jeffrey was up in his bedroom doing homework, and Samantha was cooking dinner while watching Oprah on the small television set she kept on the kitchen counter. Oprah had just promised to reveal the secret of inner peace, when the show was interrupted by a special bulletin. A local commentator announced that a developing situation in Bridgeton had police on hand.

Heart in her throat, Samantha sank down onto a chair and watched as a camera panned the facade of an apartment building located on the other side of town. The camera moved from the building to the surrounding neighborhood. A shaky sigh of relief escaped her throat when she saw that Carlo was not among the uniformed policemen stationed around the area.

"What information we have is sketchy," the commentator said, "but it appears that twenty-six-year-old Michael Blevins, an unemployed social worker, has taken refuge in his apartment and refuses to come out. He is reported to be armed and has threatened to kill himself and anyone who tries to interfere. Blevins's mother warned the police after he called her to say goodbye. We've been informed that, fifteen minutes ago, Bridgeton police chief Carlo Garibaldi went inside the building to see if he could talk Mr. Blevins into surrendering."

"No," Samantha moaned, terror filling her. "Not again." Carlo had been back to work barely a week, and already his life had been put in danger.

The truth about the foreboding that had shadowed her for

the past seven days hit her between the eyes. She was terrified she would lose Carlo. The way she had lost both her father and James.

What seemed like hours later, but was probably no more than five minutes, Carlo emerged from the building with a shackled Michael Blevins in tow. The crowd that had gathered let out a cheer.

Samantha didn't cheer. How many times? she wondered, a dull ache squeezing her heart. How many more times would a scenario like this be played out? How many times would Carlo's luck be tested? Realistically, how many times would he walk away, unscathed?

She was playing with fire, she realized. If it were just her, she might be able to take the risk. But it wasn't just her. She had Jeffrey to consider. He'd already lost his father, and it had nearly destroyed him. If she let the relationship between Carlo and Jeffrey continue to grow, and something happened to Carlo, what would it do to her son?

She'd seen the way Jeffrey looked at Carlo, heard the admiration in his voice when he spoke of their time together. It would take only a small nudge for Jeffrey's admiration and hero worship to turn to love. A very dangerous nudge, given Carlo's profession.

Samantha had already lost her husband and her father, she couldn't lose her son. And the man she'd grown to love, the man she respected and admired above all others? Could she bear to lose him, too? For Jeffrey's sake, she had no other choice.

Fighting back tears, she closed her eyes and prayed for the strength to do what she knew she had to do.

Chapter 13

It was after ten o'clock when Carlo finally came to her door. Looking tired, but elated, he drew Samantha into his arms and kissed her soundly. It was all she could do to hold herself aloof and not respond with all the love she had inside her. The only thing that kept her stiff in his arms was the knowledge that, if she did, she'd never have the strength to let him go.

The light in his eyes, and the fervency of his embrace, told her that he was flying high after his victory that afternoon. He'd been put to the test and had passed with ease. As a result, he'd gotten a good deal of his confidence back.

It was wonderful to see him this way. In charge. Purposeful. Fulfilled. Happy. He was a man who, after a great deal of agonizing and soul-searching, had refound his place in life.

Since he'd given her every indication that he wanted her to share that place, there was a strong possibility, once she had her say, that she was going to rip away a major portion of his renewed confidence. Could she really do that to him? Did she have any other choice?

"I'm glad you're still up," Carlo said, a puzzled look in his eyes at her lukewarm response. "Sorry I couldn't get here sooner. I've had a busy day."

"I saw." At his raised eyebrows, she added, "Michael Blevins. It was on the television. They gave it quite a bit of coverage."

He shrugged. "Must have been a slow news day. Otherwise, I can't imagine them giving much air time to our little crisis."

"I don't know about that. From where I was sitting, it didn't seem so little to me."

She felt rather than saw the quick look he shot her. Instead of meeting it, she busied herself helping him out of his leather jacket. Studiously avoiding his gaze, she hung the jacket in the closet.

"Can you come into the den?" she asked. "There's something we need to discuss."

"Sounds serious."

"It is."

His gaze bore a hole in her back as he followed her down the hallway, but to her relief he didn't ask any further questions. After seeing him and being overwhelmed, as always, by his presence, she needed time to compose herself for the coming confrontation. Knowing Carlo the way she did, he wouldn't go down without a fight. This was one fight she couldn't afford to lose.

In the den, she indicated that she wanted him to take a seat on the sofa. When he complied, she deliberately sat across from him in an armchair, thereby placing the width of the coffee table between them. She didn't want her wavering resolution to be swayed by the heat of his nearness. Lacing her fingers together, she stared down at her lap.

"What is it, Samantha?" he asked. "What's wrong?"

The concern in his voice brought a sting of tears to her eyes. There was really only one way to do it, she decided. Like Carlo had urged her the night she'd summoned him here to seduce him, she needed to get it over with, and get it over with fast.

"I'm sorry," she said, "but we can't see each other anymore."

A long, taut silence stretched between them. A silence during which she steadfastly stared at her hands and listened to the ticking of the mantle clock. She couldn't risk looking at him. Not just yet.

"Is it because you've discovered you don't care for me?" he finally asked in a low voice.

How easy it would be if she could just lie and say yes. If she did, she knew his pride would prevent him from protesting further.

But she couldn't lie to him. Aside from the fact that she was an abysmal liar, after everything he'd done for her and for Jeffrey, the least she owed him was the truth.

"No."

"So you do care for me?"

She felt her lips curve wryly. "I think I've made that more than clear."

"No, Samantha," he contradicted. "Other than a brief indication that you would consider taking our relationship to a deeper level at some unnamed point in the future, the only thing you've made clear over the past couple of weeks is that I excite you physically."

She raised her head and met his gaze. "Then let me leave you in no doubt," she said softly. "My feelings for you run deeper than just physical attraction."

Emotion flared in his eyes. "As do my feelings for you," he said seriously. "So, if we both care for each other, what's the problem? Why don't you want to see me anymore? Is it because I told Jeffrey about us? If so, I'm sorry. I knew you weren't ready for him to know. But I couldn't lie to him when he asked me. It wouldn't have been right."

She hadn't known he'd told Jeffrey about them. Her son hadn't said a word.

"No, Carlo, it's not that."

"Then what is it?" Frustration edged his voice.

"This afternoon."

"What about this afternoon?"

"The situation on Washington Street."

He looked genuinely confused. "What about it?"

"I was worried about you." An understatement, if ever there was one.

His expression gentled. "I'm sorry, Samantha. But you needn't have worried. We had everything under control."

"The reporter said Michael Blevins was armed and dangerous."

"The reporter didn't have all the facts. Yes, Michael Blevins was armed, but he was really only a danger to himself. He was feeling suicidal, but he really didn't want to go through with it. If he had, he wouldn't have called his mother. He wanted someone to intervene."

"And you were that someone," she said.

He nodded. "Yes. After consulting with his mother and his psychiatrist, it was agreed that I should go into the building and try to talk him into coming out. I went in. He listened to what I had to say. Then he came out. At the arraignment, the judge will remand him to a psychiatric facility, and he'll get the help he needs."

Why did she think it wasn't really as simple as he made it sound?

"That's really not the point," she said.

"Then what is?"

"You were in danger."

"I just told you that I wasn't."

She spread her arms. So he was going to split hairs about it.

"Okay, fine. You weren't in danger today. But can you guarantee that, tomorrow, or sometime in the future, you won't confront a situation where you might be in danger?"

"You were the wife of a cop, Samantha. You know I can't guarantee that."

"I do know that. Which is why we can't see each other anymore."

"I don't understand," he said slowly.

Samantha fought a silent battle against the yearning that urged her to throw herself into his arms and agree to anything he said. She had to do this. For Jeffrey. And for herself. No matter how much it hurt.

"It's very simple, really," she said. "I can't go through each day, terrified that you might not come home at night. That wouldn't be good for either you or me. More importantly, I can't risk Jeffrey's peace of mind. I just got him back. I won't take the chance of losing him again. The only thing I know is that if I let the relationship between you and Jeffrey continue to grow, and if anything happened to you, my son might not recover."

She drew a deep breath and expelled it slowly. "I can't allow that to happen. After tonight, Jeffrey and I can't see you anymore."

He looked stunned. The pain in his eyes was almost more than she could bear.

"Just like that?" he asked, his voice raw with emotion.

"I have to do what's right for my son. He's the number one priority in my life. He always will be."

"And what about my promise to him that, no matter what, we would always be friends?"

"You can always be friends," she said. "Just…long-distance ones."

He threaded an unsteady hand through his hair. "We live

twelve blocks apart, Samantha. That's hardly long distance. What will you do when he asks why I'm not picking him up on Saturday for our weekly outing?''

"I'll make excuses for why you can't see him."

"Will those same excuses apply for why I can't talk to him on the phone?"

"Yes," she agreed.

His lips twisted. "You'll blame it on police work, you mean."

"Yes. Jeffrey will understand. After a while, he'll get used to not having you around."

"And eventually he'll forget all about me," Carlo said bitterly.

That was the goal. Still, it hurt like no pain she'd ever experienced to say the word.

"Yes."

"Tell me, Samantha, will he forget his father, too?"

She knew her next words were cruel, but she said them anyway. Best to make the break as clean as possible, for all their sakes.

"You're not his father, Carlo."

He flinched. "No, I'm not."

Samantha had to bite her lip to hold back the words of apology that lodged in her throat. He didn't know it, but his pain was her pain.

It wasn't the pain of burying him, she reminded herself. It wasn't the pain of knowing that the world would be dimmer without his presence in it. That was a pain she didn't think she could bear. Not again. As for her son, if anything happened to Carlo, she was terrified he would retreat to a place where no one could reach him.

"Will you forget about me, too?" Carlo asked.

She could sooner forget her name. But she could get on with her life. Before she cared too much. Before Jeffrey cared too much. As the days, weeks and months passed, the power of his hold over her would fade, and she would be left only with pleasant memories of their time together. After all, it had only been five and a half weeks since they'd met. Surely that wasn't long enough for one person to become indispensable to another person.

"That's not the issue here," she said.

"No, the issue is my being a cop. Would you change your mind if I left the force?"

For a minute Samantha was so overwhelmed by emotion she couldn't speak. "You'd do that for me?"

"In a heartbeat." Reaching out, he leaned across the coffee table and gathered her cold hands between the warmth of his. "You and Jeffrey are more important to me than any job. If that's the only thing standing between us, I'll hand in my resignation first thing in the morning."

It was the closest a man could come to saying "I love you" without actually uttering the words. A part of Samantha thrilled to the knowledge of how deeply he really cared for her. And she cared for him, too. If he left the force, everything would be okay. If he left the force, she wouldn't have to worry about him. Jeffrey wouldn't be at risk.

She was tempted. Oh, how she was tempted. Then she recalled the look of satisfaction in his eyes when he'd arrived earlier. And the expression on his face when he'd come out of the building with Michael Blevins in tow, the purposefulness in his step that had been lacking until then.

Gently, she pulled her hands from his. No. She couldn't let her emotions, her weakness, her need for him, distract her from doing what was right. For her and for Jeffrey. And, ultimately, for Carlo, too.

"What will you do with the rest of your life?" she challenged. "You were on a leave of absence for six weeks. You had a lot of time to think. During that time, did you come up with even one feasible idea for how you would support yourself outside police work? Did any idea give you half the thrill and satisfaction that being a cop does? And don't tell me about your whittling. We both know that was just a time filler for you.''

When he didn't reply, she gave him a sad smile. ''You're a cop through and through, Carlo. It's in your blood. You wouldn't know how to be anything else. You'd only end up hating me if I forced you to stop doing the thing you love.''

''I could never hate you, Samantha.''

''And I could never come between you and your job.''

Stalemate.

''It's that easy for you?'' he asked, his voice sounding raw.

She shook her head sadly. ''It's never easy to do what is right.''

''And what is the right thing to do in this situation?''

''Protect my son.''

''At all costs?''

''At all costs.''

''You can't protect Jeffrey from everything, you know.''

''I realize that. But I can do my best to eliminate the obvious risks.''

''Don't do this, Samantha,'' he pleaded, the undercurrent of pain in his voice sending a rush of pain to her heart. ''Don't shut me out this way.''

''I'm sorry, Carlo,'' she said heavily, struggling to hold back the tears that threatened to flow. ''But I have no choice.''

''Have you spoken to Jeffrey about this?''

''Why should I?''

''You say you have to do this for his sake. Maybe, if you spoke to him, he could reassure you that your fears are unfounded, that he's strong enough to take anything the future has to offer.''

''And maybe he'd just say that because he cares for you and doesn't want to lose you.''

"I don't want to lose him, either. Any more than I want to lose you."

Rising to his feet, Carlo began pacing back and forth in front of the coffee table.

"This isn't about Jeffrey, you know. Jeffrey's found the courage to live again. This is about you and your fears. Can't you see that you're doing what Jeffrey spent the last year doing, what I did when I took my leave of absence? Can't you see that you're withdrawing from me because you're afraid of loving again?

"Where does it stop, Samantha? Will you ultimately pull back from your mother, from your friends, from Jeffrey himself, because you can't risk the chance of any more pain? Can't you see that turning your back on what we have will ultimately cause you more harm than it will Jeffrey, if something happened to me?"

It took an effort, but she hardened her heart against the pull of his words. "Where cops are concerned, I'm a two-time loser, Carlo. I don't think I'm a good risk."

"I'm willing to take it."

"I'm not."

He stopped pacing. Facing her, he held out one hand.

"You helped me, Samantha, in my time of need. Let me help you now, in yours."

"Help me what?" she cried. "Forget I was ever married? Forget I had a father? Both my husband and my father died in the line of duty, Carlo. So don't give me that old song and verse about lightning not striking twice in the same place. I'm living proof that it does."

"And because it did, and because I'm a cop, you're willing to say goodbye to all that we could be?"

If the pain was this bad now, she could only imagine how much worse it would be in the future.

"Yes." The word rang with the conviction of her feelings.

Carlo's hand dropped listlessly to his side.

"So that's it?" he said heavily. "It's over? We're over? Jeffrey and I are over? Because you're afraid?"

"It's over because it's the right thing for everyone concerned."

"In that case," he said, turning on his heel and heading for the front hall, "I suppose I'd better be going."

He didn't look at her when she handed him his leather jacket. She thought he would leave without saying anything else, but at the door he turned to face her.

"A word to the wise, Samantha. I suggest you don't fall in love again. With any man. You see, sooner or later, he *will* die. Sooner or later, we all do. It's just a matter of when. Personally, I prefer to live for whatever time I have left. You, it appears, prefer to hibernate. Merry Christmas."

It was only after the door had closed decisively behind him that she allowed the tears to fall.

For the third time that morning, Carlo attempted to draft a memo to the town council requesting funds for a stoplight at a busy intersection. And, for the third time, he was less than satisfied with the results. Wadding the piece of paper into a ball, he threw it across the room with as much force as he could muster.

Sighing heavily, he watched the paper bounce benignly off the wall and onto the floor. What he really wanted was to punch something. Hard. And it wasn't the lack of a needed stoplight that had his temper raging. The real source of his frustration was that, like the request for additional funds, he couldn't think of an adequate argument to make Samantha change her mind.

For the past four days, since she'd told him he had no place in either her or Jeffrey's lives, he'd been consumed with a paralysis that had left him reeling. He hadn't felt this helpless when he'd assumed total responsibility for James

Underwood's death. Hell, in a weak moment he'd even unloaded his woes onto his sister's shoulders.

What truly tormented him was that he understood Samantha's reasoning. He even empathized with her feelings. And he agreed with her. To a point.

But she was dead wrong when she said it was solely for Jeffrey's sake. She was the one who was running. From the past, and from a future that could be so promising for them both.

Wrong or not, it didn't change the outcome. She wanted him out of her life, and he had no choice but to comply with her wishes. To continually confront her and try to get her to change her mind would turn him into a stalker, and that he couldn't allow. She was the one who would have to come to him. Not that he was holding his breath.

The irony of the situation was that the only place he didn't feel a sense of hopelessness was at the police station. Work really helped. To pass the time. To give him a sense of purpose. To help him—at odd moments, anyway—forget his pain. The job that had lost him the woman he loved had become his solace.

A call came in, and he welcomed the distraction it would provide. Samantha had been right about one thing. He was a cop through and through. No matter what, he would always be a cop.

Which meant he couldn't have her.

Samantha was in the middle of making a notation on a patient's chart, when the pain and sense of loss hit her and took her breath away. Closing her eyes, she expelled her breath slowly and rode it out the way a laboring woman rode the crest of her contractions, willing it to abate to a manageable level.

The pain always hit her like this, at odd moments during

the day, usually when she least expected it. There were times, like now, when she didn't think she could go on.

It wasn't supposed to hurt this much. After all, she hadn't known Carlo that long. She shouldn't be experiencing the same feelings she had after she first lost her father and James.

The pain was just temporary, she told herself. It would get better. Soon. It had only been five days. With each day that passed, it would get easier. Before she knew it, she'd hardly think of Carlo at all.

Unfortunately, it wasn't going to be as easy for her to forget the confrontation with her son the day after she'd asked Carlo to leave.

"Is Carlo coming for dinner tonight?" had been the first words out of Jeffrey's mouth when her mother had dropped him off at dinnertime that evening.

"Not tonight," she answered, swallowing her dismay. Because she hadn't wanted anything to dim his joy in the festive season, she'd hoped to put off telling Jeffrey about Carlo until after the holidays.

"What about tomorrow night?"

"Not then, either."

"Why not?"

She took his coat and hung it up in the closet. "Carlo's very busy, now that he's gone back to work. It's going to take him some time to catch up."

To her relief, Jeffrey nodded as if he understood. "Okay."

Thinking that all was well and that the subject had been dropped, Samantha headed for the kitchen. Jeffrey's next words stopped her in her tracks.

"He will be coming for Christmas dinner, though, won't he?"

Slowly, she turned to face her son. "No, Jeffrey. Carlo's not coming for Christmas dinner."

"Why not? He told me he didn't have to work then."

She drew a deep breath and braced herself for the showdown to come. "The truth is, he's not coming over anymore. We won't be seeing him again."

For a long minute, Jeffrey didn't say anything. Then, a look of hurt and bewilderment in his eyes, he asked, "Doesn't he like us?"

"Of course he likes us. He likes us very much."

"Then why won't we be seeing him again?"

This was it. Like it or not, the time for evasion had passed. "Because I asked him to stay away."

"Why? I thought you liked Carlo. I thought he was your boyfriend."

Samantha bit her lip as she searched for the right words to say. Oh, this was hard. This was much harder than she'd ever anticipated.

"Relationships don't always work out, Jeffrey. That's what happened here. Carlo and I have decided not to be boyfriend and girlfriend anymore."

"Why?" Jeffrey demanded.

"Remember how you were after your father died?"

Jeffrey nodded.

"Carlo's a cop, you see," she explained. "And you two are growing very close. If anything happened to him, I'm concerned that you might act the way you did this past year. That's why I asked him to stay away. For your sake."

"But," Jeffrey protested, "he promised me we would always be friends. Even if you weren't boyfriend and girlfriend anymore."

"Some promises," Samantha said softly, "are meant to be broken."

"That's not what you told me," Jeffrey retorted, his temper flaring. "You said it was always important to keep your promises."

"I know you don't understand, Jeffrey. But you're just going to have to accept that I know what's best."

Jeffrey stomped his foot. "Well, I don't accept it. It's not fair! Carlo's a promise-breaker, and you're just mean. You're even meaner than the Grinch. I hate you both!"

Sobbing, he raced up the stairs and into his room. The slam of his door echoed in the silence.

Samantha had opened her mouth to call her son back, before deciding to say nothing. She wasn't going to change her mind. Jeffrey was angry now, but he would get over this. She'd done what was best for the both of them.

As she finished making her notation on the chart, she realized that truth had been borne out over the past four days. Jeffrey hadn't withdrawn again, the way she had feared he might. Oh, he still wasn't speaking to her, but he was speaking to, and playing with, his friends. She'd caught it in time. She'd severed the relationship with Carlo before Jeffrey had become too emotionally involved. That was definitely worth a little silence on his part.

And the pain? she wondered as a fresh wave spread through her body. Was it worth the pain?

That was one question for which she had no answer.

Christmas Eve dawned with the promise of snow, and Jeffrey still wasn't speaking to her.

Worse than Jeffrey's silence, though, was the emptiness inside her, a jagged chasm that grew wider and deeper with every passing moment.

Jeffrey was doing well, and that was all that mattered, Samantha told herself. It didn't matter that she felt as if a part of her was missing. It didn't matter that she was looking forward to Christmas with about as much enthusiasm as she would a root canal. She'd done the right thing. With that she would have to be satisfied.

At least she had her mother's and Seamus McCracken's

presence at dinner to look forward to. That should take her mind off her troubles.

Her peace of mind was short-lived.

"Okay," Maxine demanded after a strained meal, when they were finally alone in the kitchen. "What gives? The tension in the air around here is so thick you could cut it with a knife. Why is Jeffrey so angry? What happened between you two?"

"Oh, Mom." Samantha sank down onto a nearby chair and tried not to cry. "I did something really stupid."

"Come on," Maxine coaxed. "Tell Mother. You know it'll make you feel better."

"I fell in love."

The words poured out of Samantha then. Her mother was right. It did make her feel better to confide her pain. For a minute or two, anyway.

"Oh, baby," Maxine crooned when Samantha had finished her sorrowful tale. Taking Samantha into her arms, she rocked her back and forth. "I'm sorry."

For several minutes, Samantha allowed herself to bask in the security of her mother's embrace. Then, pulling back and dashing a hand at her tears, she asked, "So what do you think? I made the right decision, didn't I?"

"I can't answer that for you. All I know is that it took me nineteen years to let myself love again. Only you, Sam, can be the judge of when you're ready."

Her mother's answer left her more confused than ever. "This isn't about me, Mom."

"Isn't it?"

"No, it's about Jeffrey."

"I see," Maxine said cryptically. "Then I just want you to know that I'll be here for you. If you need to talk, or just a shoulder to cry on, you know where to come."

The tears threatened to fall again. "Thanks, Mom."

* * *

Fifteen minutes later, with Jeffrey, Seamus and Maxine watching a Christmas movie in the den, Samantha found herself blinking in surprise at the sight of Carlo's sister on her doorstep.

"I asked you not to hurt my brother," Kate said the minute she was safely inside and Samantha had shut the door.

Were all the Garibaldis like this? Samantha wondered. Did they all blurt out whatever was on their mind the minute they saw a person?

"I never meant to hurt anyone."

The severity of Kate's expression softened. "I believe you. And I'd be really angry, too, except you look as miserable as Carlo does."

Samantha's heart squeezed in pain. "He's unhappy?"

"Of course he is. He loves you."

"He told you that?"

"He didn't have to."

"But he did tell you about us," Samantha guessed.

"He really had no choice," Kate replied. "I badgered him until he told me the whole story. I suppose he needed to confide in someone."

Samantha bit her lip. "He'll get over it," she said huskily.

Kate shot her a piercing glance. "Will he? He's in love with you, Samantha. That's something you don't get over easily. Trust me, I know. The first time we were married, Steve and I divorced after a year and a half. Another eighteen months passed before we got back together. My love for him didn't fade during that time. If anything, it grew."

"Did Carlo tell you why I broke things off?"

"Yes."

"And I suppose you think I'm wrong to feel the way I do."

Surprisingly, the expression that crossed Kate's face was both understanding and sympathetic.

"What I think is that you're just like Carlo. You're letting one tragic experience keep you from reaching out to someone you care about.''

''But it wasn't just one tragic experience, Kate. It was two. My father was also a cop. He died in the line of duty, the same way my husband did.''

''My mother died when I was ten,'' Kate replied. ''It might not have been in a hail of bullets, but the outcome was just the same. I didn't miss her any less. And my first child, a beautiful baby girl, I lost her, too.''

''I'm sorry,'' Samantha murmured. ''I didn't know.''

''How could you?'' Kate said gently. ''The point is, we all suffer losses. And, hard as it is, we all have to go on.''

''That may very well be. But Carlo's and my situation is unique.''

''How is it unique?''

''He's a cop. He puts his life on the line every day.''

''And I could walk out this door a minute from now and get hit by a bus.''

''Buses don't run in this neighborhood.''

''You know what I meant,'' Kate said patiently.

''And do you know how many cops were killed last year in the line of duty?'' She didn't wait for Kate to answer. ''I'll tell you how many. One hundred and seventy.''

''Do you know,'' Kate retorted, ''that the leading causes of death last year were heart disease and cancer, followed closely by age, kidney disease, Alzheimer's and AIDS? You have to go way down the list until you reach work-related injuries and deaths, and they're just a tiny fraction of the total number. Kind of gives you a whole new outlook on probabilities, doesn't it?''

Samantha was taken aback. ''How do you know all this?''

Kate shrugged. ''I'm a journalist. I've done a lot of research, read thousands of statistics. The one thing I've learned is that statistics can be manipulated to say whatever the user wants them to say. But they can't come close to measuring what really matters, and that's what's in our hearts.''

Kate stopped speaking only long enough to draw a deep breath and pierce Samantha with her penetrating gaze. ''Do you love my brother?''

''Would you believe me if I said no?''

''No. Carlo loves you, too, Samantha. He loves Jeffrey. That should be all that matters.''

Could a heart break twice over the same person? Samantha wondered. ''In a perfect world, I'd agree with you. But this world is far from perfect.''

She spread her arms in supplication. ''I don't know what else I can do, Kate. I don't want to live the rest of my life in fear. That wouldn't be good for anyone, especially Carlo.''

''You can give up the fear and live for the moment,'' Kate said. ''It's not a bad way to go. In fact, I recommend it highly. Otherwise, you might as well be a turtle with your head tucked firmly inside its shell.''

''I did what I know to be the best for everyone concerned,'' Samantha maintained. ''Nothing you've said to me has convinced me otherwise.''

''And I've worn out my welcome,'' Kate said sadly. ''One last word, and I'll leave you to your Christmas. My brother is an incredible man. Whether you know it or not, you just threw away the best thing that ever happened to you. I hope it's not too late when you finally realize that.''

Chapter 14

Carlo stared at the Christmas tree he'd decorated with so much hope in his heart the week before. One delicate glass ornament teetered on the edge of a limb. He knew he should get up and rescue it, before it fell to the floor and broke, but he didn't have the strength. To so much as move a muscle would have cost too much effort. He now understood what it meant to teeter on the brink of despair. Like the endangered ornament, he was dangling as wildly over that brink.

Outside, a group of carolers passed by. He didn't go to the door to greet them, the way he normally would have. It was Christmas Eve, but he had no heart for the coming holiday, or for any of the trappings that went with it.

Closing his eyes, he let the memories come.

How beautiful Samantha had been that very first day she'd come to his house and begged him to be Jeffrey's buddy. How wonderful she had felt the first time he'd held her in his arms, the night he'd carried her up to her bedroom when she was so sick. Her laughter. Her taste. Her scent. The forgiveness and understanding on her face, when he'd confided his guilt over James Underwood's death. The look in her eyes when she'd told him goodbye.

A wave of self-disgust washed over him. What was wrong with him? First he'd given up on himself without so much as a fight, then he'd given up on the woman he loved. Oh, he'd put up a token battle, but he hadn't really pressed the issue. Why hadn't he fought harder? Why was he sitting here, wallowing in self-pity, when his family was across town?

Rising to his feet, he grabbed his leather jacket and hurried out into the night. He had to try one last time. And, if necessary, he had to say goodbye to Jeffrey.

"You're going to have to talk to me sometime, you know," Samantha told Jeffrey after her mother and Seamus left.

When Jeffrey didn't reply, she added, "Do you think Santa is going to bring presents to a boy who isn't speaking to his mother?"

Without waiting to see if her question had elicited a response, she picked up the half-eaten bowl of popcorn from the coffee table and headed into the kitchen.

Pulling the Santa card was a low blow, she knew, but she couldn't think of any other way to reach her son. As it was, she'd let things go on far too long, in the hope that Jeffrey would snap out of his silence on his own. But he wasn't snapping out of it. And she couldn't let it go any longer. She couldn't face a silent Christmas morning. It was hard enough already to face the holiday without Carlo.

A minute later, Jeffrey was framed in the kitchen doorway.

"I'm really mad at you," he said.

Samantha closed the dishwasher door and leaned back against the counter.

"I know you are. But when you're angry at someone, the best thing to do is to talk to the person about it. The silent treatment doesn't solve anything."

"You shouldn't have sent Carlo away."

"I did what I thought was best."

"I'm not a baby anymore, Mom. You don't have to protect me from everything."

No, he wasn't a baby anymore. Sad to say, but at nearly nine, Jeffrey had life experiences that many of his friends wouldn't even encounter until they were adults. He'd been through an awful lot these past fourteen months, and in many ways it had made him wise beyond his years. Even if he did still believe in Santa Claus.

"No, you're not a baby, but you are my child. Whether you agree or not, I have a responsibility to do what I think is best for you."

"No matter what you say, sending Carlo away isn't what's best for me."

"Isn't it? Remember how you were after your dad died? I don't ever want you to be like that again."

"I won't be. I'm not afraid anymore. Carlo helped me to not be afraid."

Surprise filled her. She hadn't expected this. "He did?"

"Yes." Jeffrey nodded vigorously. "He showed me that when bad things happen to people you love, you need friends and family to help you through the hard times."

"Is that what your friends are doing?"

"Yes. Matt's as mad at you as I am."

She had to smile. "What else did Carlo show you?"

"That Dad wouldn't want me to be thinking about revenge. And that I should talk to you about how I've been feeling since Dad died."

"Why haven't you?" she asked softly. "Talked to me, I mean. I've been waiting."

"Can we talk now?"

"I'd love to talk now." Samantha took a seat at the kitchen table and motioned for Jeffrey to join her.

"Are you mad at me because I didn't talk to you?"

"No, Jeffrey," she said softly. "Only sad that I was too caught up in my own pain to help you through yours. I always want to be there for you, and I wasn't when you really needed me. I'm so sorry."

"That's okay."

She reached out and clasped her son's hands between hers. "No, it's not. I let you down. Do you know how proud I am of you? You shared your feelings with Carlo, and you've come such a long way. I spoke to your grief counselor on Friday, and he said you probably won't have to see him anymore after your next session. Your father would be so proud of you."

"I miss him, Mom."

Her heart swelled. "I miss him, too. But he's here with us in spirit."

Jeffrey smiled. "I know."

"So," Samantha asked, "Am I forgiven?"

"Are you going to change your mind about Carlo?"

She hated to dash the hope she heard in his voice. "No."

Jeffrey looked down at his toes for a long minute before raising his gaze to hers.

"I'll forgive you anyway," he said seriously, "because you're my mom. And because I love you."

She opened her arms, and he flew into them.

"That's the best Christmas present I ever got," she said, nuzzling her cheek against the top of his head.

Jeffrey pulled away. "Can I say one more thing?"

"Of course."

"If you're afraid to see Carlo, then don't. But I don't understand why I can't see him."

There it was again. First Carlo, then her mother and Kate. Now her own son had alleged that she was the one who was afraid; that her fear had nothing to do with Jeffrey. Couldn't anyone see the truth?

"Does this mean you're not mad at Carlo anymore?" she asked.

"No. I'm still mad at him. He made a promise. He shouldn't have broken it."

Samantha didn't know what else to say. Taking him by the shoulders, she aimed him toward the door.

"Don't you think you ought to go to bed? Santa can't come until you're asleep. I'll be up in a minute to tuck you in."

Without further prompting, Jeffrey scooted down the hall and up the stairs. Samantha reflected, not for the first time, on the unfettered belief of a child.

She went still, and her heart started beating uncontrollably. The belief of a child.

When had she stopped believing? When had she stopped looking for the good and started expecting the worst in every situation? When, and this was the kicker, had she stopped living?

Her hand flew to her mouth. They were right, all of them. Carlo. Her mother. Kate. Jeffrey. It wasn't her fear for Jeffrey that had made her turn Carlo away. Deep down, in the dark recesses of her soul, she was terrified of loving and losing again. That had been her fear all along.

At least, when they had withdrawn inside themselves, Jeffrey and Carlo had had a valid excuse. Their behavior had been the result of a real and terrible loss. What was her excuse? She was turning her back on the man she loved over something that hadn't even happened. Something that might never happen. How ridiculous could she get?

Praying that it wasn't too late, she raced to the phone. Hopefully, her mother could come stay with Jeffrey while she went to Carlo and tried to make things right. At the very least, she could restore Carlo's relationship with her son.

Before she had finished dialing, there was an urgent pounding on her front door. When she opened it, Carlo was standing there. He looked big and strong and so wonderfully angry that she wanted to cry.

"I love you," he said, brushing by her and entering the front hallway. Turning to face her, he asked, "Do you love me?"

As she closed the door, she sent a brief prayer heavenward. Thank goodness for the Garibaldis and their impetuous way of entering a room. Especially this particular Garibaldi.

"Yes, Carlo," she said, her voice wavering with emotion, "I do."

"Then why," he demanded, glaring at her, "aren't we together?"

Her heart skipped a beat before settling into a strong rhythm. "Because I've been a fool. A blind, stupid, scared fool. I just realized it a minute ago. As a matter of fact, when you knocked on the door, I was calling my mother. I wanted her to come stay with Jeffrey while I went over to your house so I could tell you exactly how much of a fool I've been."

He looked so thunderstruck by her admission that she almost laughed. Instead, she settled her hands on her hips.

"And why," she demanded, "are you letting me blabber away like this? Why aren't you holding me tight and kissing me senseless?"

It took less than a second for Carlo to haul her into his arms and give her a kiss that robbed her of breath and left her weak-kneed.

"You were right," she said when he finally let her come up for air. With one hand, she tenderly traced the outline of his beloved face. "It wasn't about Jeffrey. It was about me and my fear to love again. My fear of losing that love. A couple of people, besides you, helped bring that message home to me."

Carlo gazed piercingly into her eyes. "So you're all right with my being a cop?"

"Yes, Carlo. I'm all right with that."

"What if something happens to me in the line of duty?"

For just a second her heart quaked before a quiet peace filled her. "If I only get one minute with you, it will be enough."

"And Jeffrey?"

She let all the love she felt for him fill her smile. "Jeffrey has the coping skills to make it through anything life can throw at him. The coping skills you gave him."

He gathered her close again. "I love you, Samantha."

"I love you, Carlo. Besides being the most wonderful man in the world, you gave me back my son."

"And you gave me back my life. Will you marry me?"

"I would be proud to be your wife."

"Mom?" Jeffrey called from upstairs. "I thought you were going to tuck me in."

"Be right there," she called back.

"Shall we go tell Jeffrey the good news together?" Carlo asked.

She put a restraining hand on his arm. "In a minute. First, you need to know that he's mad at you. He's angry because you didn't fight harder to stay."

"I see." Carlo took her by the hand and headed for the stairs. "Then I guess it's time I made things right with him."

Jeffrey was lying in his bed. When he saw Carlo, his arms went stiff at his sides, and he turned his face to the wall.

"Hello, Jeffrey," Carlo said.

"What are you doing here?" the boy muttered.

"I'm sorry that I haven't seen you this week. I know you're angry with me, and you have every right to be. I

250 Dad in Blue

broke a promise, and that was wrong. Do you think you could find it in your heart to forgive me?''

Jeffrey continued staring at the wall.

"There's something else I need to tell you," Carlo added. "I love your mother. I want to marry her, hopefully with your blessing."

Jeffrey slowly turned his head. There was no expression on his face when he met Carlo's gaze. Samantha gave Carlo's hand a supportive squeeze, and he squeezed back before moving to sit on the edge of Jeffrey's bed.

"I love you, too, Jeffrey. I know you had a wonderful dad, and I would never try to take his place. I was hoping, though, that we could still be buddies."

"I don't want a buddy," Jeffrey said.

Carlo closed his eyes, and Samantha's heart contracted with pain. *Please don't give up,* she prayed. *Give him time. He'll come around.*

"I understand," Carlo said slowly. "You need time. I'll give you all the time you need."

Jeffrey's face broke into a wide grin. "You didn't let me finish. I don't want a buddy, but I would really like a step-dad."

Samantha's heart had never felt so full as it did when Jeffrey sat up and wrapped his arms around Carlo. Tears of joy ran unchecked down her cheeks.

"I promise you this, Jeffrey," Carlo said, hugging the boy back. "I'll try never to let you down again."

"This is going to be the best Christmas ever!" Jeffrey announced.

Over Jeffrey's head, Carlo aimed eyes shining with love at Samantha. "And it's only going to get better."

*   *   *   *   *

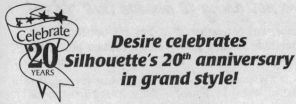
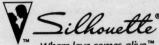

You're not going to believe this offer!

In October and November 2000, buy any two Harlequin or Silhouette books and save $10.00 off future purchases, or buy any three and save $20.00 off future purchases!

Just fill out this form and attach 2 proofs of purchase (cash register receipts) from October and November 2000 books and Harlequin will send you a coupon booklet worth a total savings of $10.00 off future purchases of Harlequin and Silhouette books in 2001. Send us 3 proofs of purchase and we will send you a coupon booklet worth a total savings of $20.00 off future purchases.

Saving money has never been this easy.

I accept your offer! Please send me a coupon booklet:

Name: _____

Address: _____ City: _____

State/Prov.: _____ Zip/Postal Code: _____

Optional Survey!

In a typical month, how many Harlequin or Silhouette books would you buy <u>new</u> at retail stores?

☐ Less than 1   ☐ 1   ☐ 2   ☐ 3 to 4   ☐ 5+

Which of the following statements best describes how you <u>buy</u> Harlequin or Silhouette books? Choose one answer only that <u>best</u> describes you.

☐ I am a regular buyer and reader
☐ I am a regular reader but buy only occasionally
☐ I only buy and read for specific times of the year, e.g. vacations
☐ I subscribe through Reader Service but also buy at retail stores
☐ I mainly borrow and buy only occasionally
☐ I am an occasional buyer and reader

Which of the following statements best describes how you <u>choose</u> the Harlequin and Silhouette series books you buy <u>new</u> at retail stores? By "series," we mean books within a particular line, such as *Harlequin PRESENTS* or *Silhouette SPECIAL EDITION*. Choose one answer only that <u>best</u> describes you.

☐ I only buy books from my favorite series
☐ I generally buy books from my favorite series but also buy books from other series on occasion
☐ I buy some books from my favorite series but also buy from many other series regularly
☐ I buy all types of books depending on my mood and what I find interesting and have no favorite series

Please send this form, along with your cash register receipts as proofs of purchase, to:
In the U.S.: Harlequin Books, P.O. Box 9057, Buffalo, NY 14269
In Canada: Harlequin Books, P.O. Box 622, Fort Erie, Ontario L2A 5X3
(Allow 4-6 weeks for delivery) Offer expires December 31, 2000.

PHQ4002